ALESSIO

THE GUZZI
LEGACY BOOK 2

BETHANY-KRIS

www.bethanykris.com

Editor: Elizabeth Peters

Proofreaders: Tracy A., Mia B., Tori W. and Felicia F.

Cover Design © Under Cover Designs

Interior Design: Under Cover Designs

ISBN: 978-1-988197-94-4

For my husband who listened to me whine my way through these boys' and their girl's love story, and yet never once complained.

CONTENTS

PART THREE
NOW

CHAPTER 1
ALESSIO

Pain taught Alessio Sorrento a lot of things.

A motivator, punishment, or a reward. In true pain, someone would find their boundaries, and the ability to go beyond their limits, too. Nothing reminded someone they were weak more than pain, and it was one of the few things that proved humans had the capability to be godlike at the same time.

Alessio hated pain.

Loathed it.

He much preferred numbness because it was a far more dangerous thing. Sure, pain made people do inexplicable, unexplainable things, but numbness? That was the flip side of the same damn coin.

In numbness, one found nothing. And one didn't have limits or boundaries, one didn't need a motivator or a reward when *nothing* was the goal. It was a vicious place to be, so numb that even happiness couldn't find its way through to one's heart.

And still …

Alessio would take numbness over pain any day. One allowed him not to care, and the other forced him to care too fucking much. He also felt like his entire life had been one huge mountain of pain, time and time again.

People said pain was growth.

Survival.

Well, fuck that trash. He'd taken enough pain to last him several lifetimes over, and now, he didn't want to feel at all.

The unfortunate thing about loving someone else was that love didn't afford the gift of numbness. Which was every reason, instead of sleeping like he should be at two in the morning, he sat on a wicker chair in the warm August air with darkness all around. A humid dampness clung to the air, reminding him where he was instead of where he might have been if this situation had been different.

The back property of the Guzzi mansion expanded a far ways into a line of forest under the moonlight. Manicured pathways veered off to a large fountain with dancing stone doves at the top, and then into the flower garden that would make anyone with a green thumb jealous. Mostly, the silence called to him late at night. He stared at the stars—had to be alone.

Things hurt less here.

There was a time when coming to this place—Corrado's childhood home—seemed awkward for a variety of reasons, and none he cared to list. Not that any one person here gave him that impression, but he wasn't used to … *this*.

They all loved.

They supported.

If someone needed something, then a few hands would be able help. The Guzzi family—just Corrado's immediate relatives—were enough to seem like a small army, and that was something else Alessio got used to. A part of him had been so used to taking care of himself for so long a family unit seemed like a foreign thing to him.

Sure, he had a family unit of his own, in a way. The situation Dare and Cree gave him wasn't the same as the Guzzis. Parenting hadn't existed for him, and his most important lessons from Cree and Dare had been learning how to take care of himself.

And still when he came here, Alessio found a sense of home. He forgot the rest of the world for a time and focused on what he needed to do the most. No one here would judge him with their *no questions asked* policy when he walked through the front door, unless he wanted to talk. He'd never told Corrado those things because he shouldn't need to, but it was true. Here, he found comfort that didn't exist elsewhere.

That was why, when he had a hundred other places to hide away and stay under the radar, he came here.

The voice coming out of the speaker of his phone dragged him from his thoughts at the same time he heard footsteps approaching him from behind. He didn't bother to end the conversation because he wasn't ready to.

"And I suppose I owe you something, don't I?"

"What's that?" Alessio asked.

"A happy birthday," Dare said.

Alessio *almost* smiled, but pain was a fucking bitch. Twenty-three years old today, and he'd forgotten. Someone else had to remind him. Appropriate for it to be Dare. At the darkest points in his life, Dare always remembered his birthday for whatever reason.

"Is it, though?" he asked.

"What?"

"A *happy* day."

Dare made a noise under his breath as Gian Guzzi came to sit next to Alessio in the wicker chair beside his. Corrado's father said nothing, dressed in his night clothes with a black robe tightened at his middle, he stared over the back property, and rested his hand along his jaw as he waited for Alessio to finish his conversation. It was late for the man to still be awake.

"Les."

"Ignore me," he muttered. "Thinking out loud."

But also not a lie.

This wasn't a happy day.

And tomorrow didn't look good, either.

Welcome to his life, lately.

"Why don't you take a break, come back here for a bit, and reset—"

"That's Alessio?"

Cree.

In the call's background, Dare confirmed what Cree asked. A shuffle of the phone sounded before more movement echoed through the speakers. Alessio heard the slam of a door before Cree came onto the phone.

"Where are you?" Cree demanded.

Alessio arched a brow over at Gian. The man didn't even glance his way. "Away."

"Doing what?"

"Thinking."

Cree let out a harsh sound. "You don't call people?"

"I'm a grown man, I can—"

"Tell the people who give a fuck that you're *safe*, Les."

His throat jumped as he swallowed back a biting retort that would have only saved his pride but hurt someone else. "I'm safe."

A second passed. Cree sighed. "Good." Then, after a brief pause, he added, "Corrado called two days ago looking for you. You should at least tell him where you are, Les. You don't have to go back—I understand things are going on that hurt you, but he's worried."

Good for him.

Because he hadn't given a shit about Alessio before.

As fast as the seed of doubt drifted through his mind, the pain following behind just as fast, Alessio tipped his head down, and shook it away. It wasn't true, and a huge part of why this happened was *because* Corrado hadn't wanted to hurt him.

Yet, here they stood.

The same result.

Alessio didn't do well with pain, and especially not if someone he loved caused it. He had a handle on this shit—this thing between them. He assumed they were comfortable, but this had taught him he had been lying to himself.

Complacent.

It took nothing to be ruined.

Nothing but a woman.

"I'm not calling him," Alessio said, "there's nothing for me to say."

Hadn't he said enough when he showed up to the penthouse over a week ago? He believed so. His words had cut with each one said—landing like knives against the man he loved to the ends of the earth and back. Alessio didn't need Corrado to tell him how much he hurt him with the things he said. He was aware.

But that was good, too.

Partly.

Why should Alessio be the only one to hurt?

He wouldn't be alone.

He needed to get his shit figured out before he went back for a second round. He didn't want to keep cutting into Corrado. As much as he hurt, it wasn't fair he continued hurting Corrado, too.

Because *he* loved.

He gave a shit.

He would have never done this to Corrado.

Ever.

"You tell him you're *safe*," Cree said, "so he doesn't do something fucking stupid, and make a scene."

"He knows, and he won't do anything. Relax."

"No, he—"

"He knows—shit he doesn't understand is what bothers him. That's Corrado, and it sounds like something he should deal with because I can't fix it."

A lot about this thing between him and Corrado couldn't be fixed by him. Too much shit had been left unsaid for years, and other things they shoved under a rug, ignoring while they pretended to be fine with the things between them.

All lies.

White lies didn't stay white when they became dirty with time.

"Les—"

Typically, he had more patience, especially with Cree or Dare, and yet he only wanted to hang up the phone. So, he did, not even bothering to say goodbye before he reached over and hit the *End Call* button on the lit up screen, ending the conversation whether Cree wanted that or not. He would pay for the decision later, but ... *worth it.*

With the phone call finished, and the conversation over, Gian turned in his chair to give Alessio his attention. Respectful, *always.* Never imposing or intruding unless they gave him no other choice.

"How much longer do you want to stay here?" Gian asked.

Alessio shrugged. "Not sure."

The answer didn't seem to bother Gian when he only nodded. "All right, you're more than welcome."

"Thanks. Shouldn't you be sleeping? Doesn't your wife get prickly when you walk the halls at night."

Gian grinned. "I have things on my mind."

"Me, too."

"Probably similar things."

Alessio scoffed and looked away from the man. "Doubtful."

"Don't. I have always worried about the two of you. I wouldn't be a good father otherwise."

"You're not my father."

Gian cleared his throat, but Alessio refused to take his gaze off the line of trees in the distance. "And yet, that never made a difference, Les."

Yeah, he knew.

"I'm *mad*."

"Mmhmm," Gian murmured.

"I really want to just do something."

Something horrible and *bad*.

Something that would make Corrado *get it*.

"Strike out, act out … *hurt*."

Alessio grunted under his breath. "But I can't … so, I'm here instead."

Gian let out a sigh, and the wicker creaked before the man came to stand in front of Alessio. He stared up at Corrado's father, but Gian looked off into the distance where the moon shone high and bright against the black backdrop of the sky.

"You are always welcome here, even if what you're here for is to hide, Alessio. But if he calls and asks me where you are—"

"You'll tell him the truth."

But that was the thing.

Corrado wouldn't call here.

He'd never think this was a haven for Les because he never told him. There was a lot of *that* between them. Secrets, and things left unsaid. And usually, when they were saying things, it was the wrong shit.

"Take the time you need," Gian said, "and go back *better*, Les."

"This doesn't get better from here."

"But it might. Go back better, and ready."

Yeah.

Right.

Ready for what?

And how should he do that when he only wanted to hurt Corrado? He could think of a million different ways to do it —ones to make the man feel the same cold ache in his chest that Alessio now had. Pain was always better when shared, right?

Did that make him a monster?

Alessio wasn't sure he cared.

And right there … that's why he hadn't gone back yet.

Not ready.

He wasn't better.

The phone buzzed on the table between the wicker chairs as Gian turned to walk away. Alessio let him go, and leaned over to check the phone, thinking it would be Cree or Dare trying to get him back on the phone.

A text from Corrado lit up the screen, reading, *Happy birthday, Les.*

Apparently, he wasn't the only one up way too late. He might have appreciated the text, and that Corrado remembered.

He still didn't.

Not when right above it rested a text, one the man had sent only two days earlier. One Alessio had been waiting for —*I slept with her*, Corrado had said.

This had never been about the sex.

The physical shit meant nothing to Les. Sex was sex to him—another urge or need to fulfill, like eating or sleeping or whatever else he needed to live. The idea of *men* sleeping with Corrado fucked with Alessio's head, and they drew the line. Women, though? He didn't care, he got off on it, really.

Rarely did he attach emotions to having sex with females, and neither did Corrado. Together was different, of course. Emotions had always been attached to their fucking when it was just them in bed together.

So, no, he didn't have a single fuck to give about Corrado sleeping with Ginevra.

It was everything else.

Everything Corrado *didn't* say.

All the things he hadn't done.

That was the problem.

~

Alessio blinked, and a week passed him like nothing at all. He didn't know how it happened, but he blamed the haze of his mind.

The *war*.

To his left, he watched the quiet, dark city street and the people passing by the bar's large bay windows as he tipped his whiskey up for another drink. Two glasses in, working on his third, and he still didn't *feel* shit.

The fucking numbness had come.

Now, he wasn't sure if he wanted it.

On the bar, his phone buzzed. Alessio ignored the device altogether. The chime of a bell somewhere behind him said someone new had come inside, and five seconds later, a presence sat next to him at the bar.

"Since when do you drink whiskey?"

Alessio made a thick noise, tipping his glass up for another sip. "Since now."

He preferred rum.

Tequila.

Vodka.

Bourbon.

Beer.

Fucking wine.

Anything but whiskey. The spirit was Corrado's drink, and Alessio didn't see the appeal. Something about the liquor made him cringe, which was amusing when he could take shots of tequila like nobody's business. The only time he liked the taste of whiskey was when he licked it off Corrado's—

Nope.

Not going there.

Not tonight.

"What do you want?" Alessio asked.

"Are you going to keep staring out the window, or look at me?"

Well …

Alessio turned on the stool to face his guest, coming face to face with Christopher. Before then, Alessio never looked at Corrado's twin and first recognized all the similarities between them. He always found the differences first because that's what he liked about Corrado.

All the things which made him different.

Today, the first thing he saw in Christopher's features were all the things that made him and Corrado identical. Right down to the way his lips quirked up at the corner when he smirked, and the gold flakes in the browns of his irises.

All it did was *hurt*.

Just like that, the numbness left, and the pain was back. Alessio didn't know which one he wanted more.

To feel *everything*.

Or nothing at all.

"How did you know I was here?" he asked.

Chris shrugged. "Dad."

"What, worried I might do something rash because I left the mansion?"

"Who knows? You might want someone else to talk to."

Alessio nodded. "Well, I don't."

"And I'm still here."

Perfect.

The phone vibrated on the bar. Alessio's gaze cut to the device at the same time Chris's did, both seeing a familiar name flashing on the screen to say a text had come through.

Corrado.

"What's that about?" Chris asked.

Alessio sucked air between his teeth, hating the taste of whiskey on his breath but needing the annoyance to help keep the numbness at bay for the moment. "I told him I'm fine … around, or whatever."

"Ah."

"And to leave me the fuck alone," he added quieter, turning to stare out the window again. "Apparently, he didn't get the memo."

Chris sighed. "Or he's ignoring it because he's worried, and he *cares*."

"*Right.*"

Cares.

A funny way to describe what Corrado had done.

"Do you want to talk about them—him and her, I mean?"

Alessio made a disgusted noise under his breath. "I don't give a fuck about them, Chris."

It was a lie.

He *did*.

He concerned himself with too much about them, what they were doing, and *why*. More than anything, he wanted to know *why*.

What was it about the woman that did it for Alessio and

Corrado? Why *her?* Why was it her who finally broke *them?* After all these years, all this time, and every female the two of them had gone through over the years in their bed … why the fuck was it *her?*

"Yeah, you get like that, huh?" Chris asked.

Alessio shot him a look. "Excuse you?"

"Indifferent. You *act* indifferent. You get in a mood whenever you don't want to deal. Corrado knows how to handle it, but the rest of us think you're being an asshole, Les."

Huh.

He stared at Chris and quirked a brow. "How is that my problem?"

Chris rolled his eyes. "You give a shit about them … or at least, *him.* Otherwise, you would have left by now, Les. You don't have to be here. Nobody is keeping you in this city. If you wanted to go, or tell my brother to go fuck himself, you would have done so. It's who *you* are. So, cut the shit, drop the attitude and the pretense, and then we can find what the real issue is here."

Alessio already understood.

Corrado lied.

They had a thing, and he fucked up.

Alessio didn't want to *deal*—he didn't know how to handle the person he loved, the only one in the world who he trusted more than himself, doing something to purposely ruin the delicate balance they had.

"And you know …" Chris dragged in a heavy breath before clearing his throat as his fingers drummed to the top of the bar. "I think he likes her."

Really?

That wasn't news.

If Corrado didn't like the fucking woman, and he had done this, it would stun Alessio. Why would he even bother?

"Obviously, he likes her," Alessio muttered before taking another drink. There was not enough alcohol in this world to deal with the darkness in his heart, he would swear on it. "Give me something I don't know, Chris."

"I meant," Chris replied, giving him a look from the side, "it's more, Les. Different. Like … him with you."

"Don't say that."

"But—"

"*Don't fucking say that.*"

The level of his tone drew the attention of other patrons in the bar, but Alessio didn't give a shit about anyone but himself right now. Hell, he'd been selfless for far too long. Time to be selfish for once.

Right?

Chris straightened on the stool but continued staring at the bar top. "Is it the fact he might care for someone else like he does for you, or that it's *you and him*?"

Alessio clenched his teeth. "Leave it alone."

Because it was both.

Except it wasn't at the same fucking time.

He didn't need this shit right now.

Chris nodded, adding, "I don't think he saw it until recently … why she made him—"

"Lie?"

Hide things from him?

Break their agreement?

Ruin them?

"I know you don't want to hear this, but she brings out the same thing in him as you," Chris said, turning to step off the stool at the same time. "And … because no one else will tell you … you should be aware. He's a happier version of him when he's with her, even if he doesn't see. It's the same thing I see when he's with you."

Alessio's jaw clicked from how hard he clenched. "Except

that's not how it is for us. That's not how *we* work. It's us, not us and someone else. Not me and him, and him and someone *else*. This isn't how it goes."

"Les—"

"Just fuck off, Chris."

Leave me alone.

He'd rather be back with his pain or numbness instead of this.

It was easier.

"You will never understand why if you don't let him explain. And yeah, it's fucked up … yeah, it hurts, I bet," Chris added quieter, "but that doesn't mean you can't find something *right* somewhere in the mess. You can't do that here, though, not alone. Let him explain, or—"

"What is there to explain?"

It was clear to him.

"Why her?" he asked around the rim of his glass.

Chris chuckled. "You could always try to find out."

Right.

Not a bad idea.

He didn't think Chris meant so in the same way Alessio took it.

Yeah, he would find out.

All of it.

Whether or not Corrado liked it.

CHAPTER 2
GINEVRA

You're a Calabrese woman—act like you know what that means and keep your eyes on the only man who'll ever be able to touch you.

Those words, said to her by her oldest brother when she first met the man she would be forced to marry, drifted through Ginevra's mind as she was reminded yet again why morning sex with Corrado was the *best* kind of sex. He had that energy—echoing around his being when he first cracked his eyes open. Like he needed to touch, and she was the closest thing he could find in his bed to do it.

She doubted her brother would approve of this.

Of this man, the way he was touching her, never mind the way she watched him as he did it all like there was nothing else he would rather be doing.

The sharp bite from Corrado found the junction of Ginevra's shoulder as she leaned down over his body, her hand pressing against his chest to keep her steady as she rode her way closer to heaven.

And what a beautiful heaven it would be.

"*Fuck*, you look good like this," she heard him say in a moan, his fingers at her waist tightening to almost a painful point. "Love it when you ride me, Ginny."

"I'm gonna—" Ginevra stiffened on top of Corrado, the wild rhythm of her hips moving against his stilling even as his continued driving into her. His fingers at her throat tightened, and she caught sight of his *oh, so pleased* sneer curving his lips as he watched her come on top of him. "*Corrado.*"

"Fuck, yeah, give me a taste of *that*, Ginny."

He only let her stay on his cock long enough to let her get the orgasm rushing through her bloodstream before his hand let her throat go. His fingers dug into her hips, and with a firm pull, he had yanked her up his body until her thighs were sitting on either side of his face. She didn't have time to appreciate the loss of his length stretching her out before his lips enclosed her clit, and he was sucking hard. She finished the orgasm off shaking while sitting on his face.

Crying loud.

Blinded.

And wishing the feeling would go on forever. She'd happily die like this. Almost numb all over, but with tingles racing up her spine, over her shoulders, and then danced over the rest of her body.

She couldn't breathe.

And it was glorious.

"Fuck, fuck, *fuck*," he groaned against her sex.

So sensitive.

Still trembling.

Way too sensitive.

Still, she couldn't move, instead rocking her hips against the lashes of his tongue taking whatever her body would give him. Fast jerks of his arm against her thigh said he was stroking his cock, and almost at his own release.

And even if she hadn't felt him doing it, she would have known by the sounds coming out of his mouth. God knew she didn't need to be in this man's bed, causing more of a problem than she already had in his life, but she'd found herself in it time and time again since the first—chasing a high, wanting to have what he gave her again.

She'd not been much for sex before—not an angel, sure, but she didn't have sex *just* to have sex. And yet, that's why she wanted to be here with Corrado doing this. Because this was so fucking good, and he kept drawing her in for more. *Sex is sex*, he'd say, and he wasn't wrong. Sex was physical, a release. It only had emotional weights when someone brought them along.

Was this emotional?

Right then?

God, yeah.

The problems those emotions might cause?

Well …

Fuck it.

Selfish?

Yes.

But why didn't she care again?

Oh, yeah, because of the man with his face currently buried between her thighs. Guilt was hard to comprehend when you still had the tendrils of an orgasm sliding through your veins. Or easier to fucking swallow.

"*You want this?*"

The gruffness of his tone dragged her back into the present with a shudder. Something about his voice changed during sex. But in a really good way. She loved the sound of his voice anytime, but it ramped up like this.

"Ginevra, do you want it?"

"Yeah," she mumbled.

She understood what he asked.

What he *wanted*.

"Now, kitten."

She slipped down his body, her hands steady against the sheets as she moved. Still spinning high, and loving the way he watched her as she took over at his cock once he'd pulled the condom off, she took him in her mouth and hands. She sucked and worked him as his fingers threaded in her hair to pull tight, and his hips flexed upward against her rhythm. Satiny and hot against her tongue, the hint of salt said he would blow soon.

Another one of those groans left his lips—heady, and deep. So fucking husky, too. Her name followed right after, and his tightening fingers stilled in her hair.

"Fuck, kitten …"

The pet name made her shiver. He'd used the name the morning after they first had sex. *Because you are*, he'd said, *as soft as a kitten during sex*. Because he was rough enough for them both.

"*Ginevra*."

He came hard, and she took every drop he gave, letting her throat relax as she swallowed him down. She released him from her mouth, but kept her fingers tight to his base as she stared up at him from his cock.

Corrado grinned back at her. "Look at you, huh?"

She smiled back.

"What's that mean?"

"You … There's something about you like that."

"Tell me when you figure it out."

Corrado laughed darkly. "I *will*. I definitely will."

She had no doubt.

"Let me clean up, yeah?"

Her lips curled up in dislike of the idea, but he only chuckled, and waved his hand. The action alone was enough to remind her that, yeah, he'd taken the condom off, and needed to handle it. She gave a little huff before rolling off him. The sound of his laugher colored up the bedroom. His hand landed to the palm of her ass with a soft crack, before grabbing the spot, and rolling her over in the sheets.

Corrado dropped a quick kiss to her lips as he climbed

over her body to leave the bed. The loss of him seemed substantial as she watched his naked backside disappear into the bathroom. But that was a nice sight, too.

Very nice.

"I have something to do today," he said, voice filtering out of the bathroom.

Ginevra sat up into a cross-legged position in the bed, dragging the sheets to cover her nakedness. She needed to cover herself. Hide what she had done again. Corrado slipped out of the attached bathroom into the walk-in closet.

"Oh?" she asked.

In his tone she found the truth.

Relief, but wariness.

Love but anger.

"Are you going to see Alessio?"

There, she asked.

Ginevra figured if she had any business being in this man's bed after everything, then she at least needed to have the courage to ask him outright about the situation at hand. Right? That didn't mean she would like the answer.

Still, she *had* to ask.

All the noise in the closet quieted, and the silence echoed. A few seconds passed before Corrado came to the doorway, still naked except now he'd pulled on a pair of clean boxer-briefs. Dragging a hand through his hair, his gaze darted around at everything except for her before finally, he met her stare.

"Yes," he said. "He wants to meet up at a place two blocks away. A restaurant, my brother's."

Ginevra nodded and stared down at the sheets bunched at her waist. "Okay."

Her voice came out faint.

"Ginevra."

Her hands became interesting.

The sheets, too.

Anything but his face.

"I hope you figure … whatever … out."

"*Ginny.*"

There were things she didn't want to ask. Stuff the two of them didn't need to talk about yet because she wasn't sure she would like what happened after. She needed to understand why Corrado would take her to bed again and again, but not seem to have an ounce of guilt. What kind of relationship did those two men have inside their bedroom?

Was *this* really okay?

She didn't have a good grasp on her own emotions here.

Dirty.

Blissed.

Ashamed.

Wild.

She felt all of it ….

That's what held her back; kept her quiet.

Ginevra dragged in a shaky breath and decided changing the topic might get them away from this for now. Oh, it wouldn't fix the deep ache in her heart, or how the bed suddenly seemed cold.

"Have you heard anything about New York—my sisters?" she asked.

Still, she stared at her hands on the sheets.

Not at him.

"Not yet," Corrado murmured, "but I can try to get a message through, and see what comes out."

She sighed. "All right."

At night, home filled her mind. About her *sisters.* When no one saw her struggle, or how she cried over things she couldn't control and the fears keeping her company, that's when she allowed herself to wonder.

All the things that might happen, and her helplessness. A rock and a hard place.

It was funny, though, how when she crawled into Corrado's bed at night, and he dared to tell her everything would be okay, she trusted him.

Her worries left.

Sleep came easier.

Or hell, maybe it wasn't funny at all.

"The building is secure, no one knows you're here," Corrado had told Ginevra before he left, "so you're fine to stay here alone. I'm trusting you not to do something to change that —yeah?"

And then he left.

For the first few minutes, Ginevra wandered the large penthouse, moving from room to room trying to find something to keep her occupied. She used to enjoy being alone, but not right now.

She didn't want to consider what Corrado might do with someone else instead of being there with her—where she wanted him to be. Because that was *most* selfish of her. She didn't have any claim here, and not over Corrado. She was the *other*.

She expected nothing from him.

Ginevra wouldn't wallow on the topic, either. It only hurt her more, and she shouldn't feel that, either.

Not now.

Eventually, she found herself in the office and library space again. Her fingers drifted along the edge of a shelf, taking in the spines of the books lined up by size. Not a single one was bigger than the other in whatever row she stared at—all matched. She often came back to this space in the penthouse because for whatever reason, this comforted her.

More than the books, and the escape provided by the words.

Something about here … she craved it; something she didn't even find in Corrado.

Soon, Ginevra found the book she had been looking for on the fourth shelf up from the floor. A book of poems by an author named only as *Anonymous*. That's what had drawn her to the book in the first place; someone didn't want to put their name on their words. As though instead of claiming their art, they wanted to *give* the words to people without the pretense of who created them, or why.

She kept coming back to the book of poems, all ranging in topics from everything like love, to the way sunlight looked on a sidewalk in the month of May. There wasn't rhyme or rhythm to them, but she liked that. She would come into the library, find the book, and read a few pages before sliding it back into the slot.

Someone else had read this *a lot* before she ever found the book. A cracked spine and the dog-eared pages told the story of someone else's appreciation of the words inside.

Opening to her last page, she always remembered the page number and didn't need to dog-ear to find her place, she became lost in words again. Time slipped by when she had a book in her hands, and nothing else to do.

She flipped to a new page—the start of a new poem— when a familiar voice came from behind her, almost making her drop the book.

Goddammit.

"What are you doing in here? Are you supposed to be alone where you might … oh, I don't know, *run*?"

Alessio.

He had a darker quality to his voice than Corrado's. She noticed that about him first. Both spoke with deep tenors that made her pay attention, but something was *different* about Alessio's.

Like he was always holding back.

Never giving *everything*.

Refusing to let the man behind her see he had scared her, Ginevra continued reading the poem as she replied, "Why would I run?"

"I'm not sure if you want to be here."

Ginevra almost laughed. "I didn't at first; I wanted to be with my sisters, but I also don't get a choice, so here I am."

"That doesn't mean you want to be here, though."

"Right now, I do."

He made a noise behind her—gruff, and *curious*. She didn't understand what to make of that, or why he came here again, although it was *his* home along with Corrado, so she focused on things that made sense.

Like the book of poems in her hand.

"Did you trick him again to come here alone?"

Alessio chuckled. "And if I did?"

"He won't like that."

"He doesn't seem to give a shit about what I like lately, either. Fair is fair, yeah?"

Ah.

Yeah.

Ginevra wouldn't argue that point.

"But what *are* you doing in here?" he asked.

"Reading."

"Why?"

"Because I like to."

Alessio made another one of those noises. "But *why?*"

"I like how others express themselves in words. Everyone

is different. I'll read just about anything—*not* a standard text-book meant to teach me something; I learn more reading things that aren't being spoon-fed like I should fit in the same box as everyone else. You can tell a lot more about someone in the way they write than in the things they say."

"Huh."

She didn't expect the response.

Then, again …

"That's not the answer I expected you to give," Alessio murmured. "But still a good one."

Yeah, she was full of surprises.

"It's the only right answer for me. That's why I majored in English." Ginevra shook her head, laughing under his breath. "Not that college matters with me here, I guess."

"You'll get back to school, eventually."

"Who knows?"

"You will. I'm sure he'll make sure of that, if it makes you happy."

She stilled in place.

Did he mean Corrado?

Ginevra turned, only enough to watch Alessio where he stood in the doorway. Not much about him had changed in the time since she had seen him last. He still wore all black, from the jeans molded to his legs, to his leather jacket, and even the black necklace with a cross made of skulls hanging down from his throat. His face, still haunt-ingly handsome, seemed carved from stone. His eyes, hiding secrets and warring emotions, nailed into her from across the room.

She stayed quiet as he scrutinized her. Not because he bothered her. Oh, he unsettled her, sure, and made her fine hairs stand on end, but she didn't *dislike* it, though. She found something familiar in his gaze and recognized it. That intensity in his gaze as he surveyed her from a safe distance was the same way Corrado liked to watch her when he assumed she wasn't looking.

That was the unsettling part.

The only thing that had changed about the man in the doorway since the last time she laid eyes on him was his hair. He lost the shaggy mane he seemed to hide his gaze behind. Shortened around the sides, but still long on the top to push the strands back, if he wanted. A touch wild, still, but more tamed.

It suited him better.

Not that she had any business thinking that at all.

Then, all at once, Alessio rocked back on his heels, hands loose in his pockets, before he came forward, closing the distance between them. Ginevra didn't know if she should keep standing there or get the hell out of his way. That concentration stayed in his gaze like he wanted to burn her to the ground right where she stood, but as though he also found her *extremely* interesting.

Would he hurt her?

Would he do something to her to hurt Corrado?

Those were things she didn't know.

The closer Alessio came, the more Ginevra teetered on a sharp edge. He wasn't the only one curious and muddled in his heart and mind. She only had to *look at him* to feel those things.

What was it about him?

There was something about him that Corrado loved—something that made him get out of bed far earlier than he normally would to chase a *chance*. What was it?

She wondered … how did they fall in love?

"What are you reading?" he asked.

Ginevra broke their staring contest to look down at the book. "*A Life Lived in Words* by—"

"Anonymous."

Swallowing hard, she peeked back up to find he stood next to her. She would still use *overwhelming* to describe this man, and his presence. Imposing fit, too, but she didn't feel like he was imposing on her or this space she adored so much.

"It's my book," Alessio said, "I found it at a used bookstore in Portugal. Figured it was … strange, spine cracked, pages smudged like someone had read the words repeatedly. One of *five* English books in that store."

"Maybe someone lost it?"

"Possibly, but I bought it, and the book made its way into this library."

Ginevra blinked. "It's yours."

"I just said that."

"No, I mean … the library here."

Alessio raised a single dark brow high, and with his new haircut, she realized how much *easier* she could see the things he had hid behind shaggy hair.

"Corrado only reads things that are legal, and he needs to sign."

Ginevra laughed. "That can't be true."

"Mostly, yeah."

"Someone needs to fix that. Did you dog-ear the pages, too?"

The corner of Alessio's mouth twitched. "And what if I did?"

"That's a crime."

"Well, it ain't your book, girl."

She narrowed her gaze at him, half-playful and yet still serious. "Or use a fucking bookmark. And you can call me *Ginevra,* or Ginny. But *not* girl."

His lips twitched *again*.

Then, he smiled.

A full-blown grin.

The first thing to come to her mind?

My God.

Because it was devastating.

Not sardonic, or sly. Not jealous, or angry.

No, just *genuine*.

And his smile was beautiful.

Ginevra's heart squeezed painfully. What in the hell was wrong with her? She had no place thinking something like that about this man.

Not at all.

Alessio's blue eyes flashed with something she didn't recognize. Another thing he was holding back.

Did he do that a lot?

Stop, Ginevra, you don't need to worry about this man.

"I didn't get the chance to finish the book," Alessio said, dropping her gaze to peek at the book again. "*And this thing, misunderstood and overlooked, vivid but understated, and which shatters and grows and is, will always be, at the heart, most human. For we love, we always love.*"

Ginevra blinked.

Stunned.

She said nothing as she flipped back the pages, knowing where to find those words he spoke. She found it easily. One of the *first* poems in the book. She remembered it, too, because she thought it was one of the best in the book. One or two, sometimes three, words to a line, three stanzas, of which he only spoke one, and yet, she felt every single syllable as it spoke of love being, at its core, *human*.

The last stanza of three stared up at her from the stark white pages, the corner dog-eared like Alessio had intended to come back to it, and the edge of the paper smudged like someone touched it often.

And this thing,
misunderstood
and overlooked,
vivid
but understated,
and which shatters
and grows
and is,
will always be,
at the heart,
most human.
For we love,
we always love.

He had known it by heart.

How long had it been since he had this book?

And he *remembered that?*

"One of my favorites in there," he said.

His fingers drifted along the edge of the book in her hands. When his fingertips brushed the side of her palm as he was pulling away, Ginevra froze. Not *because* he'd touched her at all, but because of the way it felt and what it *did*. How it warmed her and shocked her all at the same time. An energy she couldn't explain, a shift that felt *visceral*.

So fucking real.

And not at all what she asked for.

She glanced up only to find he wasn't looking at the book at all, but rather, at her. Gone was that angry, dark glint in his eyes from earlier, now replaced with *only* that curiosity she had seen.

How did the saying go?

Curiosity killed the cat.

"I don't think I wonder *why* he found something in you," Alessio murmured, "I wonder what it *is*."

Ginevra swallowed hard, confused by this man. "I didn't ask for—"

"That doesn't change that it is—it's a thing now."

Yeah.

He wasn't wrong.

Alessio tipped his head to the side, his grin deepening to something more sinful. It was enough to take her breath away, but that only left her perplexed. "Would you like to read the next one?"

Needing to break his stare, she peered down, and flipped the page without thinking. The black words printed on the white paper stared up at her, and as her gaze took the poem in, she felt her cheeks heat.

Damn.

She'd forgotten what the next one was.

> *He sounds*
> *rough,*
> *when he needs you.*
> *There is*
> *fire,*
> *as he loves you.*
> *He discovers*
> *life,*
> *as he fucks you.*

Ginevra's voice grew faint, but *hot,* as she spoke the last word. It was all of one stanza, and twenty-one words. But it felt *purposeful*, as though he'd known what the next poem in the book would be, and he wanted her to read it.

"Another favorite," he murmured.

She desperately wanted to look at *anything* but him, and yet, her gaze lifted to see what he looked like right then. So, she might know if there was something to see there that he wasn't saying.

Instead, she found him staring at her lips.

"Did you like that," he asked, his tone roughening, "watching us from the end of the hallway that night? Did you know we shared women? Us together, I mean. It was *fun* —fair game. And then there was you, and he broke the fucking rules."

"I—"

"Yes or no suffices, Ginevra. You either *liked* seeing us like that—*together*—and you want to see more, or you didn't. Yes or no."

Fine.

If that's the game he wanted to play.

"Yes."

Alessio chuckled, his thumb edging along the page in the book before raising, so he could slide the pad of the digit against the seam of her *mouth*. She hadn't expected the touch until it was right there, but she couldn't find it in herself to back away.

Not when he was looking at her like that.

Yeah …

Entirely *overwhelming*.

That's what this man was.

"If you liked that," he told her, "then you should see us when we *fuck*."

She sucked in a sharp breath.

Alessio winked before leaning in and pulling his thumb away to drop a featherlight kiss to her lips. There was something *wicked* about the kiss. How his lips moved against hers, and then his tongue swept the seam of her mouth to coax it open for him. She didn't need to be *kissing* the man whose lover she had been in bed with that morning, but she answered his kiss back.

It felt natural.

And sinful.

Then, as fast as it had happened, it was over, and he stepped back. Not that it mattered.

She felt it.

Everywhere.

The same way she could still taste him—a minty heat—lingering on her tongue and lips. Ginevra took a step back, too, needing the distance, and holding the open book closer to herself like that might stop him from doing it again. And why did she want that?

Because she liked the kiss.

As quick as it had been.

She still *liked it*.

"Why would you do that?" she asked, airless.

To hurt Corrado?

Or confuse her?

To make *this* worse?

Alessio lifted one shoulder, the hint of a smile creeping in. "I wanted to know if your lips were as soft as they looked, that's all."

She still couldn't breathe.

"That was why?"

"Does there have to be another reason?"

Ginevra wished her throat wasn't so tight, or that her heart would calm. "I think there is when the circumstances here are not—"

"If I wanted to cause Corrado pain, because I know that's what you think, I wouldn't use you to do it. I know the best place to hit that man to make it hurt, and I promise it isn't *you*. Not yet, anyway. We'll see if that changes."

"What does that even mean?"

"It means, I kissed you because I wanted to. Nothing else, so don't make it into something when it's nothing."

It didn't feel like nothing.

She was sure, to him, it couldn't be *nothing*.

"But you shouldn't—"

"I shouldn't do a lot of things I do, and here I still am, doing it."

Ginevra ran the tip of her tongue along the edge of her lips, finding more of his flavor there. "You're a complex man."

Perplexing.

And difficult, likely.

She had that feeling.

Alessio hummed low and waved a finger at her. "You're not wrong."

Well, at least he knew what he was.

That was a start.

"You should go back to the spot where I had to stop reading, and start from there," he said, turning and dropping into a nearby chair like his body was water, and it all moved at once. Hooking his combat boots one over the other at the ankles along the arm of the chair, he nodded at her. "Go on, it's been a while since someone read me poetry."

"You want me to read to you?"

"Why not?"

Yes.

That was a good question.

Why not?

Ginevra didn't have an answer.

So, she found the page he'd left dog-eared toward the

middle of the book, the last marking he had made, and read. Alessio watched her the whole time, and she felt that, too.

His gaze?

Yeah.

She felt that right down to her bones. Like he was trying to figure her out, or learn what made her tick by staring at her. But what did he think he would find?

That was the better question.

CHAPTER 3
CORRADO

What the fuck are you nervous for? It's Les. Les.

Corrado's thoughts were a special brand of his own personal hell as he parked his vehicle along the side of the restaurant that belonged to his twin. One of the few businesses Chris cared to use on his investment portfolio.

Cutting the engine on the black Porsche, he stared at the windows lining the side of the business, but the glare of the sunlight kept him from seeing inside. Where would Alessio be sitting in there? Near a window to watch people—he liked doing that—so did that mean he could see Corrado right then? Or was he sitting nearer to the front?

He drummed his fingers to the leather-wrapped steering wheel, trying to shake off that edginess. It didn't work, instead burrowing even deeper into his heart. How long had it been since Alessio showed up in Toronto now?

Two days shy of three weeks.

Nearly three weeks Corrado had spent wondering, and worrying, and ... too much. He knew Alessio needed his time, but that didn't make it any easier on Corrado even though he still tried to give his lover space.

And *now* ...

Now he wanted to close that space.

Fuck it.

Refusing to over think this more than he already had, Corrado pulled the fob, that also acted as the key, from the starter, and opened the Porsche's suicide doors to step out into the bright daylight. The humid August air wrapped around his three-piece suit, reminding him that black had been a bad choice for the day, but screw it.

He liked a good suit.

Taking the walkway along the side of the building, he entered the restaurant at the front, stepping under the entrance enclave that welcomed patrons with gold and black drapery that spoke of the truth behind this place.

Mob owned.

Specifically, Guzzi owned.

All one needed to do was look at the color scheme, gold and black. The Guzzi family colors, they showcased them on their coat of arms, throughout their businesses, and anywhere else they might be able to sneak it in. One of the few things someone was able to count on where his family's legacy was concerned. Before the Guzzis had become synonymous with crime, they had made their riches in black gold.

Oil.

Inside, Corrado greeted the woman behind the podium, but didn't bother to let her direct him inside the restaurant. She recognized his face—it matched her boss's, considering it was Chris's place, and she was accustomed to the Guzzis coming and going. Beyond the entrance, Corrado found a busy restaurant waiting for him.

Tables full.

Booths at the windows busy, too.

The breakfast bar had patrons milling around.

Exactly as he thought. It wasn't what he expected to find that irked the hell out of him, but rather, what he didn't find.

Alessio.

Corrado's gaze searched the large main floor of the restaurant, but he didn't find Alessio's familiar face. There was a small private dining area that Chris liked to use for private meetings, but he didn't think Alessio would be back in the area.

Which meant one thing …

"*Fucking hell.*"

Alessio had tricked him again.

Corrado was tiring of that goddamn game.

A quiet chuckle at his left had Corrado turning to see who was laughing, because for some reason, it felt like they were laughing at him. The universe seemed to enjoy having a laugh at his expense, so why would this be different?

To his left, he found his twin.

Chris drank from a cup of coffee with steam rising around the rim where he sat in a booth next to the window. "Looking for someone?"

"Were you aware he planned this?"

"I had breakfast with him this morning, so yes … and no."

Corrado's jaw tensed. "And you didn't give me a heads-up, or …?"

"He showed up here, Corrado. He knows this is where I do business in the mornings, and where I take my breakfast. I figured out his plan after he asked if I would be around because you might show up. Right before he left."

A sigh passed his lips.

Chris shrugged. "But hey, at least he's out of the mansion now."

That made Corrado pause. "Excuse me?"

"Ma and Papa's place—that's where he was staying."

"What?"

And his mother and father didn't think to tell him?

That irked him, too.

Sort of …

To be fair, he hadn't called his parents and asked them anything about Alessio, or his whereabouts, because he figured they probably didn't know. Why would they? And, he also didn't want to bother them with everything going on in his life, but especially the personal shit. Didn't they have enough to deal with?

Another part of Corrado found it comforting that Alessio went to his parents', out of all the places he might have hidden himself away. Like *that's* where he thought would be safest for him. *Corrado's family.*

Huh.

Chris took a drink from his coffee. Corrado figured that looked like something he should do, too. Relax for a minute and rethink this whole thing before he headed back to the penthouse to deal with the frustrating man waiting for him. Waving at a server passing with a tray of dishes she'd bussed from a table nearby, he was quick to say, "Another black coffee over here, if you wouldn't mind."

He'd add in his own sugar and cream from the table.

The server gave him a bright smile. "Sure, sir."

Chris eyed him from the side. "You're not going right home? I figured you would, knowing he's with her."

Corrado shook his head and dropped into the booth opposite of his brother. "He's not going to hurt her. Not Les's style, and all."

"I didn't assume that, either." Chris cleared his throat and dropped his brother's gaze. "I meant, more that you might be jealous the two of them are alone together."

"Why?"

"Because if someone I was fucking was alone with someone else, and the circumstances were … like yours, I might get irritated about it."

Corrado nodded. "And you're not me … or him."

Or her, but Ginevra was still a wild card here.

"I don't understand how your relationships work at all."

Corrado laughed. "You don't have to. It's not *your* relationship, and you're not the one they're fucking, Chris."

"That's probably a good thing."

Right?

"Besides," Corrado said, pulling the sugar and cream bowls closer to him as the server neared their table with a carafe of coffee ready, "the more time they spend with one another, the better it'll be for me."

Chris arched a brow at the statement, but waited until the server had poured Corrado's cup of coffee, and then left them alone before he spoke. "Why would that be good for you?"

That seemed obvious.

Corrado lifted his shoulders. "Then, perhaps I can get what I want."

"Which is …?"

"Both."

Chris let out a sigh across the table, giving his brother *the* look. They both used it—identical twins and all, right? It said he was annoyed and amused all in one breath. "That's a little selfish, yeah? You made a mess in your relationship with one, and then you dragged the other one into it without giving them the benefit of knowing what you were doing first. And now you want both like they should just … fall in line?"

"That's fair." Corrado stirred sugar into his coffee first, following up with the cream. "But it still feels right."

That's what mattered to him.

Besides, he wanted what he wanted.

Guzzis always got what they wanted.

Corrado didn't want to return to the penthouse pissed. He took his time going back. He figured … Alessio clearly wanted to do something there, or whatever. He wanted *something*, and Corrado would give him the chance to find it. It wouldn't hurt Ginevra to spend time with Alessio, if she was able to handle his swinging moods.

Corrado wasn't any better in that respect, and hell, she handled him fine. He had no doubt Alessio would be the same.

So, when he stepped inside the penthouse to *laughter*, he took a second to soak it in. It confused him, sure, and he had to listen again to make sure he heard what he thought he did … but yes, they were laughing.

Together.

Corrado didn't bother to kick off his shoes, or remove his jacket before heading down the entrance. He came to a stop at the end, staying beyond the entryway to stare into the sitting room, finding the laughter.

The first thing he noticed?

Alessio had cut his hair.

Gone was his almost *a-little-too-long* shaggy dark brown, almost black, style, only to be replaced with a shorter, but still wild, style. It never escaped Corrado's notice how Alessio was, in many ways, his opposite. Corrado was the calm to Alessio's storm. From the way they styled their hair, to the clothing they wore.

Corrado would never ink his skin.

Never pierce his body.

Alessio did those things and more.

Regularly.

He liked this new hairstyle though. It showed Alessio's eyes, even if all Corrado could see was the man's profile. Now, Alessio didn't have dark strands of hair to hide behind when he didn't want someone to look in his gaze—which was where Corrado always found the truth hiding.

Sitting opposite to Alessio on the couch with her legs

thrown over the back as she rested on her back, and played the game on the television, Ginevra laughed again as Alessio shook his head.

"That's what he's saying here, okay, it says right there in the line. That's how you know he's talking about sunlight in this one. *Streams shooting high, blinding and bright, yellows and*—"

"It could be a sh*e,*" Ginevra replied, never looking away from the game as she conversed. "You're *assuming* it's a man, and you shouldn't. Anonymous might be a woman. A lot of the poems in the book reference *men,* anyway. Sex, relationships, love ... many discuss men, and not in *first person*, either."

Alessio made a noise under his breath. "It could be a man talking about all of those things with another man, too."

Corrado blinked.

Were they talking about ...

Poetry?

"So, what you mean to say is your *bias*—because you're a bisexual, and in a relationship with a man—clouds how you interpret poems written by someone, who for all we know, is genderless, faceless, and ... well, personless."

Alessio stared hard at Ginevra, even though she wasn't looking back at him. Corrado found himself all too amused at the concentration knotting Alessio's brow as he took in Ginevra like he was trying to figure her out. *Finally*, someone to challenge this man and his need for words.

Corrado could never do it.

Reading wasn't his thing.

"How did we go from talking about whether this poem is referencing sunlight to you deciding I'm biased on the author of it?" Alessio asked, cocking his head to the side as his gaze narrowed on the woman who was still playing her game like this wasn't at all a big deal to her. "Because maybe I like to put pronouns on things, Ginny. It doesn't have to be that *deep*."

"Oh, but it does, because everything is deep, Les. *Everything* when you read, or how you interpret it, but especially poetry, has meaning. The things you find between the lines, for example. Word play. It is all important. That is the author's intention, but more so one who wrote an entire book of poetry under the name *Anonymous*, because they wanted you to consider them, or perhaps …"

"What?"

"Perhaps it was written with the intention to put yourself in their place."

Ginevra paused the game and turned to give Alessio all of her attention. A small smile curved her pretty, pink lips, and the sly glint in her eyes only added to the appeal. Alessio stared back, engrossed in the conversation, and unwilling to back away.

Good, Corrado thought. *Now he can see why … maybe.*

There was something about Ginevra.

Something that *fit*.

Not just him.

Alessio, too.

"Maybe, it was written like it was," Ginevra said, "because the author wanted to write it for you, for me, the man walking down the street, or the woman sitting on the bench in the park … for my friend at college, or the professor at the front of the class. For *anyone*. So, every person could see the words and put themselves there. Because once a name gets attached to a book, whether we mean to, we put a face and a person to who wrote it, or what we *believe* about the person who wrote it based on the penname they chose, and what it means. Like this, we read it differently."

Alessio relaxed into the couch, considering. "Huh."

"And they could still be talking about the color yellow, and not something else, so …"

"It's sunlight, Ginevra."

"Says you. Not once, in any of the four stanzas, does it reference the sky, clouds, the color blue, and it doesn't even use words like *overhead*, or *up above* to make us think *high*, like the sky. So, no, it doesn't have to be the sun just because you want it to be."

Her argument made, she went back to her game, unpausing it and clicking away at buttons on the remote.

"Jesus Christ," Alessio muttered, turning his attention away from her only for his gaze to land on Corrado in the hallway. For a brief second, something unknown flashed in Alessio's eyes, almost like he didn't know how to feel about the fact Corrado was there, watching them. Just as quickly, something else replaced it. *Cunningness.* "Looks like we have a visitor, Ginny."

She peeked around the edge of the couch, craning her neck just enough to see Corrado in the hallway, before going back to the game. "Seems so."

Corrado put his focus on Alessio, for the moment. "The haircut is new."

"I like to come back with something new, don't I?"

Ginevra passed a look to her companion on the couch. "What does that mean?"

"It means he changes his appearance with different things when he's away on …" Corrado considered his words, and how he wanted to say *that*. "… a job. That's how he got the piercing in his nose, the ones in his nipples, the second sleeve of tattoos, and more. Sometimes, he keeps them, and other times, he doesn't. All depends."

Alessio grinned over at Ginevra. "Reminds me of where I've been."

"Except you didn't *really* leave, did you?"

Just like that, Alessio's smirk faded away as his gaze turned back on Corrado. "I wasn't *here*. Same difference."

"According to you. How are my parents?"

"Fantastic."

Corrado nodded. "Good. And, if you want to be here, you don't have to trick me away, Les."

"Or you shouldn't keep falling for it."

The snickers from the woman on the couch made Corrado narrow his gaze. Alessio's smirk was back in place, like he enjoyed this.

"What are you two doing?"

"Reading poetry," Ginevra said, although he couldn't see her now she'd slid lower on the couch.

"And gaming," Alessio added, "or she is … she beat your score, too."

Corrado glanced at the television.

Ginevra had done that, playing the online version which connected her to his account which he'd been working on back in Vegas.

Dammit.

He worked *months* for the score.

Oh, well.

He couldn't be mad.

Right?

CHAPTER 4
ALESSIO

"Could we chat for a minute?" Corrado asked, stepping closer to the two on the couch as he nodded his head toward the back hallway leading deeper into the penthouse. "If you're ... not busy here, I mean."

Alessio might have enjoyed the sight of seeing Corrado confused—but also amused?—but he figured, this was going to happen, too. Them *talking*, like it would change what needed to be said.

It wouldn't.

Alessio wasn't ready for that.

"Why not?" Alessio tossed the book of poems to the couch before standing. Then, to Ginevra, he said, "And it's still talking about sunlight."

She grinned but didn't look away from the TV.

"Probably," she returned, "but we don't know for sure, do we?"

He arched a brow, considering those words. She wasn't wrong, but he thought she also didn't realize how her words could be applied to a lot of other things in his life currently. Like *this*, and Corrado. Them, and whatever the hell they were doing.

He was here because he needed to be.

A part of him searching for something.

Another part wanting to *fix it*.

Yet, he wasn't sure if those things were possible. Would

he find what he was looking for here, and could they fix the mess they were now in? He was going to try for both, but he didn't know anything for sure.

"Also," Ginevra said while Alessio rounded the couch, "if you two could just *talk*, and not … you know, do what you did before while I sit out here alone, that'd be great. I would appreciate it."

Alessio passed Corrado a look, smirking a bit at the sight of his lover's face brightening with his surprise at Ginevra's frankness. Did he not get that from her a lot? Because Alessio found Ginevra was straightforward when she wanted to be, and he enjoyed that.

More than he should.

"Oh, she's sassy," Alessio said, heading for the hallway, "and you know how I like that."

Corrado's sigh echoed.

Alessio's laughter chased behind it.

He took the first door in the hallway, to the master bedroom. Not five seconds later, Corrado followed behind Alessio, although he didn't close the door. The sheets on the bed had been thrown aside. Rumpled and messy.

Two people slept here.

Fucked there.

"I thought you didn't want to be in here because I was—"

"It's not about the sex," Alessio said, turning fast to face Corrado where he stood just beyond the doorway. "It was never about the fact you wanted to fuck her, Corrado."

"Yeah, I know." Corrado stuffed his hands into his pockets as Alessio took a seat in the chair near the far window. There, he could watch Corrado's reflection, but also enjoy the cloudless sky overhead. "Did you want to be alone with her today—this was purposeful?"

"Yep."

"Could you try *not* being an asshole, or make any trouble, because you're in your feelings right now? This is bigger than us—it's about her safety, too. That's why she's here in the first place, to stay out of sight, and be somewhere safe while Andino Marcello handles her family in New York."

Alessio's brow dipped. "Do you think I'm that petty?"

"Pardon?"

He stood from the chair, deciding he could do without comfort while he handled this *thing* Corrado was dancing around. Closing the space between them with wide strides, Alessio came toe to toe with Corrado, and only then did he speak again.

"Do you think I am so petty I would put her in danger because you *like her*? Is that the man you believe I am, Corrado? Because if so… we need to have a different discussion."

He let that hang between them.

It was Corrado's move now.

God knew Alessio didn't come here because he wanted to shout and fight again. They'd done that already—he said enough shit to last them a lifetime. That's not what this was about, now.

He was *trying*.

Corrado needed to try, too.

"I know *exactly* what kind of man you are," Corrado murmured, holding Alessio's gaze, and refusing to drop it, "but I also know when you're hurt, you act out even when you don't mean to, Les. So, if you're still working on *that* … let me know. Her safety here—not from *you*, not like that— is a priority for me."

Alessio made a noise, deep and dark. "And what other priority does she have?"

"See, like *that*."

Okay, so Corrado wasn't wrong.

Alessio put his attitude in check.

"I'm working on it," Alessio said simply. "It's the best I can do."

"All right."

Alessio broke their stare first, instead finding a spot on the wall to focus on as he said, "I'm here because it's more than just her right now. It's us, too. You owe me that—to decide this, and what we're doing together. You owe it to me, Corrado."

"I do."

"That's all you want to say?"

"That should be all I need to say. Is it confusing and a mess? Yeah, Les, I know. But you're *here,* so I can deal with the rest, and we can figure that out as we go. I can't change the circumstance, and even if I could … I don't know if I want to."

"Right, because you're *happy* with what you did. You're pleased with what you've got here right now. A woman you want to keep, and a man you can't let go of—with you in the middle, huh?"

"And you seem to think that's *easy* for me. Like this mess doesn't keep me up at night wondering what the fuck happened, or why, and you're wrong. Because I know what I did, but I'm the only one trying to figure it out or fix it right now."

"No, I'm here. *I'm here.*"

That should mean something.

Shouldn't it?

Alessio thought so.

"I just … want to know why," Alessio said, shrugging one shoulder and still focusing on that spot on the wall. It was easier than looking at Corrado because when he did that, his emotions came into play, and he couldn't compartmentalize the anger and sadness and betrayal with the parts of him that didn't want to feel any of those things at all. "Why her, and why *this*. But also, why she has you like this … why you did this *now* … after five fucking years, you did this now."

"Do you want to know?"

"*Yes*."

He figured that was obvious.

Or it should be.

"But do you *really*," Corrado pressed, making Alessio's attention snap back to him at the deeper tenor his tone took on. "Because you've always been touchy, Les, about me, what's yours, and when you think someone is encroaching on things that belong to only you. Yeah, you don't make it obvious sometimes, but you still do it. And don't act like you didn't come here because you felt like someone was *encroaching* on me, and you didn't like that."

It was the challenge in Corrado's stare that kept Alessio silent—the unspoken *I dare you to lie right now* that Corrado wouldn't say.

"Well?" Corrado asked.

Alessio swallowed the thickness in his throat. "You're not wrong."

It was his favorite way to say someone was right *without* showing his whole ass even if it irritated Corrado to no end.

"She's not a man," Alessio said, "so I shouldn't have felt that way at all, but I did because you *hid her* and your intentions. You put me in this position, in this fucking head space I don't want to be in, and I can't jump right out of it because you snap your goddamn fingers and tell me to."

"I don't expect you to."

"But I don't know what I want to do now, either," Alessio muttered, "and that pisses me off more. You didn't give me a choice here, Corrado. I'm here, or I'm *gone.* Those are the options I have … five fucking years with you, and those are the options I'm left with. To stay here, and watch you *be* with her because you want to, or walk away alone. It should be an easy choice—I'm tired of what we've been doing, but I've still got *you*, right?"

"Until I die, yeah."

Alessio sneered, angry again just like that. "So, yeah, you put me back there like you did five years ago. Where I have to make the choice between keeping you, because at least I get a part of what I love, or walking away and having none of it. So thank you for that, really."

"Les—"

"Just, don't."

Corrado dragged in a heavy breath and dropped Alessio's stare. "It's only like that because you don't want me to tell you what you want to hear right now because she's involved. If she wasn't here, you'd let me say and tell you *all of it*. The shit I didn't say five years ago, the issues you kept running from, and I ignored … I'd say it but she's here, and that changes it for you again."

Again, he wasn't wrong.

Alessio shook his head. "I want to understand why it was her. Why now?"

They weren't even questions.

Mostly because, he didn't know if there were answers.

"I can explain it, but once I do, when it's all out there, everything will change again. Is that what you want to happen? Because I will, Les. I'll say what you wanted me to say for the last five years, but I will say something about her, too, and it will change things. So, if that's what you need, and you want to handle all of it, then let me know."

Alessio stayed quiet.

He heard what Corrado said.

He knew what it meant.

And fuck …

"Not yet," he said under his breath. "I don't think I can

understand yet, and I know it's important to you, and *this* ... I need time."

"Just tell me when."

Time for Alessio also meant space—he needed *both*. Which was fucking hilarious, the world was laughing at his stupid ass, because at the same time ... he didn't want to leave here. He needed to *be* here. Something inside told him he wouldn't find what he needed *away* from Corrado, and this home.

"I'm staying here, though. In this penthouse, I mean."

Corrado shrugged like he expected nothing different. "Our names are on the deed. It's your home, too. You good?"

"Not even close."

"I'm sorry."

But all it took was Corrado's hand coming out from his side so that his fingertips could glide along the inner skin of Alessio's wrist. A *soft* touch, something he wasn't at all used to with this man when they were doing their thing. He expected roughness ... but never in their quiet moments, he knew.

Never then.

Alessio let out a slow stream of air, flipping his hand around, and let his fingers weave with Corrado's. The touch was brief, with featherlight pressure, and he didn't look at his lover, but he needed that.

A *them* moment amid everything else.

It was good.

Right.

Then, Alessio let Corrado go, and moved to head out of the bedroom, but stopped beside him first to say, "And I kissed her earlier, so you know."

Corrado cleared his throat. "Did you?"

"I did."

"Hmm." Corrado glanced to the side, cocking a brow

when his gaze met Alessio's. "Was that because you wanted to hurt me, confuse her, or something else?"

Alessio smirked.

Really?

"One—I don't need to use her to hurt you. *Ever.*"

"Fair," Corrado replied.

"Two—that woman is a lot of things, but confused isn't one of them when she's getting something she wants. And she wanted that."

"Be careful with that, she's not used to this thing like we are." Then, Corrado nodded, his tongue peeking out to run along the edge of his bottom lip. "So, your reason for doing it was the *something else?*"

"I wanted to kiss her. That's all."

"And you always take what you want, don't you?"

Alessio winked. "That I do."

Back in the living room, Alessio took his position on the couch he had vacated earlier. Ginevra looked his way as he picked up the book, too, but continued playing her game like nothing was happening. Corrado hung back in the hallway like he hadn't decided whether he wanted to join them.

"So," Ginevra said, still watching the screen, her tone playful, "where is everyone sleeping?"

The black Cartier watch on Alessio's wrist ticked past twelve at night as Corrado stepped into the penthouse's home gym. Corrado found Alessio perched on top of the bars they used for chin-ups. The single, smooth bar of metal secured between two beams wasn't the most comfortable place to sit, but it gave him a better view out of the windows, and made him seem unavailable to conversation.

Which he was because—

"Is that the book Ginevra was reading?" Corrado asked.

Alessio rolled his eyes and peered up from the words on the page. "The poems, yeah."

"Didn't she take that to bed with her?"

Why was he asking questions?

It was easier *not* to ask.

Alessio didn't want to explain that he'd felt the strangest urge to sneak that book from Ginevra's bedside table and take a peek at where she left off before falling asleep.

"I'll put it back before she wakes up," he muttered.

That was way too defensive, asshole.

Corrado's brow lifted, but he said nothing in reply to that. "Just curious."

"I noticed she's not in *your* bed," Alessio said.

"You're here," Corrado replied. "I left the option open, if she wanted, and I think her conscience sent her across the hall."

Right.

"Or her morals, yeah?"

Corrado sighed. "Are they not the same thing?"

"Not really. One means she might feel guilty, and the other says she thinks it's wrong to have sex with someone in a relationship with someone else, Corrado. Guilt is a byproduct of an action."

"I don't think the latter is the problem, all things considered."

"Or it becomes a problem when the other person is using the bedroom down the hall."

"I didn't come find you to talk about where Ginevra is sleeping," Corrado said sharply.

Ah.

Who's defensive *now*?

"Well," Alessio said, shifting and dropping to the floor

eight feet below soundlessly, "I suppose that means you're sleeping alone then, doesn't it?"

Corrado gave him a look.

Alessio just shrugged.

That was his way of telling his lover he wouldn't be joining him in bed, either. And if there was anything Corrado hated the most, it was sleeping alone. Maybe it was because he'd become used to Alessio sharing a bed with him over the years, or because he woke up ready to fuck as soon as he cracked his eyes open.

It could have been a lot of things.

"You should suffer a *little*," Alessio murmured as he came to stand in front of Corrado in the doorway, "for what you did. Take your penance, Corrado."

"You're an asshole."

"Do you have something new to tell me?"

"I have a question."

Alessio tipped his head to the side, tucking that book under his arm as he shoved his other hand into his pocket. "Give it to me, then."

"Why did you go to my family when you needed time alone? I think I know … I want to hear you say it."

Alessio's shoulders tensed at the question, his heart thundering with sharp beats that ached all the way through his bloodstream. If Corrado owed him certain things, then he might as well admit there was shit he should give back to the man, too.

"They remind me of you."

Corrado's gaze drifted over Alessio with slow intent. He wanted *something*. To be close—*closer*—to touch, or to fuck. To have the thing he wanted, or one, which was Alessio. It was his gaze that always told the truth when his mouth didn't.

"Oh?" Corrado asked, his stare coming back up to meet Alessio's.

"And even when I hate you, Corrado," Alessio said, his words a whisper before he leaned in to press a quick kiss to Corrado's mouth, pulling away just as fast to add, "I still love you."

He left Corrado alone in the gym.

It was for the best even if it was the last thing he wanted. They could fuck this out like they did other fights they had in the past. They could find a familiar comfort in the physical side of this together. The thing was, it would only work for so long. More shit swept under a very dirty rug.

It wouldn't *fix it*.

Sometimes, the right choice was the hard one.

Including walking away.

CHAPTER 5
GINEVRA

Tucked into the checkered pattern bucket chair, with her feet resting on the ottoman, Ginevra was more interested in the two men across from her rather than the movie. Alessio, comfortable in a chair, set his arms along the recliner, and Corrado, on the couch next to him, kept glancing over at the other man.

Something was bothering Corrado … She could tell in the way he kept shaking his head subtly, and his gaze kept narrowing back on Alessio every twenty or so seconds.

Ginevra couldn't figure out what.

It could be anything, really. A week after Alessio decided he was *staying* in the penthouse, and she wasn't sure what any of them were doing together, or what was happening. They all gave each other a wide berth of space, safe conversation was a must, and nobody stepped on anyone's toes.

She was back to sleeping alone.

So were they.

They all moved around each other like they were familiar strangers, as if that was possible. Nods in the mornings, and hellos at the table. Little else, though. She was sure Alessio and Corrado hadn't worked out their issues, and *she* hadn't settled herself with everything happening here, but for now … this was what they did.

Nothing.

It was awkward.

"Jesus Christ, will you give me those?" Corrado snapped.

Alessio turned his attention from the television, a smirk playing at that edges of his lips as he did so. "Does it bother you that badly?"

"*Yes*, it's annoying. You know I hate it when you let them get like that."

What were they going on about?

Ginevra tucked herself tighter under the blanket she was using while watching the movie. This way, she could hide her grin because for a brief second, Alessio and Corrado looked like lovers arguing with one another, and not … whatever in the fuck they had been for the last week.

She liked this sight of them more.

And that only left her confused.

"Fine," Alessio muttered.

In a blink, he flipped his wrist over, placing it across the arm of the couch where Corrado was sitting at the end. Ginevra watched, fascinated and amused, as Corrado seemed too pleased while he untangled the thin, black braided bracelets on Alessio's wrist. Maybe fifteen. All twisted into a mess of a knot because of the delicate design.

Corrado worked in silence, his gaze lifting to check what was happening on the movie, before he went back to untangling again. Alessio, as though this was normal and something Corrado did, paid the other man no mind.

Did they do this often?

Sometimes, she thought they forgot Ginevra was in the penthouse with them. They often had silent conversations, even when standing across the room from one another. Shared looks, and quiet noises she didn't understand, but they seemed to comprehend from the other just fine.

It was yet another testament to her about just how long these two men had been together. That their lives, even if on the outside they seemed entirely different, were very intertwined. They fit better together, but for now, they were still too far apart.

And she was right in the middle.

It took all of five minutes.

Alessio pulled his arm back when Corrado released his wrist, all the braided cords sitting nicely against each other instead of the mess they had been. "Better?"

Corrado shrugged. "Getting there."

"Hmm."

Ginevra raised a brow, wondering what in the hell she had just watched. "How did you two meet?"

Corrado stilled on the couch, but didn't take his gaze away from the screen. Alessio tipped his head sideways as he peered over at Ginevra.

"Work."

"Easy," Corrado muttered.

"She asked."

"That doesn't mean she needs to know."

"Except that's exactly what it means."

Corrado let out a sigh and pushed up from the couch. He didn't even bother to say goodbye, or explain what he was doing before he left the sitting room, and disappeared into the hallway. Ginevra was still staring at the spot where he'd left when Alessio grunted under his breath, gaining her attention instead.

"What was that about?" she asked.

Alessio clicked his tongue. "He doesn't *talk* well."

"He talks perfectly fine."

"Okay, his communication is sometimes shit."

Ginevra considered it. "Yeah, that's fair."

"And he's in a mood."

"I figured. It's the whys."

Alessio chuckled. "He's sleeping alone, and he isn't getting to fuck first thing when he wakes up. He doesn't have quiet time in the morning because when he does roll his ass out of bed, there's already two other people in this house that have been up for hours. Oh, and he doesn't like to run on a treadmill, but he hates jogging on a city street, so all he has is the gym here. He ran out of his favorite whiskey he likes in his nightly coffee three days ago and hasn't gone out to get more. The current ringtone on my phone irritates the hell out of him, but he won't tell me to change it. You sat on the chair instead of next to him when we started the movie. Pick one, Ginevra."

She blinked.

He … *knew* all of that.

Like he'd been keeping a tab.

"I'm very out of place here," she murmured.

Alessio's amusement faded. "Or you need time to learn." He waved a hand, adding quieter, "He's moody, difficult, and *fickle*. Constantly. His mornings often determine how the rest of his day is going to go, and God knows it's better for everyone when it goes well. And yet, he puts up with my shit, too, or the fact he has to turn on the heat in the penthouse at night because you won't sleep under a blanket."

Ginevra guffawed. "That's—"

"The truth. Everybody's human, and it's not the flaws that make up the person … we all have those, and it's only a small portion of what defines us. Corrado isn't easy to deal with, but I'm not perfect, either, and neither are you. If you want to know why he gets into his moods, then pay attention. You'll figure it out, too."

They stared at each other, but neither spoke. He had offered her something—the confirmation she was *wanted* here, by at least one. And she was kind enough not to point it out to him.

Alessio had his pain, after all.

"So, will you tell me how you met?"

She figured a change in subject was needed.

Alessio let out a steady stream of air, his smile growing again. "The League."

"What is—"

"An ... organization," he interjected carefully. "Do you want me to be frank, or color it up with goodness for you?"

"I'm sorry?"

"I know where you came from—who you are. So, you're aware of *some* things about this world, and how it works. You recognize things are not always black and white because some of us, like me and Corrado, or the people you come from, live in shades of gray."

"Corrado told me he was worse than them once. Made men, I mean. The mafia."

Alessio nodded. "He's not wrong, either."

She stilled, a chill running down her spine. "But what does it mean?"

"The League trains people—we walk in one way and walk out another. Think of it like this ... a man comes back from a war, he has a *very* specialized set of skills that is no longer useful to his country, and won't help him in civilian life. What's he to do?"

"I'm not sure."

"The League does. They'll train him, and he'll either become an independent contractor for the organization, or he'll be auctioned off to a buyer who will decide, depending on his skill set, what kind of jobs he might do. Recons, hits, robberies, recoveries ... more. It all depends on what someone needs, and what the person with the skills is capable of. The training takes place over a year, it's intensive, and it's *hard*."

"That's ..."

"Overwhelming, isn't it?" Alessio asked, chuckling. "It's a lot to take in. Sounds like a fucking movie, huh?"

"Like it's not real."

"Except it is, and from the time I was ten, it's what I've done with The League. I've been to twenty-eight countries, I have taken out the potential leader of a major rebellion for a government who couldn't have it on paper, and I have been on a team that went after a politician's daughter to remove her from the traffickers who took her from a family vacation on a cruise. I killed a mob boss's rival because he was causing too many problems, but he couldn't be attached to the hit. What do you think I do for a living, Ginevra? Or Corrado?"

"Hitmen doesn't sound like the right word."

Alessio scoffed. "Not even close."

"What would you call it?"

"Well, everybody likes to call it something different, but The League likes to say they train assassins. Highly skilled, dangerous, and useful depending on who has deep enough pockets to buy one of us."

Oh, wow.

Ginevra had another inkling even as the chill in her spine grew colder. "So, why is Corrado *guarding me,* then? Seems like a waste of his time if you all do … other things."

"He owed a favor."

"Oh." Ginevra pulled the blanket down and eyed Alessio. "Ten, you said?"

"Yeah, it's about when I first came to the people who started and control the organization."

"That's very young."

"My father had been dead for years, and my mother might as well have already been six feet under what with the way she needed drugs to get her from the bed to the floor on an hourly basis. The League was a far better choice for me, trust me."

God.

Her heart hurt.

No child should feel unloved by their parents. Ginevra missed her mother more than anything in the world, and thoughts of Marie filled her mind late at night when she couldn't sleep. The pain of losing her mama would never go away, but she realized as she stared at Alessio, she would much rather deal with this kind of grief than the type he faced every day of his life.

They both hurt.

One seemed … more painful.

"Your mom, well, you don't talk about her with fondness."

"Because I felt none."

"I'm sorry."

Alessio shrugged and grinned again. "Thing is … I'm grateful for her, which puts me in a strange place, right? She might as well have abandoned me, like my father, and everybody else around me, too. But if not for her, then I wouldn't be here. I wouldn't have The League."

Ginevra cleared her throat. "Or Corrado, right? You said it's where you met him."

"Yeah, and him, too."

Ginevra heard his wariness. Like he wasn't sure whether meeting Corrado had been a good thing, but he didn't sound like he wanted to change it, either.

God knew she understood the feeling.

Far too well.

From her position on the chair, Ginevra was able to see the credits for the movie scrolling past, but Alessio was the most fascinating thing. She wasn't sure when he'd rested his head in his hand, and closed his eyes, but at some point, he fell asleep during the movie.

Usually, the man gave off an intensive vibe. Like he was vibrating with energy, some of it dark and enthralling, but it had nowhere to go. A simple conversation with him left her doing a deep dive through her mind and heart because even talking to the man was overwhelming.

She wasn't sure what to make of him.

What to think …

Alessio hadn't touched her since the day in the library. He hadn't even tried, really, but he observed her all the time. Similar to the way Corrado did, too. Like he both enjoyed what he was seeing, and, there was something about her that he couldn't quite figure out.

It put her on edge.

And she liked it.

Which only confused Ginevra *more*.

Like she needed this problem.

Wasn't being entangled with one of these men bad enough? For her, yes. She had enough shit to consider about Corrado without adding Alessio on top of the mix, too, but that's what a single kiss had done.

A kiss.

A few words.

Poetry.

Sharing the same space.

All of this made her consider Alessio.

Refusing to go down the damn rabbit hole again, Ginevra stood from the chair, gathering the blanket into her arms. Corrado hadn't come back after he left the living room, and she wasn't sure how to turn off the movie using the game system remote, so she let the credits play as she headed out of the space.

Not that she needed *more* shit to wonder about before bed, Ginevra still lingered in the doorway of Corrado's bedroom. He milled about the room, shedding his clothes, undoing his wristwatch, and leaving the bathroom like he wasn't at all bothered about her staring.

Finally, he turned to give her a look as, in nothing but boxer-briefs, he came up to the side of the bed, ready to get in. "Are you sleeping in the room across the hall again, then?"

Ginevra blinked.

His frankness never failed to surprise her.

"I shouldn't be in here," she said truthfully.

Corrado raised a brow. "I would prefer you in my bed."

Wow.

And he didn't pull punches, either.

"And if you think," he continued, not giving her the chance to speak, "you sleeping in my bed is a problem for Alessio, you're wrong … you're not giving this enough consideration, Ginevra. He doesn't care if you're in my bed, or if I'm fucking you in the shower first thing in the morning. It's not about *sex* for him—oh, he fucking loves that, yeah—but it's something more for him about this.

"The physical side of a relationship is probably the easiest thing for him to deal with, if I'm being honest. He can compartmentalize and comprehend all the *whys* I want to fuck you, doesn't see a problem, and because of that, doesn't care. It's not the real issue."

"Seems strange. I would imagine that part of this would be the hardest to deal with."

"Not for him, or me." Corrado shrugged one shoulder, pulled the blankets back, and slipped into the bed as he said, "It's not about the sex, and it doesn't matter how much you *think* it is, it won't change that he doesn't give a shit."

"He told me about where he came from, his mom, and stuff. After you left earlier, I mean."

Corrado made a noise under his breath, dark and irritated. Over what, though, she didn't have a clue. It could have been something hurt Alessio, or that they had a conversation. Because frankly, Alessio was right.

This man was *shit* at communication.

He needed to work on it.

"Stem it back to that," Corrado said, gesturing between them, "for this, huh? You want to understand what his problem is here—it's *that*. It's about being vulnerable to someone else for Alessio, him giving something willingly when he doesn't give it to fucking anybody."

"Loyalty. Trust."

"That, yeah. And I abused it, in a way." Corrado leaned back against the headboard, using his arms crossed behind his head as a pillow while he watched her with that stare of his, so penetrating and vast. All it took was a look, too. "So, again, if you believe this is about sex, or the fact you're in my bed might piss him off, you're wrong. It's not even a fraction of the problem."

"It's good to know, but it's not why I came in here to talk, either."

Corrado nodded at her. "What do you want, then?"

"I want to ask some things."

"*About?*"

She shifted on her feet, tightening her hold on the blanket like it might make it easier to say the words drifting through her thoughts. Because, if she wanted to *think* about two men, their relationship, and her interest in both, then shouldn't she voice those same feelings, too?

What was it her mama told her years ago?

If you suppose you're mature enough to have sex with a man, Ginevra, then you best be ready to talk about it, too.

Right.

"How long have you been together?"

Corrado smiled a little. "Five years, or so. Almost from the day we met, but it was a shaky thing for a while."

Huh.

"And you … love him?"

"Even if he doesn't want me to say it, yes."

"Is what he told me true?"

Corrado gave her a look, murmuring, "I have no idea what he told you, Ginny."

"That you … share women and—"

"Yes."

"Often?"

Corrado laughed. "I mean, not as often as you might assume. We didn't prowl the streets every night looking for someone to take home to fuck, kitten. If it came up, then it did. We did our thing together, too, and we slept with different women alone without the other involved."

"Sounds … messy."

And *intriguing.*

She had so many more questions about that part of Alessio and Corrado's relationship, especially where other women came into play. But she didn't want to mull it over right then, not that her body was giving her much of a choice. She was glad she had the blanket hanging from her arms, so Corrado wasn't capable of seeing the way she shifted on her feet because the spot between her thighs was hot and aching for reasons she didn't care to admit.

"And that's what you want to keep doing with him?" she asked.

Corrado stilled on the bed, his gaze drifting from the black and gold trimmed comforter to where she still stood in the doorway. "No, not at all."

"I don't understand."

"I found what I want, even if I didn't realize I was looking for it. I don't need to look elsewhere when it's all right here, I need everybody else to figure it out now."

Well …

That only made her more confused.

"He kissed me," she blurted. "The day he came back, I was in the library, and he kissed me."

Corrado nodded like he already was aware. "And did you like it?"

What?

She stayed quiet.

Corrado gave her another pointed stare. "Well, did you?"

"I did."

"Good, think about that, and what it means," Corrado said, gesturing at her doorway to add, "And if you're not sleeping in here tonight, then leave the door open when you leave. Good night, Ginny."

That was it—*done.*

Not that it left her with any more answers.

And she still didn't know what to do.

CHAPTER 6
ALESSIO

Are you sure you want to do this, Les?

Dare's words from their earlier phone call drifted through Alessio's mind as he flipped over another sheet on the contract spread out across Corrado's desk. Placing his hands to the edge of the curved, smooth wood, he took in the words in black ink, their ramifications not lost on him should he put his name on the dotted line.

It will require Subject One to commit to four years under contract with WHICHEVER bidder wins the bid on his or her person. No circumstances will void the contract before the four-year term is up unless or until the buyer is deceased, and in which case, Subject One may be transferred to someone of the buyer's choice, if made before passing.

Four years of his life.

Auctioned to the highest bidder.

All the skills Alessio worked to hone over the years with The League came down to a ten-page contract that laid out every detail for him so that he had no questions left to ask. Until now, his career with The League had been as an independent contractor. A choice Dare and Cree allowed him to have because of their attachment to him, and it meant a lot.

Others didn't get the same treatment. Mostly, people came to The League knowing what their fate would be—one year of training, and then the auctions came up where very rich and dangerous people bid on the members for four-year contracts. That's how The League's *real* money got made.

Alessio never had much interest in the auctions. Working alone, or with The League's team that Cree had made, gave him enough freedom to do whatever he wanted. Something had changed over the last year, though, and he leaned towards the auctions as the yearly date neared for them.

Hence, the contract.

And his need for a decision, considering in two months, the auctions would happen. Dare would need to get his paperwork settled and put him on the roster for potential buyers to peruse before they went into the auctions. It was typical for a buyer to settle on which member they wanted before they ever even stepped foot inside The League's building.

"With your varied skills," Corrado said from the doorway of the office, "you'll cause a bidding war, likely."

Alessio had known Corrado was standing there from the moment he entered the room even if the man hadn't made a noise. So was their fucking life together. He wasn't able to even consider this alone because he had to consider everything else, too.

"Yeah, possibly," Alessio muttered, "but that's not a bad thing. Thirty percent of the final buyer's cost goes to me, and the rest to The League. After four years, I wouldn't have to take another job, if I didn't want to. I could do … anything."

"You have enough money to do that now."

Another thing that wasn't a secret between them. Alessio didn't even hide how much fucking money he had spread across several portfolios because Corrado had details for all that shit, too.

"What do you want?" Alessio asked.

"To know if you will sign that and go up on the auctions."

"Considering it."

"I don't want you to do it," Corrado said.

Alessio's shoulders tightened at that. "I've been saying for a year I wanted to do this, Corrado. It shouldn't be a surprise now that I have the contract in front of me. If you had an issue with it, then you should have said something *months* ago. Not now."

"Months ago I would let you do whatever you wanted to make *this* better for you. And sometimes, that meant you running away from me, right? Fucking off to work, or staying away from me because you didn't want to deal with the shit you didn't like at home."

"Where in the fuck do you—"

Alessio turned to tell Corrado to go fuck himself, but stopped when he realized the man had crossed the office to stand right beside him. With Corrado *this* close, there was no mistaking that look in his eye.

That *glint*.

He wasn't hiding shit.

It was all on the table, now.

"You only want to do this to get away from me," Corrado said, not pulling any punches with each word he threw at Alessio, "the same way you take extra jobs, run with the second team when Cree allows it … you have to keep running away, Les, because you're scared of what might happen when *I* catch up to you—when this shit between us comes to a head, right?"

Alessio straightened to his full height, realizing his pride could sometimes be just as much of a bitch as Corrado's. "Or I want something *different*, yeah? Not everything is about you, Corrado, even if you want to make it that way."

Low blow, Les.

He knew it.

That was the thing, though, if Corrado wanted to say shit

that hurt Alessio, then the man better be damn ready to have it thrown right back at him, too. Alessio no longer understood how to survive the mess they'd created together, otherwise.

Was it healthy?

Not at all.

Not that it mattered.

The words were out there, now.

He blamed his attitude and mood on the fact he had been tiptoeing around Corrado for almost a week and a half. Shit was always better, *and far easier,* between the two of them when they were together, and close. Sure, those issues still existed, but at least he was able to tuck them away when they had each other to focus on.

Right now, they were focusing on the wrong shit.

Or it was right.

It just wasn't easy.

Corrado didn't seem bothered by Alessio's words. He came back stronger for the second round, saying, "It's true, you didn't want all of this—our problems, the shit you weren't getting from me—to come to a head, either, because you're terrified of what might come after. So, you keep busy, you keep running … it keeps a distance between you and me, yeah. But then, you come back, and we have two weeks together."

He let out a bitter laugh, so fucking dark and hurtful, adding, "But then we're too busy focusing on being *together*, Alessio, because neither one of us like being apart, instead of all the shit that weighs us down. That's why you want to do it."

Fuck.

More than anything, Alessio wanted to deny what Corrado said to him. He wanted to tell him to shove his fucking assumptions up his ass and get out of his face.

Except he couldn't say any of that shit at all, even if he was mad—and *Christ*, he was so mad—because Corrado wasn't wrong.

Nothing he said was a lie.

"You want to do the auctions because you need a new way to run, instead of staying here and handling the issues we've unpacked from the baggage we've been carrying for five fucking years," Corrado uttered. "If you can do it to me, then the least you can do is *say it*, too. Just admit it."

God.

Alessio dragged in a lungful of air that burned all the way in. "And if we didn't have all this shit going on if we were *good*, Corrado ... then what would you say about these auctions, and me going up for a buyer?"

Because that mattered, too.

"I would still ask you not to do it."

Alessio's jaw ached from how hard he was clenching his teeth. "Why?"

"Because they won't give a *fuck* about you. You will be a tool, something for them to use. They will tell you where to go, and what to do. They will determine your worth, and the value of your life, by how valuable you are to them. You might die because someone figured you were just collateral, and that contract says it *doesn't matter.*"

"Corrado—"

"That contract says someone can take you from me, and there's not a fucking thing I will be able to do about it because you signed your goddamn name on it. And right now, the only reason you want to take that risk is because as much as you like to throw my bullshit at my feet, you're still not ready to deal with your own."

Why did he have to be like that?

Why did he have to be *right?*

"Okay?" Corrado asked. "Was that what you wanted me

to say? Because fuck knows you still won't let me tell you I love—"

Alessio's hand hit the papers on the desk, sending them scattering everywhere. He didn't let Corrado finish his statement before he spun on his heels and left the office without a look over his shoulder.

No, Corrado didn't get to say those words.

Not yet.

They still struck like a fucking weapon.

Alessio wasn't ready for the impact.

The music filtering out of the tiny speaker on the middle of the kitchen island had Ginevra dancing to the beat, a wooden spoon swaying with the rest of her body in her grip. She didn't seem to care at all that Alessio sat at the right side of the island, a thriller opened in front of him, while she cooked and danced.

In fact, she barely paid him any mind at all.

He was sure Corrado had found the speaker for her and let her steal his phone for the *massive* music playlist he kept on the damn thing. Not that he cared to ask at the moment, because despite how interesting his book actually was, Alessio was far more concerned with watching Ginevra.

A curious thing.

Smart, and quick.

She didn't miss a beat.

Innocent, but sinful.

Sly, but sweet.

He found it odd he was able to sit down and have an intellectual conversation with her about things that no one else ever wanted to talk about—like his appreciation of the written word. She calmed his constant, *excessive* energy, and brought him back down to earth with nothing more than a conversation. On the flip side of that coin, he watched her handle an uptight and stiff Corrado, and make him more playful than Alessio had ever seen.

He had yet to grasp how to deal with it. Unlike every-thing else, compartmentalizing this woman was impossible. It was how Alessio liked to deal with anything in his life. Things fit in neat little boxes inside his mind, and he handled them accordingly.

Ginevra was not the same.

At all.

There were too many facets to her personality, and he couldn't unveil them all before another one came along to make him do a double-take of her yet again. He was still trying to find that *thing* in this woman that had made Corrado change the landscape of their relationship, but the longer he searched for it, the more Alessio realized something else.

He liked Ginevra.

Finding the parts of her that had Corrado spun up in the woman became *almost* insignificant when suddenly, Alessio had his own interests in her.

And that was a goddamn problem.

He didn't ask for that.

None of it.

"Want to try it?"

Alessio blinked to find Ginevra had stopped dancing and came to stand on the other side of the island from where he sat. On the wooden spoon in her hand, a red sauce coated the concave tip. A rich red, and smelling like spices, his mouth watered as she held it out like it was a treat she might tease him with.

That cunning smile on her lips said the same.

"Well?"

"Who taught you to cook, hmm?" he asked.

Ginevra grinned. "My Mama."

"Oh?"

"She worked a lot, so I had to look after my little sisters. They didn't like things that came from a box when our mom wouldn't dare feed them something like that, so I had to learn how to make them what they liked."

"And you liked that."

She arched a brow. "What do you mean?"

"Taking care of your sisters."

He didn't miss the way her throat jumped, or how a sadness dimmed her eyes. "Of course, I did. I love them, Les."

"You haven't seen them in a while, huh?"

"Too long. I don't like to think about it. There's nothing I can do about it. I can't talk to them, they can't be told where I am, so ... I don't bother."

Yeah, he could tell.

The emotion in her eyes, and the thickness in her tone, that made him lean forward to take her sauce. Perhaps then, she would go back to smiling and dancing, and his chest wouldn't feel like a fucking elephant was sitting on it because she was *sad*.

Yeah, fuck.

He didn't ask for this.

Alessio shouldn't have *any* emotion for this woman.

Yet, he did.

More and more each day.

He did.

That would be a problem.

Alessio took the sauce on the tip of the wooden spoon Ginevra held out to him, surprised at the richness and varying notes that glided across his palate from just *one* taste. Leaning back on the stool, he nodded.

"It's good."

She gave him a look. "*Just* good?"

One breath in.

Another breath out.

He had to remind himself to breathe with her, too.

"It's wonderful," he murmured. "Really."

A lot like her.

And that's enough.

Alessio liked this woman—did he need to say that again? —and he hadn't planned for this at all. It wasn't why he came back here, not even a thought until it stared him right in the face and *laughed* at him.

The universe having another joke.

He wasn't ready for it.

He was pissed, but not at her. Ginevra hadn't asked for this situation, and mostly, she gave him and Corrado as much space as she could to work out their issues *without* her stepping in. That's why she still slept in a separate bed even though he didn't give a fuck if Corrado was fucking her.

Because she had a heart.

She gave a shit.

Even though this hurt her.

Alessio needed to be *mad*. Mad this became less and less about why the fuck Corrado had done what he did—more about why Alessio thought he was doing the same fucking thing.

He pushed off the chair, despite Ginevra's confused expression, and turned to leave the kitchen without an explanation. Corrado, standing in the entryway, and watching their exchange with an amused smile *really* sent his blood pressure spiking.

Like the man just knew what was happening—expected this.

And he *liked* it.

Fuck that noise, too.

"Les," Ginevra said, a question lingering in her tone, "are you okay?"

Not at all.

Not one fucking bit.

He left the kitchen in a rush, sliding past Corrado who met his stare, before he tried to put distance between him and them. That was the problem with him deciding to stay here.

There was no space.

Only an illusion.

"I didn't mean to upset him," Ginevra said, her tone quaking but faint. "What did I do?"

"Nothing," Corrado replied. "I doubt it was you, Ginny."

"But—"

"Everything is all right, keep cooking."

Alessio didn't want to see them—didn't want to smell, or hear, or *feel* them. He went to the only place which might give him some sense of privacy, if only for a short time, to clear his fucking head. Maybe that was his biggest mistake; he thought he could stay here, and not change anything.

He found the solace he needed in the attached bathroom of the bedroom he'd been using. Three bedrooms, and three bathrooms, the penthouse gave them all their own personal spaces, if needed.

Not that it helped.

Clearly.

Alessio wanted to do and be nothing. He wanted to be able to ignore the fact his cock was hard as he stripped out of his clothes, all because he'd enjoyed the sight of Ginevra dancing in far more ways than one.

Another goddamn problem.

Stepping under the too-hot water after he'd spun the taps on, Alessio let steam and heat drag him from the hell of his thoughts. Except, it didn't last. Once the sting of the hot water dulled beating down against his head and back, his mind filled with nonsense again.

Of *everything*.

Them.

This mess.

His *feelings*.

Fuck, he hated that the most.

"*Les*."

Corrado's voice had him tensing under the water, but he didn't answer the man back. Instead, he kept his hands pressing against the cool tiles of the shower, happy with pretending like he had gone deaf.

It was easier than explaining his behavior.

Making sense of *this*.

"Les," Corrado snapped again.

Still, he said nothing.

And *shocker*, that wasn't good enough for Corrado, because when the man didn't get what he wanted verbally, he yanked open the frosted glass doors of the shower, and stepped inside, fully clothed. At his side, Corrado stared hard at him, barely fazed at all by the large shower heads raining down on them from several directions. Soaked to the bone, and *waiting*, Corrado said nothing. Alessio didn't move or speak, either.

Finally, he uttered, "Get out."

"No."

Alessio let out a dark sound. "Get the fuck—"

"Not until you tell me what that was about."

"You fucking *know*."

"Maybe I want to hear you say it."

"Fuck you," Alessio mumbled, shaking his head under the water, droplets sliding down his face to fall to the tiled floor. "I didn't come here for *this*—for her. We're supposed to be figuring shit out, but we haven't even done that, and you know what's happening with me because that's what you fucking wanted to happen."

He would not spell it out for Corrado.

The asshole could read between the lines.

"It wasn't *us* with someone else, Corrado," Alessio said under his breath. "That's not what this ever was, but you didn't let me choose—*you did.* And you knew what would happen if I stayed here long enough ... if I was around her long enough, so fuck you for that, too."

Every word he threw at Corrado cut like knives. He was sure when they stabbed into Corrado, it hurt like hell. He wanted that clear, though, because it's how this shit felt to him. Someone decided something else for him, and he didn't get a say either way.

He could be pissed about that.

That, he could choose alone.

"Get *out*," Alessio snapped at Corrado when the man just kept standing there.

"Les—"

"*Go.*"

Corrado didn't leave like Alessio wanted him to. He never had understood boundaries, or possibly, a part of Corrado sensed when Alessio struggled, even when he said he wanted to be alone, he needed someone there more.

He'd been alone for most of his life.

A vicious circle.

Corrado often reminded him he wasn't navigating life by himself so that just made this worse. It made the pain of it all amplified because *God* ... Alessio handed him everything, and he ruined it.

Instead of leaving, Corrado backed him against the shower wall. Alessio tipped his head back to the tiles, letting the coolness of the marble press along his jaw and cheek when Corrado buried his face into his neck. His lips touched his skin, soft and quick, silent apologies following the featherlight kisses.

He didn't need to have it said.

He knew what Corrado didn't say.

"I didn't *find* her," Corrado muttered against his skin. "I didn't seek her out—she just *was*, and I didn't get a choice, either. You don't want this to change, and I get it, Les. You get too close, you give a shit, and then what happens, huh? It's someone else that can leave you, right?"

"Fuck you," Alessio mumbled.

Fuck him for knowing.

For being right.

For doing all of this.

It wasn't fair.

"It's like you fucking tricked me, like you manipulated me," Alessio said, his voice a rumble under the noise of the shower. "This is what you wanted, right?"

"I did nothing. I let shit happen."

"No, you did."

"Les—"

"That's what it seems like, Corrado. And it makes it harder, it makes this worse."

"Why would I do that to someone I lov—"

Alessio turned his head fast, his lips crashing against Corrado's. He still wasn't ready for those words, still didn't want to hear them, not when he was trying to deal with everything else too. It made it more difficult, because part of him wanted that more than anything, he wanted those words for so long, and now, Corrado *needed* to say them, too.

But all it took was that kiss, the hard work of their lips moving against one another's, and they lost the words. Oh, the anger was still there, visceral and vicious. Tinging every swipe of his lips against Corrado's. That anger colored the roughness in Corrado's hands when they slid down the sleeves of tattoos on Alessio's arms.

Still, it was a background thought.

Fading away with the flavor of Corrado when Alessio's tongue teased the seam of his lips. He had far more he wanted to say, all those warring emotions battling for a presence, but he didn't want to feel anything at all.

Instead, he found somewhere else to go—a better place to be. He found it in the wet clothing covering Corrado's hard lines as he crowded closer to Alessio. He reveled in letting the anger drift away when a firm grip found his cock and stroked him fast. Teeth cut into his lower lip, giving him a shock of pain with the hot licks of pleasure climbing his spine with every pull of Corrado's hand along his length.

It'd been too long.

Hell, he hadn't even touched himself in *weeks*.

Too caught up in their shit, this mess, and everything else. Sex came secondary, and he didn't care for the release when it would only be fucking *empty*. And yet, he was begging for it, now. *Craving it*, so bad.

"Jesus Christ," he growled against Corrado's kiss.

That palm on his dick tightened.

God, yeah.

"Let me say it," Corrado murmured, "just fucking let me *say it*, Les."

"*Shut up*."

"Stop using that to *punish me*."

Never once did Corrado's hand slow. Those strokes came faster, and the next kiss bruised. It's what Alessio needed, what he wanted more than anything, and when he came … *fuck*, it ached as much as it relieved. His semen spilled between them, hitting the tiles just long enough for the water to wash it all away. A broken sound tore from his chest, breathless and harsh, as Corrado's hand slowed but his fingers tightened at the same time.

Corrado's gaze lifted to meet his, but Alessio was already turning his head to look away again. Now, they had switched places, he thought. It wasn't *him* that wanted something from Corrado that his lover wouldn't give.

The shoe was on the other foot.

He didn't mean for it to punish; love wouldn't hurt anymore.

Corrado released his hold on Alessio, his palm coming up to snap hard against the tiles of the shower when he still wouldn't return his stare.

He couldn't.

Not when he was mad again.

"So, what if this thing of ours has to change?" Corrado asked. "What if it makes it better?"

Alessio didn't reply.

Corrado stepped back from him, letting the cold air wrap around Alessio as he moved out of the shower. He left behind a mess on the floor from the water dripping off his clothes, closed the shower without a word, and exited the bathroom with a slam of the door.

Only then did Alessio breathe again.

What if it makes it better?

Right.

Because it sure as hell couldn't get worse.

CHAPTER 7
CORRADO

Rolling over, because Corrado could no longer ignore the sun coming in through the windows of the bedroom, his hand slid across the top of the bedside table. Soon, he found the device he was looking for.

His cell phone.

He dragged a hand down his face, willing away the grumpiness he *always* felt first thing in the damn mornings, and pulled the phone closer to his face. He blinked, making the screen come into focus when he turned it on to check for something.

A missed call.

Any texts.

A fucking *smoke signal*.

Not that the last one was possible, but anything would be better than what he had been getting, which was nothing. Anyone else, he called or sent a word to, and they were quick to get back to him.

Andino Marcello was an asshole.

And he did not care.

Out of everything Corrado knew about the man, he was quite aware that Andino being an asshole was the most truthful. It was obvious Ginevra was missing her sisters, and that she worried about what was happening back home in New York. Regularly, Corrado had sent a message to check in with Andino just to make sure he was still where he needed to be, so was Ginevra, and that nothing had changed.

He never got a response.

Ever.

Corrado didn't know why that was except to say Andino was being his usual asshole self and didn't want to return a fucking call or message. What other excuse did the man have? Through the contacts Corrado had with his twin in the Guzzi Cosa Nostra, if Andino or any other Marcello was dead, then he would know it.

They were alive and well.

Except that one's husband.

Cella Marcello, was it?

A bystander, Chris had told Corrado. Wrong place, wrong time, but it looked purposeful, too. Not that it made any fucking difference to Corrado either way.

If the Marcellos wanted to go to war in New York, then they could do that. He would rather keep Ginevra here with him while they did it, so she wasn't another innocent bystander in their goddamn feud with her half-brothers' organization.

And even so, she continued to worry.

Silently.

So, he kept sending messages.

Frustrated at the lack of a response from Andino—yet again—Corrado threw the phone to the blanket and rolled over so his back was against the headboard. Through the opened door of his room, he could see the empty bedroom across the hall from his. That wasn't unusual, either, considering Ginevra was often up and around long before he ever was.

Same with Alessio.

He was not rolling his ass out of bed before nine if he wasn't doing it to fuck someone. He didn't make the rules of life—like needing sleep to survive—but he could sure as hell decide what he did about it.

It took Corrado too long to get out of his bed and make his way to the attached bathroom. He did his business, wishing he had just stayed in bed the entire time. Mornings were not his thing, and the less time he spent around other people, the better the rest of it went for him.

Why pretend?

The only exception to that rule was when someone was in the bed *with him*. And since that wasn't happening, either, because both people he wanted to fuck decided they would rather sleep in their beds that weren't his, then his ever-present pissy mood was a constant in the mornings.

What could he do?

He dressed, opting for gym shorts and runners because once he stuffed his face full of something suitable for breakfast, he would hit the gym in the penthouse. Corrado slipped out of the bedroom with his head down. He expected to find Alessio and Ginevra in the kitchen, making their usual noise and waiting for his moody ass.

Instead, he found it empty.

Well, mostly.

A plate of eggs, bacon, and toast waited for him in the warming rack of the oven. Still hot, and ready for him to eat. *Huh.* He pulled it out, ignoring the nagging sensation in his chest because *fuck*, he was selfish as hell, and yet, one of those two still thought about him and made sure he would eat.

Probably Ginevra.

Alessio didn't cook—he ordered.

Corrado, balancing the plate in his palm and using a fork to stab into the eggs, he decided to go find the two. He figured they were likely in the library, pouring over a book because that's what they enjoyed first thing in the morning, and it let him have quiet time after he woke up. Something he needed when he first woke up.

Bad moods, and all.

Corrado entered the hallway leading to the office, main bathroom, the gym, and the one spare bedroom Alessio was using at the far end. The connecting hallway led to the other bedrooms, his and Ginevra's. He'd focused on getting out of bed, he hadn't bothered to look around the corner when he came out.

Alessio leaned against the doorway of the gym, staring inside. Corrado set his fork to the plate, and picked up a strip of bacon, shoving half into his mouth while his brow furrowed at the sight of the man standing there, dressed, staring into the room like he was considering whether he wanted to enter.

"What are you do—"

Alessio waved the hand at his side, never looking Corrado's way. He made an annoyed noise, passing the office library and realizing, it was empty. Ginevra wasn't in there, either.

He figured out where Ginevra was when Corrado came to stand next to Alessio's side. Inside the gym, the woman had slipped on the headphones Corrado liked to use when he was running in the mornings—it helped to distract him from the fact he wasn't running on a trail—as she jogged on one of the four treadmills lining the far windows. *Four* treadmills, because each one served a different purpose, and did different things.

"So, she jogs," Corrado said to Alessio.

Alessio nodded. "But for an hour or more?"

Corrado raised an eyebrow as he took in Ginevra again. *No*, that was unusual. Typically, if he woke up early enough to see her go into the gym, she jogged for twenty to thirty minutes, jumped in the shower, and then went about her day.

Oh, he liked watching her run, sure. He would not pretend like her lean form didn't have his cock perking under the satiny cloth of his gym shorts, but he figured Alessio was trying to tell him something right then, and his lust could wait.

"That long?" he asked.

Alessio let out a hard breath. "Yeah."

Huh.

"Something is on her mind—it's bothering her," Alessio murmured.

Corrado gave the man a look from the side. "Les, her whole life is a mess. Congratulations, you're just realizing she is *really good* at compartmentalizing shit like you do. She tucks it all away, lets no one know she's having a rough go, and continues on with her life. Between this here, New York, being without her sisters … I would be shocked if she wasn't one step away from a nervous breakdown."

"So, we … let her do this?"

He looked back in the gym, noting Ginevra's pace hadn't changed. She focused, working through whatever nonsense was in her mind by making her body tired, and pushing it to its limits.

"Because I don't like that," Alessio added quieter, "I don't like it when she's upset, even if she doesn't say that."

"That's a step forward, ain't it?"

Alessio scowled. "Could you not?"

"I'm just saying."

"Well, don't." Alessio sighed, shaking his head. "It bothers me she's—"

"Hurting," Corrado interjected, handing his plate over to the man, which Alessio took with a question in his stare.

"You figured out what my problem has been these last three weeks."

"What?"

"With you. Excuse me."

Corrado left Alessio in the doorway, and entered the gym, still hungry but willing to put it off for a little while. He crossed the space, and jumped onto the treadmill beside Ginevra's, turning it on and starting a pace good for a warmup.

She peeked over at him.

"Faster?" he asked.

Ginevra grinned, faint as it was. "Yeah, sure."

Five minutes later, Alessio joined them, too. On the opposite side of Ginevra, he started the treadmill he preferred because he'd pre-programmed paces into it, from a slow jog, to a sprint, and then to a full run before switching all the way back again.

She didn't want to talk.

Fine.

They would still be there.

They would still do this.

A month was a blink in time for Corrado, but especially when he wasn't doing anything. Days melted into one another, turning into weeks, and then changing into a month before he even realized what had happened.

An entire month with the three of them sharing the same space. And hey, nobody had ripped anybody's head off yet. He took that as a win.

Corrado only realized the date because his father said it in his ear, and he checked the calendar on his desk to confirm that Gian was correct. Surprise, he was.

"How is everything over there?" his father asked on the call.

"Better."

Gian chuckled. "You know, I never realized how nosy I was until one of you five boys had something … interesting going on in your personal lives."

Corrado wasn't stupid—that was his father's sly way of asking about their situation. Mostly, his father allowed all his children their privacy and space.

Sometimes, though, he didn't.

Like now.

"It's a complicated thing," Corrado said quietly, eyeing the open doorway of his office. Ginevra had been playing a game in the sitting room, and Alessio was in the gym again, beating the hell out of a punching bag. "But then again, it was a complicated thing before she ever showed up, too."

"And delicate, I imagine."

Corrado cleared his throat. "Yeah, that, too."

"I'm sure you'll get it figured out. You got that message from your mother, *oui*?"

"I did. She's like you—*elle est trop curieuse*."

He only got to speak French with his father, and Corrado tried to sneak it because he could. None of his brothers, except for Marcus, had picked up French from their father like he did. Just bits and pieces, but not enough for him to hold a proper conversation. He liked to use it when he could.

"She is not *too* curious, Corrado. That is not why she asked for lunch."

"Right," Corrado said fast before his father could make up another excuse for Cara, "not at all."

"Maybe that's the case, but she also gets whatever she wants, and what she wants right now is to spend time with—"

"Oh, I'm sorry."

Corrado's head snapped up, and he found Ginevra standing in the office's doorway. Her gaze drifted from him to the bookshelves lining the wall at the left of his desk.

"I'll just give you a minute," she said. "I didn't mean to interrupt."

"It's fine," Corrado told her, and then back on the call, "I will call you back, Papa, and *yes*, tomorrow is a go. Tell Ma."

"Will do, son."

Once Corrado had ended the call, he gave Ginevra his attention. She continued standing in the doorway not coming further into the room or moving away.

"You need something?"

She pointed at the bookshelves. "I picked out a book yesterday, but I didn't take it with me. I hadn't finished my other one, so …"

Corrado nodded and gestured at the shelves. "Go ahead. This space is as much yours as it is ours while you're here."

She passed him a curious glance, but Corrado didn't bother to ask what for. He figured it was better he talked like Ginevra had to share the same spaces he and Alessio did daily because it was true.

She belonged here.

With them.

They needed to figure it out, too.

Ginevra moved into the office, and crossed the space with quick, quiet steps. She bent down to pull a book from the third shelf, like she had known where she left it, and straightened back up with it in her hand, ready to leave.

Before she did, she flipped it open to the title page, and a soft noise of surprise escaped her. That gained Corrado's attention again, but she wasn't even looking at him. Instead, her focus was on the book in her grasp.

"Something wrong?"

Ginevra glanced up, a soft smile curving her cheeks. "No, I … there's a note here, is all."

"Pardon?"

She turned the book around so that Corrado could see what she meant by *a note*. There, a yellow sticky note with familiar handwriting scrawled across it stuck to the page. He was unable to read what Alessio had written on the note, but he still recognized the bold cursive lettering.

Corrado felt his smirk growing. "From Les."

She shrugged. "Seems so."

"What does it say?"

"That I will like the second half more, and to skip the first," she said, laughing. "He gave me the page numbers of his favorites, too. It's another book of poetry—that's all."

Not at all something Corrado enjoyed.

Or appreciated.

Yet, Ginevra and Alessio shared that, and he found it fascinating. "Did you show him that book when you picked it out yesterday?"

"No, I came in and looked it over before putting it back."

Right.

But those shelves …

All those books.

They were Alessio's. He'd picked every single one and decided where they should go on the shelves. He recognized them front to back because not a single book went into his library if he didn't read it cover to cover. If one of those books moved, Alessio would know about it.

Which meant …

He'd been watching for which books Ginevra picked out on her own.

"I'm sure it seems silly," Ginevra said, rolling her eyes, "But … it's nice."

He didn't think it to be silly. No, he didn't appreciate

books and words and poetry like the two of them did, but he grasped what Alessio had done here.

"It means he likes you," Corrado murmured.

She scoffed, giving him a roll of her eyes. "Lately, he barely speaks to me. He keeps a distance, not that I blame him. Oh, he watches me sure, but so do you. But *likes me*, Corrado, that's a stretch."

Oh, it was way deeper than that.

"You should have figured out by now that nothing with Alessio is simple or obvious. Think about it," he said, leaning back in the office chair to watch her over the steepling of his fingers, "you hadn't told Les about the book which means he sought what you read, so he would be aware, and keep up with you. It means he's thinking of *you*, Ginny, in his own way."

Corrado shrugged, adding, "So, he keeps a distance, and he's quiet. *That's Alessio*. He's working through his own shit, and when he does that, he isolates as much as he can. It's not about you, even if it is *for* you."

He didn't miss the way her fingers tightened on the edge of the book, or how her throat jumped at his words. She shifted from foot to foot, too, refusing to meet his gaze. All those nerves of hers, he saw it all.

And Corrado *hated* that.

Out of all the things happening here, he did not want her nervous about this. Not about Alessio, or him, or what might come of it. Some things should be *easy* and them falling into step together needed to be one of those. There would be more than enough of it that would be hard, surely.

"Come here," he whispered, tipping his head to the side.

"What?"

Corrado pointed at his side. "Get over here."

Still tittering in her anxious way, Ginevra closed the book, and came to stand next to Corrado's chair behind the desk. Staring down at him, he thought she looked sweet, and a little sinful. Expectant, but hesitant.

Exactly as she should, really.

Reaching up, he caught one of her stray waves of hair between his fingertips and twisted the strands around his index finger. "I like you closer, Ginny. You understand that, don't you?"

Her tongue peeked out to wet her lips when he tugged on the strands of hair, making her lower until she bent over at her middle, and the two of them were at eye level with each other. Here, he only had to lean forward and *kiss her*.

Still, he held off.

For a moment …

"Do you?"

"Hmm?"

"Like me closer."

"More often than I get you, *chérie*."

Her gaze dropped to his mouth before snapping back up to his eyes. He didn't miss the way her lower lip trembled like she had something to say, but held it back.

"What is it?" he asked. "Say it, kitten."

"You still call me that."

"Because you are, soft but with sharpness. It's perfect."

Like her.

Ginevra let out a slow breath and glanced away. "I'm not sure what to do here, Corrado."

"With what?"

"You, and … him. I don't know what to do, or how to act. I didn't ask for any of this, and it's hard enough handling *one* man who has an interest in me, let alone two. It's confusing and—"

"I get it," he interjected. "He knows that, too."

She gave him a look again.

That look.

Annoyed, and amused at the same time.

"What?" he asked.

"It doesn't bother you at all?"

"I need more to go on, Ginny."

"To think someone else might want me—to touch me, *fuck* me? Or I might want to do that to someone else that isn't you?"

Corrado blinked.

Straight to the point, then.

That's what she worried about?

God.

That was the last thing he worried about with the three of them. It would probably be the easiest part of it all. Sex was sex, and when that was good, shit, everything else came a hell of a lot easier.

"No, actually," he said, smiling as he leaned in closer to her, nearly able to kiss her as he spoke, "the idea of that, the person I love, and the one I'm falling in love with might love each other, too … why would that bother me?"

She blinked.

Still and quiet.

Corrado wasn't sure if he liked that more than her frankness in this discussion, or not. Quickly, he added, "And it turns me on."

Ginevra made a soft noise.

Airless, he thought.

And hot.

"A bonus for you, I bet," she said.

"Or the way it *should be*."

"I don't think this is that easy, Corrado."

"No, some of us want to make it hard, I suppose." His gaze dropped to her pretty, pink lips and their natural pout. "I'd like to kiss you."

He hadn't touched her.

Gave her space.

Didn't *push*.

It stopped now, but he needed her okay, first. Their game had becoming tiring. He'd sacrificed and suffered because of what he'd done, and he took that penance, as Alessio had once said.

He'd gone without.

Waited.

He wanted from afar.

"Do you?" she asked.

"I do."

Ginevra swallowed audibly, her lips pressing together before she said, "Then, do that, Corrado."

He didn't need further permission. The second those words slipped out of her sweet mouth, he closed that inch of space between them. Catching her lips with his own, he reveled in the softness of her mouth against his own. It'd been far too long since he had a taste of this woman, and he soaked in every single second.

The way her lips worked against his, slow but *sure*. How her tongue struck out first to tease at the seam of his lips, asking for more. The little gasp she gave when he nipped at her with his teeth, and how her tongue slashed with his, not giving him even an inch of control in this battle between them.

He loved it all.

Wanted it all.

Corrado stroked the side of Ginevra's cheek with the pad of his thumb when he pulled away, although part of him wanted to just stay right there, with her caught up in him and those thoughts of Alessio running through her head.

Because yeah, he knew that's what was happening.

And he was fine with that.

"My mother called this morning," he said, holding her gaze strong, "she wants to have lunch with you tomorrow."

Ginevra's gaze widened. "Why?"

"Because she found out you were still in the city with me, that Alessio is also here, I imagine she has questions, and she knows better than to ask me. Oh, and because she thought you made quite an impression on her, which means she *likes you*. Surprise, someone else that thinks you're amazing."

"Corrado. Stop it."

"But it's not a lie."

And it wasn't.

"We Guzzi men try to give our mother what she wants," he added, "or we have to deal with our father. You're safe to leave the penthouse, even if you haven't asked to go further than a shop for clothes. No one knows you're here, so if you want to do lunch tomorrow—it's not negotiable, Cara decided, so—then you can do that. Chris promised Ma he would come to pick you up, so you wouldn't be late because they don't trust me to let you out of here, apparently."

Ginevra grinned slyly. "Oh?"

"Seems so."

He let her go, and Ginevra stood up straight. A happiness lingered in her smile, but he found something else dimming her gaze.

"What's wrong?" he asked.

She shrugged. "I just … have you heard anything about back home, or my sisters?"

He didn't tell her about the calls and messages he'd made because Corrado didn't want to get Ginevra's hopes up only to watch them crash and burn when he got no response from Andino. She had enough to deal with, and that didn't need to be something else on her plate.

"No," he said.

"Will you try?"

Corrado sighed.

Ginevra frowned. "*Please*? I haven't tried to leave, or use the phones or your laptop to contact anyone. I've followed all the rules, haven't I?"

Jesus.

Why did she think he would say no?

That it depended on her behavior?

He would do it because he cared—he had been doing it because of that. Nothing else.

"I'll see what I can do," he said.

"Thank you."

Quickly, she leaned down and pressed another quick kiss to his lips, winking before she turned away from his desk, and headed out of the office without a look back over her shoulder. She was gone all of four seconds before someone else came to stand in the doorway.

Alessio.

"Were you spying?" Corrado asked, never looking up from the papers on his desk. He had things to do. "Because you know, you're more than welcome to *join* the conversation, Les."

"And if I was?"

Corrado chuckled. "The door is open. I leave it like that for a reason."

He met Alessio's gaze.

Questions stared back.

Curiosity.

How much had he heard?

Corrado didn't mind waiting to find out.

CHAPTER 8
ALESSIO

"Give Ma my love, yeah?"

Chris nodded at his twin where he stood next to a waiting Ginevra. "I will." Then, the man's gaze lifted over Corrado's shoulder, drifting to where Alessio stood leaning against the wall further down the hall. "Les, it's been a while."

Had it?

A little more than a month, he supposed, since he sat with the man in that café.

"Chris," Alessio replied. "Get her there safely, yes?"

He hadn't meant for the statement to sound threatening, and yet somehow, it did. Except there wasn't anything he could do about the looks coming his way now because the damn words were already out of his mouth.

Ah, well.

Corrado cleared his throat, passing a pointed look over his shoulder at Alessio. A quiet, *hey, now, that's family.* Alessio only shrugged back.

"No worries," Chris said, shaking his head as he turned to offer a hand to a grinning Ginevra. "She'll come back in one piece."

She better.

At least, that time, Alessio kept the thoughts inside his head. It wasn't lost on him that his sudden protectiveness over Ginevra was for more than just him. He also felt protective of her for Corrado, and he didn't want to get into it.

Not yet.

Once Ginevra and Chris had exited the apartment, Corrado turned to face Alessio with a raised brow. "You don't need to go full-on asshole to Chris, right? It's *Chris*, Les."

"Gotta make an example out of everybody, or nobody will care, huh?"

It reminded him of that whole saying *if you stand for nothing, then you'll fall for everything*. In a way …

"It's still *Chris*," Corrado said, laughing under his breath.

Yeah, yeah.

Alessio didn't need his nonsense pointed out to him when he was glaring at him right in the face every time he looked in the fucking mirror. He changed the conversation, because all too soon, the two of them would go right back to shit that had them snapping at one another's throats again.

Wasn't that the way, lately?

Well …

"I've been here a little more than a month," Alessio said.

Partially passing him in the hallway, Corrado's walk came to an abrupt halt. He looked over at Alessio and nodded. "Yeah, I figured that out yesterday. Passed quickly, didn't it?"

He hadn't realized he had been here with Corrado and Ginevra that long, and he'd barely left other than to take his morning jog, and pick up a coffee from that place he liked down the street.

He took a second.

And then another.

Alessio couldn't remember a time when he had stayed in one place for longer than a month. Or rather, two weeks. The longest was for a *job*, and he had been alone on that one. He stayed home for a while, and then he took off again. And sure, he recognized why he did that, but it was still the urge he had.

Well, the urge he *didn't* have.

Not here.

With them.

He didn't want to run like he'd been doing for years—trying to out run his problems, their issues, and just *life* because it worried him what might happen when it caught up to him. He wanted to be here with them, even if it meant pain and facing his own baggage because God knew he'd been throwing Corrado's at him for so long, now.

Alessio wanted to be here.

Even if it wouldn't be easy.

Even if it didn't end well.

He still wanted to be *here*.

"Les," Corrado said.

He lifted his gaze from the top button on Corrado's dress shirt he'd been using as a focal point to ignore the man's stare. There, in his lover's eyes, he found an understanding reflecting at him.

Corrado always had known Alessio better than anyone, and he wasn't fucking perfect ... that was one thing about Corrado that Alessio had never denied.

This man in front of him wasn't perfect.

He was *flawed*.

So difficult.

Selfish, sometimes.

But he was still Alessio's.

And he loved him, regardless.

He always would.

"Are you going to call Andino for her?" Alessio asked.

Corrado smirked a bit. "So, you're admitting you spied yesterday on our conversation instead of joining?"

"Are you going to answer the question?"

"I have been calling. Three times this last week, in fact. He ignored my calls and messages. You're informed on how Andino Marcello can be."

"Rivals you for the biggest asshole, doesn't he?"

Corrado flashed his teeth when he laughed. "Yeah, a bit. I asked Chris to see what he might find for her, and about her sisters, though. I figured ..."

"Cosa Nostra, made ... connections to New York, yeah," Alessio said, "I get it."

"It's the best I can do right now."

"Is it?"

Because if Corrado really wanted to, he would make a trip to New York himself, pay a visit to Andino, and get business *done*. Like Alessio had done when he wanted details about what in the hell Corrado had gotten himself into here.

It's who they were.

Rules be damned.

Corrado sighed and glanced away. "For once, my pride isn't playing a part here, Les. She needs to be safe more than she needs to be informed on what's happening there ... doesn't she? *Yeah,* I could go there, get what she wants, and come back, but it's a risk. I don't take risks with people I love."

Alessio blinked.

Corrado stared back, silent.

Alessio thought hearing Corrado say those words would have more impact when they hit him with their reality— their blinding truth. Though he had been watching this man fall in love with that woman for an entire month ... a month after Corrado had already spent time alone with Ginevra before Alessio even showed up, he still hadn't allowed himself to *think* Corrado loved her.

He didn't want to think it.

Not when he *wanted* to hear Corrado say it.

"I expected a different reaction when I told you that," Corrado murmured, "something other than ... silence."

"I already knew because I saw it coming, and I understand why."

Corrado nodded. "And you're not hurt or—"

"Was I the first person you told? Not *her*?"

"Of course, you were."

Alessio's brow dipped. "Why?"

"Because that's what we do, Les. That's what we're supposed to do, and I didn't do that before. *I'm sorry*. So yes, you were the first person I told. Anything else you want to hear me say right now? Anything else you want to ask about that conversation I had with her yesterday, or no?"

A lot.

But he was still trying to unpack all that shit he'd compartmentalized over the years. One thing at a time, and he was trying to handle this *thing* in the present. He couldn't go back to the past.

"I want to talk about now, *really* talk," Alessio said.

"Her, you mean?"

"Why you did this, yeah. You said when you told me, there would be no going back. That it would change everything. I want to know—so talk."

"*Koi no yokan*."

"I have no idea what that is."

Corrado smiled, staring down the hall. "You wouldn't unless you favored Japanese writings, and you don't."

"Because I can't understand the language."

"*Anyway* ... I learned what the phrase meant days before I came to The League with my father and brother; when I met *you*."

"That doesn't tell me what it means."

"It is the knowledge upon meeting someone that, eventually, you will fall in love with them."

"Sounds like bull—"

"Except I felt it with you," Corrado interjected, his gaze snapping back to Alessio's in an instant. The truth he found staring back kept Alessio from saying anything more. "And somehow, I believed you would change everything for me. You did, by the way."

Alessio dragged in a hard breath. "And you mean to tell me … what, you felt it with her, too?"

"Almost instantly."

Huh.

Alessio ran his tongue along the seam of his lips, considering and unsure of what to say. Mostly because *yes,* he was still angry this had happened. He became so attached to this thing they had created between *only* them; he didn't know what it would be like after.

Because this would change.

Corrado's feelings, even if Alessio's were not there yet, determined that for them. Would the rest come along, too?

That was yet to be determined.

"You get she's not like us, right?" Alessio asked in a murmur. "She hasn't been in this kind of relationship, Corrado. This *poly*—"

"Or are you scared she might be perfect for us, but then that leaves you vulnerable again, Les?"

"Unfair."

Not everything boiled down to Alessio's *issues.*

Sometimes, shit just was.

"Why, because I understand your baggage like you get mine? Is it only okay when you want to throw my baggage at my feet for us to unpack together, but not when I throw yours back at you to do the same?"

"All of this still doesn't change you didn't tell me from the start about her, Corrado. The one thing I asked for with us, and you abused my trust."

"I understand. I'm trying to fix it."

"It's still hard for me."

"I didn't assume otherwise."

"As long as you're aware."

Corrado laughed huskily. "And nice deflection—you *still* haven't answered my question. Anything else you want to ask me about my conversation with Ginevra?"

"Good catch."

Because the man wasn't wrong.

Alessio just figured this was something he should work out on his own, but especially his darker urges that seemed to want to come out to play more often. It'd been too long since he'd fucked, and he sat on an edge like never before. It was strange how something like sex could drive him up the wall, becoming a focal point in his thoughts.

"I get you—you already have me. Despite all of this, that hasn't changed. I swear, we won't ever fucking change, Les."

Seemed not.

"Okay," Alessio said. "Did you mean that when you told her it didn't bother you at all to think of me being with her —*fucking* her, Corrado, or having her with me?" Corrado opened his mouth to speak, but Alessio was quick to jump in with, "She's not the same as when we shared women before. This is *different.* Feelings are at play here—emotions. She's not the same to you."

Corrado remained quiet.

Alessio continued on with, "Can you mean what you said knowing that?"

"Yes."

There was the truth again.

Staring him right in the face.

Corrado grinned in his way—cocky and dark. The sight

alone was enough to get Alessio's cock perking to life. How long had it been since Corrado leveled the look on him, and *fuck*, he'd missed it.

The man inched closer to Alessio, closing the bit of small space between them until they were eye to eye, one with his hands in his pockets, and one with his arms folded across his chest. Corrado looked calm with his easy, arrogant stance, and Alessio was trying to keep a wall built up around him with his.

They were hard to let down.

"What do you want to hear, huh?" Corrado asked. "About her, Les. What she tastes like after she's come a few times? The sound of her screams in the morning when she's still hoarse and raw? The way she looks on her knees when she's got you buried down her throat?"

Fuck.

"*Ask*," Corrado added, his tone dropping, "and I will tell you."

He could ask a lot.

So many fucking things.

He fantasized far more than he should. To punish himself, and because he *wanted* it. Wanted her, wanted her with Corrado, and wanted her between them. Everything else was hard.

That would be easy.

"Well?" Corrado asked.

"What does she look like when you're fucking her?"

Corrado flashed a smirk. "Of course, that's what you ask."

"You've always known what I like."

"Watching me work."

Alessio shrugged a shoulder.

Why deny it?

"She looks like art," Corrado said, "she always looks like art."

A centimeter closer, and he'd be able to taste the lust right from Corrado's mouth. He was a breath away from closing the distance, but the ringing in his pocket broke their staring contest, and the conversation.

A familiar ringtone.

Dare.

The League.

Corrado dropped his stare, and so did Alessio. "You should get that, yeah?"

Alessio nodded.

He needed to breathe.

To reflect again.

Corrado's presence made those things hard.

Even when it hurt.

"I have calls to make," Corrado said, stepping back as Alessio fished the phone out of his jeans pocket. "Say hello for me."

"Probably not."

"Yeah, Dare is likely in a mood, anyway."

Where was the lie?

Alessio answered the call as Corrado disappeared down the hall. Not that he sensed the man's loss, because it was still imprinted on Alessio's entire soul. Corrado never left, even when he wasn't seen.

"Dare," Alessio greeted, putting the phone to his ear.

"Les, how are things?"

"Better."

It wasn't a lie.

"Oh?"

"Yes."

"That's ... good," Dare replied.

Didn't sound like he meant his statement, though.

"I have information, or rather, confirmation," Dare said.

"On what?"

"The upcoming Albanian job. We were waiting for the call, the *right time*, as the client said. They're nearly ready to give the okay, and it should come up anytime over the next few weeks. You need to be ready to pick up whatever and leave. All right?"

Shit.

This hit had been years in the making, according to the client. Alessio had taken the job a few months back even though the client wasn't ready to see it through back then. Semantics, and details wouldn't line up quite right.

"Any way we can change the member for the job?"

"Not possible," Dare said, "I have signed the contract to you. Those are rules I don't bend or break, not even for you, Les."

Right.

"Got it, Dare."

"Are you sure everything is well?"

"Yes."

Or it would be.

Soon.

"Oh, and Les?"

"Yeah?" he asked.

"I need the contract for the auctions signed and faxed over soon to include your portfolio for the potential buyers."

Yeah, damn.

"I, uh … I'm not going to the auctions, actually."

Dare was silent for a moment. "Because of him?"

"It doesn't matter why."

"Whether I want you to do the auctions is not important, but I don't want you *not* doing something you've wanted to do because Corrado Guzzi has more control of your life than he should, Alessio."

"Dare—"

"You seem to forget you're not an extension of him, Les. You're not his shadow. Don't forget you were somebody long before you even knew he existed."

Yeah, but Alessio liked life better *now*.

He could never go back to *then*.

CHAPTER 9
GINEVRA

"Ma," Chris greeted, leaning over the table to kiss a waiting, smiling Cara on her pinked cheek. Ginevra, standing next to the man, wasn't offended that he said hello to his mother before he even considered pulling a chair out for her at the table. "Corrado sends his love."

"I bet he does." Cara's gaze turned on Ginevra and lit up even more. "And I managed to get you away from that penthouse, hmm?"

A laugh escaped her.

"Thank you for asking me to lunch."

Cara waved a hand. "Oh, it's a little thing. Chris, help her sit."

"Right, right."

Chris pulled the chair across from Cara at the table out for Ginevra, and she made herself comfortable at the table. Once he was sure she and his mother were fine, he said his goodbyes, and said he would be back later before disappearing around the partition wall keeping them hidden from the rest of the restaurant.

And what a place it was.

Gold draperies, matching tablecloths, napkins, and dark-colored rugs under each modernly decorated table. Large golden chandeliers hung above every table, making Ginevra think she was underdressed in the simple black dress she had thrown on for the lunch date with Cara Guzzi.

"This place is …" Ginevra trailed off, unsure of how to describe it.

"A little much, yeah?"

She passed Cara a look.

The other woman only shrugged.

"My husband likes to go over the top," Cara explained, "and since this restaurant is one of a few he owns, you can always tell when Gian has had his hand in the design. Lots of gold, a spattering of black, the sense of wealth all over … it all screams Guzzi."

Ginevra hadn't considered that, but now Cara had said it, she realized the other woman was correct. Like their mansion, or even the aura the couple and their sons gave off, it very much appeared like she was sitting in an excessive show of wealth.

Not that it was uncomfortable.

Just … very *there.*

Present.

Unashamed, maybe.

Cara waved a hand, and the woman that had been standing at a table nearby, but without staring at them, made her way over with the crystal pitcher of a pinkish liquid. She poured the juice—at least, that's what Ginevra assumed it was—into the two glasses on the table, and then turned to give Cara her attention.

"The usual, Mrs.?"

Cara nodded. "Yes … gives us a few options."

"Sure."

It was only once the server left around the partition wall that Cara turned her attention on Ginevra again, a glimmer in her eye as she asked, "And how are the boys?"

Boys.

As in, both.

Ginevra didn't miss that.

Cara smirked when Ginevra didn't answer right away. "I know about them, you know, and about things I am sure Corrado would tell me are none of my business, too."

Great.

Ginevra's cheeks heated, but still she answered with, "It's complicated with the three of us."

"I imagine."

"I'm not sure what else to say about this other than that."

"Nothing," Cara replied, winking. "Complicated sums it up pretty well."

Didn't it?

Conversation turned to a safer topic as they waited for their food. The designer of the dress Ginevra was wearing, one of the many outfits that were delivered to the penthouse from the same boutique that Corrado seemed to favor when she needed something special to wear.

"Why all the gold?" Ginevra asked.

"Oh, that's just a Guzzi thing." Cara shifted in her chair, flicking out one napkin to ready it on her lap. "Blood made of dirt and gold, they like to say. It's been a thing for a few generations, and started before they were … a *famiglia*," she said, choosing her words carefully, "the family had made their money in black gold."

"Oil."

"Yes." Cara peered around their private section with a soft fondness in her gaze. "And as much as this restaurant seems like too much, I still love it the most out of all the ones in the city."

"Why is that?"

"My husband bought it after a date we had here, although back then, it didn't look like it does now. They had the best poutine I had ever tasted, and Gian took that to heart. As he does with most things."

Ginevra laughed lightly. "Really?"

"Yes. Have you ever had it—poutine?"

The memory of the one time she had tried the French dish of fries, cheese curds, and dark gravy seemed to come to the forefront of her mind with a heaviness, taking with it all of her happiness.

Cara didn't miss Ginevra's change in expression. "Something wrong?"

A typical mother.

Caring.

Concerned.

Loving.

Like hers.

"I had poutine once," Ginevra said, "with my mother and sisters. Mama made it because Greta saw a recipe on the internet—looked fun, I guess."

Cara quieted for a moment. "Ah."

"I liked it."

"Ginevra."

She peeked up through her lashes, but Cara's soft smile faded. Instead, she found sympathy and understanding in the older woman's gaze. "I'm aware of your current circumstances, and what brought you here."

"Oh."

"I'm so very sorry about your mother's passing. You are too young to be without your mother, and I bet that because you have two younger sisters, you feel you need to fill that role for them now. Except being here makes that impossible, doesn't it?"

"Entirely." Ginevra shrugged. "And thank you. I try not to think about it … it's easier."

Well, mostly.

"Once," Cara said, "there was a time when I, too, was a woman who did not want the legacy of the mafia following me, or the life I was just *given* and told I belonged to. I know what this world can sometimes make you sacrifice for this, and I'm sorry that they took your normalcy from you for the benefit of men who do not care what will happen to you because of their choices."

Ginevra dragged in a burning breath, surprised at the ache in her chest. "I didn't ask for what my half-brothers did. But I had no choice—if not me, then my sisters. I was willing to be whatever they needed for me to be so that my sisters didn't have to."

"And you worry for them now because you're not with them to stand in where they might have to," Cara replied. "I can hear it in your voice."

"Every single night. I worry for hours. I can't sleep."

Cara sighed. "I am not supposed to talk about the things my husband knows, or his contacts with other crime families outside of his own. Not our way, you see."

"I suppose."

"*But* ... I will make an exception for you, Ginevra." Cara smiled, that twinkle back in her eye as she said lowly, "From what I understand, and from what Gian has gathered, New York will be a better place for you and your sisters when this ends ... one side is winning, and it's the one you want to win."

Ginevra straightened on her chair, taking that statement in, and what it meant.

"And for now," Cara added, "no one will blame you for focusing on yourself, and your own happiness. Because there is nothing else you can do when these men ... they make our choices. We make the best of it and say to hell with them when we can. You didn't ask for this life, but you can do amazing things with it, Ginevra. I hope you're aware of that."

The server came around the table, stopping the two from saying anything more on the topic. Food piled high on a silver platter that the woman balanced on her arm had Ginevra's stomach rumbling.

She could absorb Cara's words later.

When she was alone …

"Have you pried as much information from her as you could, Ma, and can I take her home with me now?"

Ginevra and Cara spun around from the piece of artwork they had been admiring behind the restaurant's bar. Done with their lunch, Cara had called, so Chris could come back around to pick up Ginevra anytime he was ready.

Someone else came instead.

Cara grinned at the sight of Corrado standing behind them with his hands tossed into the pockets of his suit's slacks. "Is that the only reason you assume I wanted to have lunch with her?"

Corrado's gaze drifted to Ginevra; his usual intensity colored by a clear affection. "Of course not, Ma. She's amazing without all the other interesting bits with me and Alessio. She doesn't need us for *that.*"

"And you would be right," Cara said.

Ginevra smiled and stared down at the floor.

"And yes, we're done," Cara added, "so you can sneak her back, and hide her away from the world, Corrado."

"Thank you, Ma."

Cara pointed a finger at him, her gaze narrowing. "I do, however, want to see more of *you,* if you will be staying in this city. It's not acceptable for you to be here for two months, and I see you all but *one* time. I don't like that."

"I will fix that."

"Make sure. Oh, and Alessio, too. Although, I have seen far more of him than you … pick up the slack, huh?"

"Noted, Ma."

Ginevra hid her grin at Cara chastising her son by continuing to stare at the floor. She only looked up when Cara touched her arm with a soft touch.

"Thank you for joining me today," Cara said, winking, "and we will do it again soon. I promise."

"I can't wait."

It wasn't a lie, either.

"Your driver is outside, if you're ready to leave, Ma," Corrado said. "I chatted with him before I came in."

Cara nodded. "Good. I have errands. Take care of this woman, Corrado."

"Will do."

Corrado leaned down to press a quick kiss to his mother's cheek when she stopped at his side before passing him by. A simple wave of her delicate hand over her shoulder was all Ginevra saw of his mother before Cara disappeared out the front of the business.

Just like that, her focus was back on Corrado.

And that sly grin of his as he stepped closer to her until she had to walk backward from his closeness. Not that she went far—her back hit the edge of the bar, and she was cornered. Except it didn't *really* feel like he cornered her, not when she liked being caught by Corrado.

He stared down at her, his brown eyes darkening before he dropped a quick kiss to Ginevra's mouth without asking if he could or should. She didn't mind that, either, taking his kiss and reveling in the way he owned her.

All too soon, he was pulling away.

But he didn't move away.

Corrado's thumb stroked her bottom lip, and then drifted over the edge of her jaw as he asked, "Did you enjoy yourself?"

"Very much."

"Good. My mother loves you."

"She's … amazing, too."

Corrado cocked his head to the side with a curious eye. "She is, and so are you."

"Do you lay that charm on for every woman that catches your eye, or am I a special case?"

"I never tried."

She appreciated his frankness.

"And you're quite special," he added, winking.

Ginevra laughed. "You came to get me alone?"

"I did. Today has been long … Alessio needed time alone. I'm giving it to him."

"Did something happen?"

"Nothing that didn't need to happen."

Ginevra wasn't sure if that was a good thing, but Corrado also didn't seem like he would give her the chance to figure it out. Not before he leaned in, and found her lips with his own again in a soft, slow kiss that had her entire body heating as sparks lit up all of her nerve endings.

Damn this man.

"And I wanted to spend time with you," he murmured against her lips, his forehead touching hers, "because I don't do that enough."

"We spend all day together. We're living in the same place, and we don't leave it often, if at all."

"It's not enough. It's easy to be with you, Ginevra. *Too easy.*"

Yeah, she understood the feeling well.

And still when she looked in his eyes, she was sure something else lingered there, too. His need to have someone else with them, too, but that person wasn't there.

Which was also strange …

Because she felt that, too.

What were these men doing to her?

CHAPTER 10
ALESSIO

"I want coffee."

Alessio didn't bother to look up from a new set of knives Corrado had laid out across the desk for him to admire. "Then, make one."

"No, from that place down the street."

Corrado peeked up at Alessio to smile. "Ah, the café down the block. She thought it was cute when we drove past yesterday."

"Yeah," Ginevra said in the doorway, "that place. Can I walk down—"

"No," Alessio said.

"But ... it's a block away. And no one even knows I'm here."

Alessio turned away from the knives all at once, done with them now that something better had his attention. Ginevra, that was. "If you want to walk down to the café, then that's what we'll do. Let's find your coat."

"You're busy."

"And Corrado's middle name is Paul," Alessio said, because it was as ridiculous as her statement. "What does it matter? Now, I'm not busy. Let's go."

He didn't give her the chance to argue it further before heading past her in the doorway with a wave that demanded for her to follow. He wasn't so busy that he couldn't come back to the damn knives another day, no matter how nice they were. If she wanted coffee from the place down the block, then that's what they would do.

"Pick me up one of those Danishes!" Corrado called after him.

"Diabetes in a paper bag, got it."

"Fuck off, Les."

"But not a lie."

"Wait for me," Ginevra muttered, jogging to catch up with Alessio in the hallway. "I'm just saying, I could have walked down by myself."

"And then if something happened—"

"It wouldn't."

Alessio shrugged. "Well, it won't *now*. Will it?"

She huffed in the front hallway.

He pulled her coat from the hook and handed it to her with a grin.

"Besides," he added, "I need a walk."

"What, like a restless puppy?"

His grin turned playful in a blink.

"Exactly like that."

Mostly.

"Really?" she asked.

Alessio made a noise under his breath. "Listen, if I can't fuck my issues out, I might as well walk them out, huh?"

Ginevra's cheeks pinked.

God.

He had no clue how this woman was both innocent and sexy.

"Let's go," he said, yanking open the penthouse door.

"Should we get you a leash?"

Her teasing tone had him shaking his head. The sassiness, though? Definitely his favorite.

~

"Les?"

"Hmm?"

The sky, a bright blue for the second of September, stayed clear overhead. He hadn't been spending enough time outside.

When Ginevra didn't respond to his prompt, Alessio gave her all of his attention. He didn't miss how she tried to avoid his gaze by using her to-go cup of coffee as a shield in front of her face when she sipped from it.

"Ginevra, what is it?"

She peeked over at him. "Well …"

"Say whatever, woman."

"Why haven't you kissed me since the day in the library?"

Alessio blinked, surprised at the question. "I'm … not sure."

"Oh."

Her dimmed tone made a tightness clench in his chest. Mostly because, to him, the sound echoed with rejection. She had to realize that was the furthest thing from the case with him and her, *and* Corrado.

"Is that what you want?" he asked.

Ginevra laughed and glanced away. "I asked *why*, if you might have a reason."

"And that's not an answer to my question, Ginny."

"Because I don't know, either."

Alessio chuckled, stepping closer to her side as they continued their walk down the street. Close enough to wrap an arm around her side, hold tight to her waist, and pull her into his body. Like this, he was able to press a quick kiss to her temple, which he did to have the softness of her skin and her scent against his lips.

Only a *tease*.

A promise.

A hint of what he wanted to do.

"I've been busy unpacking my shit," Alessio murmured against her skin, tightening his hold on her waist, "and it had nothing to do with you on a *personal* level. Your presence, yes, but not you. But yes, I think about you, and what I would like from you, often."

"Do you?"

"More than I should—feelings make things dangerous, Ginevra."

"It always comes back to that for you, right?"

"Pardon?"

"How you *feel*, or what feeling something might do to you."

He stiffened.

She wasn't wrong.

"Yes," he said, "and I needed to make sure what happened here, with *you*, had nothing to do with him."

"I don't understand."

"I don't want to have you only because he does, Ginny. And I wasn't sure if that's what was happening here, or not."

She stopped their walk, turning, so both faced each other. He didn't mind because now he saw her eyes, and she had all his attention. His truths were always in his stare.

He wanted her to *know*.

All of it.

"Maybe I lied," she whispered.

Alessio arched a brow. "Oh? Hard to believe."

"I want you to kiss me, and *more*, but this is overwhelming, and confusing for me. It's easier for me to do the simple thing because I don't have to overthink, or worry about the consequences of what this all means. And—"

Quite enough of that.

Her rambling.

He only needed *I want you to kiss me*, and would happily give her what she wanted. Right fucking now, honestly.

Alessio liked to give everyone their space, but especially this woman and Corrado because shit was easier.

He was tired of easy.

The only way the three of them might figure this out was if they closed all the distance and opened every single door. *Wide open*, right?

Yeah.

Alessio leaned down and grazed his lips against Ginevra's with a gentle kiss. *At first*. Enough to taste her, and the lingering bitter sweet coffee she'd been sipping on during their walk. And that's all it took for her to inch closer, for her hand to snake up against his stomach before her palm laid flat to his chest, pressing hard.

Not to move him back, no.

To keep him right *there*.

The russet stare of hers locked on his as his tongue snaked out to strike against the seam of her lips, testing and promising. *Give me a little more,* he wanted to say*, and let's see what might happen here, Ginevra.*

Instead of talking, he let the kiss say what he needed to, and what she *wanted* to. God knew he found more than what he expected in the way she stood there on the sidewalk, tight to him, her tongue slashing against his as their lips worked a familiar beat together.

Somehow, the kiss seemed familiar. Like it *should be*, as though it had always been.

Ginevra pulled back from the kiss first, her ragged exhale whispering across his lips when she breathed, "You should do that more often."

"I will."

"And you know …"

"What?"

"Those feelings, Les," she whispered, "It's not just about me, but Corrado, too. If being here has taught me anything

... well, loving someone is not a *vulnerability*—it's courageous."

"What makes you say so?"

"What else would you call handing over a part of yourself to someone else when it means also accepting that being alone is a possibility? And yet, you're still willing to take the risk. Loving may make you vulnerable to being hurt, but it's courageous to love all the same."

"And you think that's what I should do here?"

Ginevra smiled, her fingertips drifting over his jaw with a soft touch. "Not with *me* ... no one but you knows what you want with me. I meant with him—it hurts you more when you're not doing what you want to do with Corrado, when you're not *with* him."

"How can you possibly—"

"All someone has to do is watch. I have had a lot of time to do that, haven't I?"

Why should he argue?

Right was *right*.

"You realize me being with Corrado means we would be—"

"Loving again?"

Alessio wet his lower lip. "You think that man and I have *love* in the mess we made together?"

"You two might not love the way everyone else does, but it's yours. That's what matters, isn't it?"

"I still haven't decided if that makes it right, though."

Or *healthy*.

"I think it's where you're meant to be," she said, shrugging one shoulder, "together, Les. When you're apart, even when you're standing in the same room, everyone else senses the distance, too."

"Or only you do."

"Doesn't change that it's true." Ginevra sighed, dropping his gaze. "I haven't figured out yet where I fit in here."

"I know exactly where you fit in."

Her head snapped up, and those wide eyes of hers, always so expressive and deep, found his with a million and one questions reflecting back. "Do you?"

"Yes."

With them.

She belonged with them.

Except this was all on her, and she had to make those choices on her own. It wasn't something they could do for her. He only controlled what he wanted to do with Corrado, and Ginevra was right. Closer had always been better for Alessio with Corrado. Being *together*, despite the things separating them, would forever be right when everything else seemed wrong.

Alessio leaned in and pressed a quick kiss to Ginevra's lips again. "Thank you."

"For what?"

"Being you, Ginny."

∾

Alessio knew exactly how he'd found himself like this—his back straight against Corrado's leather-wrapped headboard, a hand tight around his throat to keep him pinned in place. Corrado's mouth worked against his, kissing him hard and deep as his cock fucked him the same way.

Strange, that.

And fucking wonderful, too.

Corrado's kiss was the same as his beat with every thrust and pull against Alessio's body. Brutal, and *so fucking good.* Each snap of his hips had the firm lines of their forms driving against one another. Alessio's cock, painfully stiff, felt the brunt of their weight, grinding against his length in the best way possible.

It was too much.

It wasn't fucking enough.

How long had it been since the two of them were like this? Since Alessio just *woke up* in the night, needing Corrado? Far too long, he realized. He'd understood that better than ever tonight when he woke up, alone again, in a bed that didn't belong to him. Like one side was far too empty, and he needed to fix it.

Nothing was ever right like that.

He could still remember the cold floors chilling the pads of his feet as he drifted through the penthouse, needing to find that thing he'd been missing. *Corrado, Corrado, Corrado.* It had become a mantra in his mind, until he slipped into Corrado's room, then his bed, and finally … *this.*

"Too long," Corrado mumbled against his mouth.

His thrusts were coming faster, now.

Harder, too.

Like the hand at Alessio's throat, those fingers tightening and loosening almost rhythmically. His voice was fucking hoarse, so deep, full of air and lust and *love.* He'd realized that, too, now. He didn't need to be told those words to know they were true.

They were *words.*

Not actions.

Or behavior.

Or their *life.*

It was just words.

Alessio had put far too much weight into words, and less trust in the man he had known from the time he was seventeen years old. So, no, he didn't give a fuck about words.

Not tomorrow.

Not yesterday.

And not right now, either.

"Look at me."

Alessio's gaze snapped up, pleasure racing through his bloodstream with every pounding beat of his heart, to find Corrado's eyes locked on his. His lips hovered above Alessio's, ragged exhales coming out fast between them, their kiss broken.

"Fucking missed you," Alessio said, words husky.

"God, yeah."

He was going to come.

Soon.

The sensation teased in the tightness of his balls, and in the heat shooting up his spine. Every slam of his lover's body into his, stretching him open in the best way as fingers dug achingly into his thighs, and he tangled his into Corrado's hair.

He couldn't stop it.

"*Jesus Christ, Corrado.*"

Alessio stiffened, a loud groan escaping from his lips before Corrado slammed his mouth against his to swallow it up. Their tongues clashed, warring like their hands pushing and grabbing far too tightly as his come spilled between them.

"Come on," Alessio urged Corrado, his tongue snaking out to taste the salt on his lover's jaw as those words tumbled out. "Fucking give it to me, then."

"*Fuck.*"

Teeth scraped against his stubble, a sting following the same path. The ache of Corrado's hands, one still at his throat, and the other now pushing firmly against the hard ridges of Alessio's abdominal muscles, only want more.

"*Come,*" Alessio goaded. "*Fucking come.*"

The control Corrado always had snapped, and nothing was better than that, too. The wild darkness he found in the man's gaze under the dim lighting of the one bedside lamp which was still on. The way he bared his teeth and met that challenge staring back.

After all these years that was still the same.

Sex was still their war.

There were no losers here.

It didn't matter if he was *fucking*, or the one being fucked. This was their battle that only got better with time. The one place they found the most solace together. Quiet, alone, lost in each other, and nothing else.

Fuck, he forgot how much he missed that.

How much he needed it.

The husky moan that escaped Corrado as his next thrust brought him to a full stop against Alessio, his grasp stilled before it trembled like the rest of his body, brought him out of the remnants of his own orgasm to watch his lover fall into his.

Corrado's head dipped down, his forehead pressing to Alessio's chest over the tattoo of a crowned heart, as his back tensed, and a curse fell from his lips. Nothing sounded better, and nothing would ever calm him more than this.

Of that, he was most sure.

Seconds passed.

Silence echoed.

Alessio sighed. "Too fucking long, Corrado."

"*Yeah.*"

"Shit still won't be perfect," Alessio warned.

He figured, the man needed to hear that.

He did, too.

"But it is right now," Corrado replied, tone low.

"It is right now."

Their reminder.

They could have this. It would be there, present and effective like they needed it to be. That didn't mean it would fix everything. Sex didn't work that way, not for them. But it helped.

Alessio stared at the ceiling above him, body thrumming and sensitive in the best way. "I could love her."

His words were soft in the darkness. Like maybe if he didn't say them loudly, then they wouldn't come true yet. He wasn't sure if he was as ready for that as he had been for this.

He heard Corrado's swallow.

Audible, and weighted.

Like the rest of this, too.

It was all too fucking heavy.

"I could," Alessio said again.

"You should. *You should.*"

CHAPTER 11
CORRADO

Alessio shifted around Corrado in the walk-in closet, reaching past to grab the folded pair of black jeans sitting in a pile of other plain, black jeans. It was almost amusing because even Alessio's clothes had remained in Corrado's room, although the man didn't.

Corrado slipped a watch onto his wrist, already mostly dressed after their shared shower. He wasn't soon going to forget that, or the night before, either. It always led to far better mornings when he woke up next to the person—people, now—he wanted. Last night seemed like it was for him *and* Alessio, and this morning … well, it was only for Les.

From the second the man backed him against the shower wall, to the way his teeth had found the back of Corrado's neck when he fucked him.

Like that, they connected better.

It was *easier.*

"Yeah, this is gonna have to do," Alessio muttered.

Corrado eyed him from the side, smirking. "You're practically naked."

In nothing but black jeans, showing off inked, tanned skin, nipple rings, and the hard-cut V of his groin, Alessio stared back at Corrado like he didn't see the problem. He hadn't even bothered to pull on shoes or socks. He worked on affixing his row of bracelets and his favorite watch to his wrist as he asked, "*And?*"

Corrado shook his head. "And nothing."

It spoke to their differences again.

The things which make them unique.

Corrado was up and dressed in slacks, his usual silk button-down, and ready for the day, bad mood not included. He couldn't be in a bad mood after a night and morning like the one they had. It had been a long fucking time coming.

Alessio liked a bit of laziness when he first woke up after a night like the one before. Half-dressed, partially awake, still happy, all things considered, but not sure if he wanted to start the day or not.

Leaning against the row of shelving in the walk-in closet, Alessio said nothing as Corrado pulled a silk tie from the rack that matched the navy blue of his shirt. He didn't mind the man's attention, because it wasn't unusual, but he still figured after the night before, maybe Alessio had things to say.

"What?" Corrado asked.

"Nothing."

"You sure?"

Alessio grinned. "Just thinking I missed this, is all."

Corrado stilled as he threw the tie around his neck, the ends hanging down. He peeked up, meeting Alessio's stare to hold it as the silence echoed all around them. Not that he needed to repeat or confirm what Alessio had said because he heard it fine. He didn't think Alessio needed Corrado to say he felt the same, either.

Wasn't it obvious?

And yet, he still murmured, "Me, too. Every fucking day, Les."

Because this was *them*.

Their life, routine, and *thing* together. Morning, noon,

and night. For five years, there were things about them that had never changed. And when one became comfortable in the mundane parts of life with someone else at their side, like getting dressed together first thing in the morning, it was like missing your left hand when you had to do it alone.

Corrado *hated* that.

He needed Alessio to feel right.

Normal.

"Yeah, me too," Corrado said again, moving to leave the walk-in closet.

Alessio stopped him with a hand that shot out fast to slip around Corrado's neck to stop him. His fingers threaded into Corrado's hair line at the nape of his neck, tightening just enough, before he yanked him forward for a kiss.

He took that, too.

Happily.

It was softer than their moments had been the night before, or even that morning. Slower, too, like Alessio wanted to enjoy it.

Corrado didn't mind at all.

His teeth dragged along Alessio's lower lip as he pulled away with a wink. "We're good?"

Alessio nodded. "We're *better*."

He'd take that.

It was something other than what they had been.

"And I'm still not fucking getting entirely dressed yet," Alessio grumbled when Corrado turned to leave the closet. He laughed, hearing the pattering of Alessio's footsteps following behind him. "I want pancakes."

"Cook them."

"I don't ... *cook*."

"You should learn. Why do I always have to feed *you*? It should be the other way around occasionally, yeah?"

Alessio made a noise under his breath.

Corrado just chuckled.

"Fine, I'll cook them, but if you die from it, you can't blame me."

"I'll help."

"Thought so."

He ignored the smugness to the man's tone as he found the shoes he'd slipped off next to the bed before climbing in the night before. Sitting on the edge of the mattress, he shoved his feet into the supple leather loafers, glancing up to find Alessio leaning against the small dresser between the bathroom and closet doors.

"I'm not signing the contract for The League's auctions," Alessio said without prompting.

Corrado took those words in before responding. It was Alessio's choice, but after saying his piece that day in the office, he decided there wasn't anything else he needed to do.

Like everything else in their relationship.

Corrado didn't have to like it all.

"And how does Dare feel about that?" Corrado asked.

Alessio shrugged. "It's not his choice."

"That's not what I asked."

"I'm aware."

It didn't matter, Corrado decided.

Alessio was right.

No one else but Alessio got the final say.

Standing from the bed, ready to start his day in a far better mood than he had in a month or more, Corrado turned to face the doorway of the bedroom.

The *opened* door, he realized.

He blinked, staring across the hall to the open doorway of the bedroom just across from his. There, Ginevra slept on top of her blankets, like usual. There was nothing strange about that, and yet, it still seemed like he was missing something.

"Hey," Alessio said behind him. "We cooking food, or not?"

Corrado didn't move. "Did you close the door last night?"

Alessio didn't answer.

Because he didn't need to.

A sound escaped Corrado, wary and curious at the same time. "*Les?*"

"I can't remember, and I don't, no. That's *your* thing, not mine. Someone is in the bed, you close the door. I came in, Corrado, and we didn't get out of the bed."

"I didn't open it this morning."

"Me, either."

They had yet to leave the bedroom. So yeah, the door had been open all night.

Had Ginevra's also been open?

Fuck.

"If your first ten calls and messages went unanswered," Andino Marcello said, his tone cool in Corrado's ear on the other end of the call, "then maybe that should have been a clue to you about the fact I wasn't willing to chat."

Corrado stiffened, trying to subdue the urge to tell this asshole where he could fuck himself, and with what tool to use to do it. "Despite this ... *favor*," he said, choosing his words carefully although he wanted to make himself clear, "I don't answer to you, Andino. When this is all said and done, remember that, yeah?"

Alessio peeked over his shoulder, arching a brow in silent question. Corrado shook his head in response, not wanting the man to worry about it. They would talk about this after. Alessio needed to focus on *not* burning the pancakes.

Because apparently, standing next to the stove while he cooked was too big of a hassle. That was every reason Corrado was standing behind him while on the call to make sure Alessio didn't move from his spot.

That, and he wanted to be close.

"I have nothing to tell you," Andino snapped.

"She would like to speak to her sisters."

"Absolutely not. As far as they know, she is missing, and dead. I want them to keep believing that. They are too young to understand the consequences of outing the fact she's still alive."

"They think *what*?" Corrado hissed.

Alessio's hand drifted behind him, his fingers twisting into the fabric of Corrado's shirt like he assumed holding onto the man would keep him calm. It helped; he wouldn't lie about that. So much so that Corrado moved closer to Alessio. Close enough to share the warmth of Alessio's sculpted back molding against his silk-covered chest.

"You're not serious, right?" Corrado asked, his tone calmer.

Not by much though.

"I need people to rely on what I tell them," Andino said, sounding as though he was just about done with this conversation. "And I don't care if you, or she, or anyone else, fucking likes it. As long as I get what I want that's what matters."

"They're teenagers. You're *traumatizing* them, likely. Their father died a while back, then their mother, and now they think their sister is—"

"Is there something I can do for you, or did you keep calling me so you could bitch about shit that won't change soon, Corrado?"

His jaw ached. That's how hard he was clenching his fucking teeth. It was likely the next time he had a face-to-face moment with Andino, well, it would not end well. Corrado would guarantee it wouldn't end badly for him, though.

"Easy," Alessio murmured as though he was reading Corrado's mind. It was far more probable he was feeling Corrado's body cues that spoke of his anger, and he was reacting to that. "Try to get *something* you want from him. Something to give her, Corrado. It's the best you can do. We can handle his stupid ass another day."

Right, right.

When had Alessio become the voice of reason?

It didn't matter.

"Just …" Corrado cleared his throat and pinched the bridge of his nose to settle the fury swimming in his bloodstream. Some people just had that effect on others. Like instant anger right to the fucking vein. Andino was one of those. "How much longer before she might come home?"

Although that thought alone was enough to make Corrado want to rage all over again, but for different reasons. Ginevra had a life away from here … people to take care of. And God knew he would never deny her those things, even if he had fallen entirely in love with the woman amidst this mess with him, the favor to Andino, and Alessio.

Still, he loved her.

At some point, she would go back.

Corrado didn't like it, but that didn't make it any less true. He figured, when the time came, then they would all handle it together. Him, Les, and her. However they wanted to work that out, then they would.

"When?" he asked again, firmer the second time when Andino said nothing.

"I'm not sure."

"Jesus Christ. And they want *you* to be the next boss of that organization there?"

"Out of line," Andino murmured, "and now you're pissing me off."

Oh, really?

That was nice.

So fucking nice.

And Corrado didn't give a shit.

"You've been pissing me off since—"

Alessio pivoted and snatched the phone right out of Corrado's hand. He put the device to his ear at the same time his palm came to rest flat against Corrado's chest, a silent order for him to stay. He wasn't even pressing down to keep him from moving, and Corrado's blazing gaze didn't seem to bother him in the least.

"Andino," Alessio said into the phone, never looking away from Corrado's severe expression as he did so, "it's Alessio—yeah, you remember, right? Say hello to Pink for me, I'm sure he needs the reminder, too."

A beat of silence passed.

Alessio grinned. "And your point is? Because here's our fucking point—we need a timeline, something to *give* this woman here who did everything you asked of her even when you gave her fuck all in return. She followed *your rules*. She did what you wanted. Not once has she stepped out of line, and every single day, she continues to do these things hoping that back there, the people she loves—who no worries, we know you don't give a shit about—are still okay. And so, if you can't tell me things I need to know here, I will come find it."

A hum sounded from the speaker.

Loud and dark.

Alessio seemed unaffected. "That's nice, and I also don't care. Because while we're aware that to you, Ginevra is a means to an end, *here* … here she means something. So, you give me something to tell her, or I will come cut it out of your fucking mouth. You hear me?"

Corrado grinned, glancing away because *right*, he was the one who needed to keep himself in check. Not at all Alessio.

No.

Alessio's fingers tapped against Corrado's chest, drawing his attention back to the man as he nodded. "Within a couple of months? Not firm, but likely. Got it."

He hung up the phone without a proper goodbye and handed it out to Corrado accompanied by a pointed look. Corrado took the device, shaking his head at the same time.

"He's hoping to have *everything* finished within a couple of months," Alessio said like Corrado hadn't heard the conversation already. "We'll see how that works out."

"Still nothing for her to have about her sisters, though."

Alessio shrugged. "They're alive, Corrado. You can tell her they are still alive."

Yeah.

What good would that do, though?

"It's the best we can do."

"Right," Corrado agreed.

Not that it made him feel better.

Alessio turned back to the stove, his pancake bubbled in the center to say it was ready to flip.

"Turn it over," Corrado said. "And try not to make a mess."

"I am doing *fine*."

"I didn't say you weren't."

Alessio made a noise under his breath but did flip the pancake. Corrado wasn't sure how long the two of them stayed like that, close together against the stove as Alessio made an entire stack worth of pancakes that were decent, and not at all burned, but the minutes ticked by.

In their closeness, he found home.

In their silence, comfort.

A part of Corrado hoped the two of them were getting back to what they had been before this whole thing happened. Oh, he wasn't stupid enough to think it would be the same, but it could be better.

He wanted that just as badly.

Corrado pressed a quick kiss to the top of Alessio's wide shoulder. His head turned, his gaze finding Corrado, but he said nothing. Not that he needed Alessio to say anything—all he ever needed was the man to be *there*.

In Alessio's stare, he found familiarity.

Understanding.

Corrado figured Alessio still had shit he needed to work through here, and he was more than willing to allow him whatever he needed to do it. Now, at least, they could get back to *them* while he did it, and that made all the difference.

It always had.

Alessio turned his attention back to the last pancake on the frying pan, saying, "Someone should go wake Ginevra up. She'll want to eat, too."

"She's up."

Corrado glanced to the side, and sure enough, found Ginevra standing in the kitchen's entryway watching them. He'd sensed her presence from damn near the moment she came to stand there, even though she hadn't made a single noise the entire time. She hadn't been there long enough to overhear the phone conversation with Andino, but she had been watching Corrado and Alessio interact together for quite a while.

Alessio looked her way, too.

Ginevra's cheeks heated as her stare drifted between the two. He didn't find shame there ... at least, not to say she might be embarrassed despite her blush. A bright curiosity blazed in her eyes, and he bet she didn't have the first clue what to do with that at all. And then she turned to dart out of the entryway, leaving air and shadows in her wake. Corrado let out a hard breath, a heaviness climbing up his spine.

Her reaction was all he needed.

The door had been open.

He bet she knew what happened the night before and had a front-row seat for at least *some* of it.

Alessio dropped the spatula to the counter. "Let me go talk to her, yeah?"

That … wasn't a bad idea.

"You should."

Alessio sidestepped Corrado to leave the stove. "All right. Keep the food hot."

"Sure. And, Les?"

"Hmm?"

Corrado shrugged one shoulder. "*Be easy*. You're a bit overwhelming at first, but especially like *that*."

A sinful smirk curved Alessio's lips in the most wicked way. "You don't know that's what—"

"Be easy." Corrado pulled open a drawer on the island, and in a flash, tossed an item to Alessio that he caught without hesitation. He stuffed the foil packet into his back pocket. Alessio didn't know whether he was offended or aroused that Corrado was sure enough about what would happen between him and Ginevra that he pulled out a condom from one of their many stashes, or if it should irk him. "A *just in case*, yeah?"

"Right."

CHAPTER 12
GINEVRA

"Ginevra."

Oh, God.

Alessio's voice calling out behind Ginevra had her wishing she could crawl into a hole and disappear. She thought, *surely*, she could act like nothing had happened the night before. Like she hadn't woken up in the middle of the night to the sounds of two men *fucking*. Like she hadn't been able to tip her head up and see *everything* happening across the hall because Corrado slept with a goddamn lamp on.

Not that it bothered her.

That was a lie.

It *bothered* her.

But in strange ways she hadn't expected. For one, because a part of her wanted to join them. For two, because she was out of her league here with these men, and their brand of love. Not only had she found that she couldn't look away the night before, a part of her hadn't wanted to, either.

That wasn't *her* moment.

They weren't fucking *her*.

She had no business watching them together, and yet, she hadn't been able to stop, either. Somehow, she'd went back to sleep … but not until they finished. And not without an ache between her thighs she was sure wouldn't *ever* be satisfied.

"Ginevra!"

A few more steps that's all.

Then, she could tuck herself away in the bedroom, close the door, and pretend like this hadn't happened at all. She wasn't ready for what was happening here if she couldn't stare those two men in the face the next morning without reliving every single detail of the show she got the night before.

So, she needed to avoid it.

Entirely.

Right?

"Would you *stop*? Christ, woman!"

Ginevra didn't make it to the bedroom before Alessio caught up to her in the hallway. His hand snagged her wrist and grabbed tight before she found herself spun around *fast*. The walls were a blur until everything stopped, her back hit the edge of the decorative table a couple of feet away from the bedroom doorway, and Alessio closed in on her.

She felt like a caged animal.

This man had *that* effect.

When he loomed over her, when he got close, and those eyes of his were only on her. Yeah, she felt just like a caged animal, and he was the predator that found his prized prey. Not that she minded it, but right then … Ginevra wanted to hide away.

"I want to go to my room," she whispered.

Alessio's brow dipped. "Ginevra—"

"I didn't mean to see that last night, and I'm sorry. I know I shouldn't have spied. Please, let me go."

He didn't.

In fact, he moved closer.

Pinned her harder.

Ginevra dragged in a ragged breath. "What are you doing?"

"You think we're *mad* at you?"

"I—"

"The door was open, Ginny."

She blinked at how he said those words. Like it just was, and she should have realized that a long time ago. She didn't think he was talking only about the bedroom door, either. She only had to consider it, and this last month with the three of them living in the same place.

Rarely did they close doors.

In any room.

Alessio and Corrado didn't tamper their tones when they spoke, either. It didn't matter if they were talking about the weather while running on the treadmill or shouting at one another in the office like they had when Alessio first came back.

The doors didn't get closed.

They let her hear everything.

She saw *everything*.

Her gaze lifted to meet Alessio's, and there, she found a raging blue storm staring at her, but in the middle of it all, she found truth. They'd purposely done that—never once had they hid themselves, their baggage, or the rest. To her, they stayed *way open*.

Alessio, too, she now realized. Even when he had been so mad, closed off, keeping that distance, and dealing with his own mountain of problems, he'd not shut her out physically. It was disconcerting.

Because she liked that.

And it terrified her, too.

"Ginevra," he murmured.

Still staring at him, she swallowed the nerves in her throat, saying, "I still shouldn't have done it. I ... you didn't invite me to do that."

Right?

She didn't think so.

It didn't matter she liked it, or they left their door open like they had a silent understanding between the three of them that she only now realized … that was them, and their private moment together.

"I didn't feel like an intruder, but I still think I intruded."

Alessio shook his head. "Not at all, sweetheart. That's one thing you couldn't do with us, but especially not when we're fucking. Do you hear me?"

God.

That heat climbed in her cheeks again, and shot right down to her pussy, too. It was easier to admire the grain in the wood floor than his handsome face, so she did that. His words shouldn't have sounded as sinful and inviting as they did, and somehow … he still pulled it off.

"You know," she said, her nervous energy falling out in fast words, "before you two, I used to say I was open about sex, and what people liked, or … all of that. Someone else's bedroom was theirs, and it's fine."

"And now?"

"I still think that, I just didn't consider it would be *my* bedroom someday, either."

Alessio chuckled. "Ginevra, look at me."

When she didn't do what he wanted right away, his left hand shot up to catch her under the jaw. A simple tilt of his hand, and she was staring into his eyes again, frozen in place by the intensity she found there.

"It's okay to be overwhelmed and confused," he said, shrugging one bare shoulder, "but never *hide* when you want it, too. That's the only way you can find out if what you want is worth it."

"Oh, that I don't doubt."

He raised a brow. "Hmm?"

"That this will be worth it."

It was the aftermath that made her wonder, but even then, she would brave it for them. She wasn't sure she wanted to find out what life would be like after these men had come into hers to change it irrevocably.

"Did you see me go in last night?" he asked.

Ginevra shook her head. "I woke up *during …*"

The memory flashed in her mind, thick and heady. Part of it hadn't seemed real, and yet, every inch of her body knew it was vivid and true.

Corrado had put Alessio on his knees, a hand tangled into his hair, and the other wrapped around his chest to keep the man suspended higher off the bed as he fucked him from behind. Their voices, their *sounds*, all came out husky. And even as it seemed like one had more control than the other, she found power in Alessio, too. In the way his body moved, how his hands tugging and grabbed to Corrado, seeking what *he* wanted.

She'd blinked, stunned at what she was seeing, and after they had rolled over, Alessio's back against the headboard, and Corrado was above him. They stayed close, movements frantic, and beauty covering every action between them.

And their *fucking*?

She found it familiar. Or rather, she recognized it was familiar to them. So rough, and vicious, yet she found affection in between, too. Maybe that was what had drawn her in the most …

"There's *always* affection," Alessio said.

Ginevra flew from her thoughts in a bang, her stare still locked on Alessio's, although she had been seeing him differently just moments ago inside her mind. Now, she found something hotter staring back at her, not that the night before, she would have thought anything would be more wickedly tempting than seeing those two men fuck.

Now, she'd say it was the way Alessio was looking at *her*. A lot similar to the way Corrado did when he had her pinned under him, making her beg and scream in all the best fucking ways.

"Intense, and beautiful," she said, her voice a breath, "that's what it was."

Alessio's gaze blazed with lust. "Was it?"

"I wondered …"

"Tell me."

"Does he fuck me the same way he fucks you—will *you*?" Ginevra dragged in a hard inhale, letting the air ache in her lungs at the thought. "Would either of you ever be able to love me the way you love each other?"

Alessio never blinked.

Didn't *breathe*.

"And how do we fuck—and love—each other, Ginny?"

"Savagely," she whispered.

It was true.

They hurt each other loving. Survived from it, *killed* with it, or become better for it. Was that not the most primal aspects of being *human*? Of loving as a human? And so, it seemed appropriate to say at their most base of being, in their moments of rawest need, they savagely loved.

"Savagely," Alessio echoed.

Ginevra nodded. "And I don't know if I could ever be the same to—"

"You only have to say yes."

"What?"

"*Say yes*." His hand on her thigh squeezed, making her all too aware of how close his fingers were to the tiny cotton shorts she wore to bed. The matching top rested higher above her navel, and she had on nothing underneath. There was no hiding the way her nipples had pebbled under the thin top, or the way her throat jumped when her gaze darted down to his mouth.

Not that her staring stopped there. She had never gotten

the chance to admire Alessio without a shirt. He even worked out with one on, and he didn't leave a bathroom unless he was fully dressed after a shower, not that it mattered because he had a private bath in his room.

But *now* ...

Now, she admired the strong muscles that made up the man's chest, and the hard lines that showcased his abs, and the way his pants rested low on his defined hips. He seemed chiseled from stone, a lot like Corrado. She'd watched him and Corrado put the gym to use day after day enough, so she knew why they looked like they did, too.

She took in his tattoos, the double sleeves, and the start of the chest tattoo that showcased a crowned heart. Corrado hadn't been lying, either. Straight bars pierced through both his nipples. They were opposites in that way. One showcasing his calm strength in a body that was uninked and unmarked in other ways. And the other taunted the world with his wildness through colorful designs, and piercings.

It wasn't obvious.

Then again, they'd been subtle from the start.

But she saw it.

She recognized it all.

They were Godly.

Both.

Why her?

What God had she pleased?

"I like your staring," he said, chuckling, "but I would *love* an answer more, Ginevra. A yes, or a no."

Right.

"And if I do? Say yes, I mean."

"Then you can learn what we both can do," he replied, his tone husky.

Like last night.

That memory swept in again.

She was *wet again*.

"Say yes," he urged.

How could she not?

Temptation had ruined the world before.

And she was only a woman.

Ginevra stood no chance.

Her hands shook against the table when he set her on it, yet her next word same out clear, and sure. There would be no mistake about what she wanted. "*Yes*."

She was grateful for the sturdiness of the table—its thick, long curved legs and strong, shiny top more than capable of handling their roughness.

Alessio closed all the distance between them in an instant. His mouth collided down on hers as his hand at her thigh slid higher up the leg of her shorts. The way he kissed her matched the way his fingers explored her. Soft strokes at first, his lips drifting over hers damningly the same way his fingers drifted over her bare pussy. Tentative at first, *seeking*. All it took was her moan, and the widening of her thighs as her lips parted for his kiss to deepen, and she found a whole *new* heaven.

There was something wicked about the way Alessio kissed her as two of his fingers slid into her clenching sex. His tongue curled around hers as his fingers twisted into her G-spot. At her jaw, his hand still keeping her head in place, so he watched her while he came up higher, and his thumb slipped into her mouth as he pulled back.

He watched her like that, too.

Sucking on his digit.

Riding his fingers.

Jesus Christ.

She would come fast.

It didn't matter he wasn't kissing her now, either. He cocked his head to the side, a sexy smirk curving the edges of his lips as he pulled his thumb from her mouth with a *pop*, and his hand slid down to her throat. Those fingertips of his drummed against her racing pulse as he spoke. "Right there, huh? Your pussy is holding onto my fingers so tight, Ginny? *Fuck*, are you gonna rain on me, sweetheart? Soak me?"

"Oh, my God," she breathed.

"Come, and give me some of you, yeah? Let me suck you off my fingers before I see my cock stretch you out, Ginevra."

Yeah.

That did it.

She came hard, a broken cry escaping her, and a rush of wetness pooling between her legs which she *might* have been embarrassed about with someone else, but not with this man. Alessio's gaze dropped between their bodies, and his grin deepened salaciously, pride coloring up the throaty noise he made as his fingers slipped out of her pussy.

He liked that.

"Fuck yeah, that's what I wanted to see," he murmured. "You try."

His hand came up fast, and unquestioningly, she opened her mouth to take the single finger he offered for her. Her heady flavor coated her tongue as she sucked herself from his digit, surprised at the tart undertones of her arousal.

She still trembled from that orgasm when he pulled his hand away to clean his other finger, the one still wet with only her, too. *God*. Nothing looked better than him enjoying the flavor of her.

Those next few seconds came like a blur. He moved fast, tugging her shorts down her legs so fast it stung her skin, not that she cared. Her hands worked at his jeans while his slipped under the cropped tank she wore to cup her breasts. Her gasp filled the hallway when his fingertips tweaked her hard nipples.

"Still yes?" she heard him ask.

"Still yes."

Undeniably yes.

Alessio's hands disappeared from her shirt to speed up her attempt at shoving down his pants. Although, not before he grabbed a foil packet from his back pocket.

Oh.

And did she mention he went commando?

Because he did.

Yep.

Fuck.

Her fingers circled around his length, already so fucking hard and weighty in her palm. She stroked his length, letting her fingertips drift over the vein on the underside of his cock that pulsed from her touch.

"Easy," he was quick to say when her grip tightened, "let me fill that pussy before you try to make me come, woman."

Ginevra grinned.

She got his kiss again, after they rolled latex down his length, and he widened her thighs enough that her muscles ached deep. His lips found hers as he positioned the head of his cock at her slit. His tongue stroked hers when his hips flexed forward.

She was so wet.

So beyond ready.

And still the first thrust took her breath away. Her body tensed, the width of him stretching her open fast, and hard. She loved it, though.

So much.

Still, he didn't stop kissing her, lips warring with hers as his tongue seemed intent to lick the fucking taste right off hers. His pace came swift, and deep. A brutal rhythm that held no reservations and didn't hold back.

Not for a second.

His hands were on her body again.

Pinning her in place.

Tightening to take her air away.

One on her chest.

At her throat.

Ginevra whimpered, words becoming impossible. It surrounded her in *him*. His taste, his scent, and all of him inside and on her. It was overwhelming, and exactly what she needed.

"Let me have this pussy suck me dry, sweetheart," he uttered against her cheek. "I want it, so you better give it to me, huh?"

Her desperate cry tangled with his thick groan.

That pace didn't let up.

Ginevra's peak climbed higher and faster than she expected it to. Still soaked between her thighs from that first orgasm, she fell over the cliff again. His blue eyes stayed locked on hers, and pleasure darkened Alessio's stare as he watched her come from him fucking her that time.

His hands slid down to grip tight onto her thighs, his strokes coming shorter, but still as rough even as he fucked her through that orgasm. She couldn't breathe, her vision tunneling from the intensity.

And then his head tipped down, his forehead resting against her chest as his thrusts came *faster*. Shaking, her peak waning but bliss racing through her bloodstream, as his fingers dug painfully into her thighs.

God, it felt good, though.

Still.

He had the best view like that, she realized. Looking down, watching himself fuck her. His next three thrusts came slower, but deeper than before, the final one making him still as her name tumbled from him with the rawest sound.

"*Ginevra*, fuck …"

He shook, too.

He lost his breath, too.

And she was still spinning high.

Ginevra wasn't sure how long the two of them stayed like that, tucked close, saying nothing, and letting it all sink in. A minute, or maybe two.

Hell, it might have been more.

She didn't care to know.

A throat cleared further down the hall, and Ginevra's eyes squeezed shut, *knowing*. Against her chest, Alessio let out a dusky laugh that still somehow sounded airless as his shoulders lifted with his breaths. She turned her head, unsurprised to find Corrado lingering at the end of the hall, half around corner, and half not. He didn't directly look at them, but he didn't keep his focus off them, either.

The ridge of his erection straining against his slacks was impossible to miss, never mind the way his tongue snaked out to wet his lips like he'd seen something he liked. She might have been embarrassed another time, but not then.

The doors were open here.

And she wanted to do this again.

All of it.

With both.

"Food is hot," Corrado said, "whenever you would both like to join me."

That said, Corrado turned, and left her view.

Ginevra made a sound under her breath. "What happens now? What do we do now?"

Alessio laughed again. "Nothing. Everything. *Anything.*"

Well, that told her all she needed to know, didn't it?

CHAPTER 13
ALESSIO

Sex was sex to Alessio, and he rarely, if ever—because he couldn't remember a time when it happened—felt awkward afterward. He understood why other people might feel that way, though. Which was why after he'd tucked himself away, and slid Ginevra's cotton shorts back up her legs, he helped her down from the table in the hallway, and with a press of his palm against her lower back, directed her into the nearest bedroom.

Hers.

She twisted her fingers, fidgeting as he moved around the room to pull clean clothes from the dresser before setting them on the edge of her bed. Not that she had a lot of clothes—a few things, he supposed. Enough to get her by here as Corrado told him.

"You need more clothes," Alessio muttered.

Ginevra let out a soft laugh. "And what would you know about that? You only wear black; everything looks the same."

He tossed her a heated look over his shoulder, and he liked the way she stilled when his gaze landed on her. All over again, the taste of her seemed to flood his mouth, and every sweet sound that came out of her when she was being fucked filled his ears again.

Yeah.

Alessio was screwed.

"Really, I just *always* look the same?" he asked, arching a brow.

Ginevra grinned, some of her nervousness bleeding away. "You're far too cocky for your own good."

"But *with* reason."

She didn't deny it.

Alessio pulled a white, cotton thong from the top drawer in the dresser, and tossed it to the pile of clothes, too. Coming to stand in front of Ginevra, he found her nerves made an appearance again when she wouldn't look up at him.

That was fine.

He could fix it.

Sliding his hands under her jaw, he tipped her head up, so she *had* to look at him. Those wide brown eyes of hers reflected everything she wasn't saying, and he saw it as clear as day staring back at him.

"Hey," he murmured.

Ginevra wet her lips. "Yeah?"

"Everything is *fine*."

"I know that."

"Nothing happens unless you want it to."

She nodded. "I know that, too."

He grinned. "That's all that should matter, then. Everything else is details, and noise. Don't overthink it. That's my job."

Her soft laughter had his semi-hard dick perking in his jeans again, making him all too aware that he still needed to go dispose of the condom, and clean himself up. *Fuck.* He'd much rather stay right here with her and handle whatever she needed.

Still, the bigger deal they made about this, the harder it might be for Ginevra to see *this* was all normal. Perhaps not for other people, but for them … it was fine.

"I just … what if I mess up?" she asked.

Alessio frowned. "How would you do that?"

"I'm not sure." Her fingers tittered in the air when she waved her hands. "Maybe I give him more attention, or I sit beside one and not the other. Or—"

"Stop. That's ridiculous."

Ginevra blinked, hurt coloring up her expression. "It's not ridiculous just because *you* already know how to handle something like this. *I* haven't, Les."

Okay.

"So, that's the wrong word," he said, dropping a kiss to her lips that lingered as he continued quieter, "these aren't things that matter here, I swear. Corrado and I … we can handle each other, or get what we need. Whether that's from each other, ourselves, or from you. This thing isn't a tit for tat, sweetheart. We're not keeping score."

"So, I can just … keep doing what I'm doing."

"If that's what you want. The only things that change are the things you want to be different."

"Okay."

Alessio smiled and pressed another kiss to her grinning lips. "Get dressed—you need to eat, huh?"

"Yeah."

It might not fix her nerves, but he hoped it helped a little. His fingers drifted over her cheek, tucking the wild strands of her dark brown hair behind her ears before he left her side, and headed out of the bedroom. She needed time by herself, he figured.

And he needed to get cleaned up.

After doing that in his own room, Alessio arrived back in the kitchen alone, although Corrado was already there, sitting at the large dining room table with the newspaper spread out in his hands. To his benefit, Corrado didn't look at Alessio as he came to sit on the left side of the man and reached for the plate of pancakes in the table's middle.

That didn't mean he stayed silent though.

"And?" Corrado asked, his voice a murmur, his gaze still taking in the paper.

"Give her a minute. Let her absorb it all."

Corrado hummed his agreement, then turned to peer at Alessio as he smothered a pancake in maple syrup. The thing he loved the most about Canada, next to the fact it was Corrado's birthplace, was that they didn't do that fake syrup shit *flavored* like maple.

"And what about you? Are you good?"

Alessio arched a brow. "You're right."

"Oh? I usually am, but do tell. It's not every day you say *you're right* and not *you're not wrong*. Because one is you outright admitting *you* were wrong, and the other is your way of trying to keep from showing your whole ass in a conversation."

"Fuck off," Alessio muttered, chuckling.

He peeked up from his plate, but Corrado hadn't looked away from him. Their gazes met, and Alessio relaxed in a way he hadn't before.

"Not a lie, though," Corrado said, shrugging.

"Not a lie," Alessio echoed. "And I meant … about her. You were right. She's like art."

Fucking her had been a privilege.

And not one he was sure he deserved.

Corrado made an appreciative noise under his breath, and his attention quickly went back to the paper. "I know, now so do you."

Right.

He was a quarter of the way through his plate when Ginevra darkened the entryway of the kitchen. She hesitated only momentarily before joining the two at the table, taking a seat at Corrado's right, across from Alessio.

Ginevra didn't reach for the food.

Alessio continued eating, and Corrado didn't turn his attention away from the paper in his hands. It was like any other morning, except it wasn't.

He could *feel* the change, now.

It was palpable.

Corrado flipped the corner of the paper down and winked at Ginevra. "Eat, kitten. Food is better when it's hot."

"Oh, I like that better," Alessio said more to himself than anyone else at the table. "Kitten—it's appropriate."

"Right? That's what I thought."

"Makes sense."

Ginevra let out a breathy laugh. "You two are horrible."

"But are we?" Alessio asked.

"We are a *little*," Corrado said, and then to Ginevra, "Unless you want a plate made for you. All you have to do is ask."

For anything, Alessio added silently.

He was sure they'd figure out a way to give it to her now.

Ginevra smiled. "I do like being spoiled."

Corrado tossed his paper aside before Ginevra had even finished her sentence and was already getting up from the table to do her bidding. Alessio met her gaze across the way, and winked.

See?

Fine.

Everything would be fine.

"Cree," Alessio greeted, standing from the couch and giving

the other two a wave of his hand as he left them alone while he answered his phone. "What can I do for you?"

Alessio was on the other side of the large sitting room from Ginevra and Corrado when Cree finally responded. "You're not picking up Dare's calls."

"I have nothing to say to him, he doesn't need me for a current job, and I don't like listening to him bitch at me because he's in his feelings."

Behind him, Alessio heard Corrado clear his throat. Okay, so he hadn't been quiet about saying what he had to say, even if he was twenty feet away. Not that anything he said was a goddamn lie, either.

"He doesn't want to talk about the auctions, if that's what you're worried about," Cree said.

"I have no doubt it'll lead into that, and I made my decision. It was mine to make."

"I agree, and so does he."

Alessio stuffed a hand in his pocket, turning to watch Ginevra sitting in Corrado's lap on the couch while the two of them battled one another on their war game. She whooped his ass all over the screen which amused Alessio to no fucking end. Even Corrado seemed to enjoy it, and usually, he was a sore loser.

He wanted to be back there.

Not here, doing this phone call.

"What do you want?" Alessio asked.

Better to get straight to the point.

"To make sure you are okay," Cree said. "Because otherwise, you don't fill us in."

"Because I'm handling shit I need to handle. And since at least one of you are of the opinion you get a say on how I handle my personal business, I no longer want either of you in on it."

Cree cleared his throat. "He didn't want you to do the

auctions. Dare, I mean. He wanted to let you do what you wanted. He's only in his mood now about it because he believes you backing out had to do with—"

"Corrado," Alessio interjected. "And he's not wrong, but that doesn't change it's still my choice to make. I don't want to do it, and regardless of what happens here, I still won't be doing it."

"Les—"

"The only reason Dare is in his feelings about Corrado and I is because *you* took the information I shared with you back to him."

"I don't hide things from him."

"Oh, I get that," Alessio said, "and I don't blame you, but you also can't fault me for keeping my private business *private* from here on out, yeah?"

"We worry."

"Don't bother."

"Alessio."

"Any news on that Albania hit yet?" Alessio asked.

Cree made a noise under his breath. "That's what you want to ask me?"

"I'm not talking about anything else with you, or him. Not until you both learn that taking me in when I was ten doesn't mean you're owed everything I do now, Cree."

"We don't assume that."

"I beg to differ."

Cree sighed. "Are things better there? That's all I want— that you're *happy*, Les."

A loud, happy holler drew Alessio's attention back to the other side of the room. Ginevra's hands flew high in the air as she tossed her head back and laughed in her triumph. On the screen, the words *Mission Accomplished* flashed across her character, while Corrado's only had a red *FAILED*.

"How did you beat me again?" Corrado groused.

Ginevra grinned, turning her head enough to catch his scowling lips in a kiss that had Alessio's own smile growing. He wished he was over there, sharing their moment with them, instead of on this damn call.

Because they were happy.

He was happy.

"We're all happy," Alessio said. "And you can tell Dare, too."

"I'll try to rein him in, Les. It's the best I can do."

"I would appreciate it."

He had to get back to his life.

"Stop it."

Alessio's words came out in a mumble given that his face had buried in the pillows on the bed, and he was half asleep. *Nearly there*, but not quite. He couldn't fall into sleep like he wanted when a foot away from him on the large king-size bed, Corrado kept tensing every few seconds.

It wasn't the movement, or even Corrado's sighs in the darkness, but rather, the fact his lover was annoyed. Or bothered … likely both.

Alessio didn't like that.

"Am I keeping you up?" Corrado asked.

Alessio twisted his head around, so he could stare at Corrado, or what he could see of him. "Yes, and if you want something different, go *do that*. Don't lay there and fret about it. That drives me fucking crazy."

"You don't—"

A quiet shuffling echoed outside of their bedroom, because *yeah*, Alessio was back in here a couple of days later. This was where he wanted to be, he had a better night's sleep, and didn't give a fuck about the details. Those only held him back. Corrado left the door open in case the woman across the hall wanted something other than to sleep alone in her bed. Not that she had taken the invitation yet.

But at that sound, the noise Ginevra made when she rolled over in her bed *again*—for what, the millionth time since she had gotten out of the bathtub two hours ago?— Corrado tensed again. The woman wasn't sleeping, but she was far enough away that she probably couldn't hear their quiet conversation, and he wasn't sure she had a clue that they were aware she wasn't sleeping.

Her choice to sleep alone was hers.

They said nothing.

"At night, she worries," Corrado said.

"About home, you mean."

"What else? When does her brain shut off? About her mom, I suspect, and her sisters. She doesn't tell us because who knows why ... but it's what she does. I don't like it."

Alessio sighed, and scrubbed a hand down his face, willing that sleepiness to *go*. "Just go do what you want to do. If you're going to lie beside me wondering about it, and keep me up all night, too, then I will need you to do that somewhere else."

"Well—"

"*Go get her,*" he grumbled in the darkness.

"Or this is her time, no? At night, that's when she can actually be alone without *us*, Les. It's how she deals with all the shit going on—her anxiety, and the rest, you know?"

"Except it's not dealing with it when she does the same thing night after night, is it?"

Corrado didn't reply.

"Fine," Corrado snapped.

Alessio smirked to himself as Corrado kicked the blankets off and jumped out of the bed without another word to his lover he left behind. He listened as footsteps padded across the room, out into the hallway, and faded into the room next door. A quiet *hey* echoed from Ginevra, followed by a *what are you doing* before Corrado was back in the bedroom.

He lifted his head from the pillows in enough time to see Corrado set Ginevra on the bed right in the middle. His hands scooted her over as she still looked confused before Corrado got back on his side and found his comfortable position on his side again.

Ginevra blinked. "I was fine over there."

"No, you weren't," Corrado muttered.

"I *was*."

Alessio grunted under his breath. "Lies. You twist and turn half the night, and when you fall asleep, it keeps going. Just saying, you could sleep better over here."

"We're only *sleeping*?"

Alessio would have laughed at the question she hinted at, but he didn't think now was the right time. Corrado saved him from having to say anything.

"This isn't about sex," Corrado murmured. "It's about something you need ... sleep, rest, or a recharge—letting someone else take care of you because you're dealing with shit alone when you don't have to, Ginny. Just because you think you're handling it alone doesn't mean everyone around you isn't still affected."

Sleepily, Alessio said, "Exactly." His tone deepened as he added, "But if it was about sex, though, we'd *all* be good with that."

"*Les*," Corrado warned.

"I'm not wrong."

Ginevra let out a soft laugh, but it was the *heat* lingering behind her nervous energy that took his attention the most. He looked up to see her staring back at him. The same curiosity and lust lit up her gaze.

All right.

"Is that what you want?" he asked her.

Ginevra sucked in a tentative breath. "It wasn't."

Corrado made a dark noise from the other side of the bed. "And now?"

"*Maybe.*"

"I don't do maybes, kitten."

Consent always mattered here.

Clear, unquestionable consent.

It *had* to.

Alessio rolled to his back, deciding he would settle this for all. He figured it had been one thing for Ginevra when she was dealing with these men one at a time, but when they were close like this, both near with her in the middle ... she had to get stuck in her head.

It wasn't that deep.

"Think about it," Alessio murmured, "he will tuck you against him on your side, get his hands between your thighs, make you crazy, and after, he's going to fuck you while I enjoy the show, Ginevra. That's it, that's all. And you get to fall asleep fucked, happy, and on top of the blankets the way you like. But if you would prefer to overthink it until you think it to fucking *death,* fine, we can do that, too."

Corrado chuckled. "There you go."

"I thought ..." She trailed off, her voice faint.

"What, both?"

That seemed like the obvious answer.

"A little," she whispered.

Alessio dismissed that with a grunt. "Not yet."

"Not yet," she echoed.

"Soon," Corrado added, a wicked promise lingering there. "But not yet."

That took time.

A *readiness.*

A certain level of trust and need he didn't think Ginevra was ready for yet. Oh, they would get her there, certainly, but not tonight.

Ginevra made a soft, hot noise. "But tonight—"

"If you want," Corrado said, "but that's not why I brought you over here. It's not why you're in this bed at all, and as long as you get that, then whatever you want, you get."

"You only have to ask," Alessio said.

"Okay."

Alessio peeked up at her where she still sat between their resting positions. "*Okay*, okay, or okay we will sleep?"

Ginevra grinned in the darkness. "Sleep ... later."

Yeah, that's what he thought.

"Corrado, then?" Alessio asked, wanting to be sure that was *who* she wanted. "Because I have a kink, and I like to *watch.*"

All it took was Ginevra's subtle nod, and her soft *yes*, for Corrado to reach for her. Alessio didn't plan to touch, but he reached over to drift his fingers through Ginevra's hair when Corrado kissed her. He hadn't been wrong, either.

Corrado used his hands first—stripping her of clothes and shedding his own; he did his best work between her thighs, hands spreading her legs wide before his fingers stretched out her pussy, too. All those sounds that crawled out of her throat as Corrado circled her clit with the pads of his fingers while his other hand stuffed her full had Alessio harder than ever.

Still, he didn't touch.

He didn't need that to get what he needed here.

"Fuck, yeah," Alessio murmured, "you should see what I see, Ginny. How wet your pussy is, and how you're already soaking his hands. So fucking good. How bad do you want his cock, huh? *Tell me.*"

"Jesus," Corrado grunted, "killing me here, Les."

He grinned.

Yeah, he knew.

He loved watching Corrado work.

Corrado liked hearing all the details.

"Use your words, kitten," Alessio urged Ginevra.

"*Please …*"

Her eyes flew wide, landing on Alessio when Corrado's teeth found the junction between her neck and her shoulder. She came hard, gasping into the dark room and twisting against the bar-like hold Corrado had on her body.

Alessio enjoyed every fucking second. There was nothing better than watching someone get off unless you were the one making them do it. And even that … well, he didn't mind this.

For now.

He'd get the rest later.

Her next words came out breathless, and high. "*Fuck me. Please, oh my, God … please, fuck me.*"

Alessio might have gotten his own cock in his hands just to get his own while he watched them get theirs, but she reached for him across the bed. Her fingers tangled with his to hold tight as Corrado left her long enough to grab what he needed from the bedside table. Alessio slipped across the bed, his mouth finding Ginevra's in just enough time to swallow her hard moan when Corrado filled her from behind.

And *God …*

That did sinful things to him.

Wicked things.

He inched closer, but only because her soft hands pulled at him to do it. He tweaked her hardened nipples and tasted the salt on her skin as she whispered for *more*.

Corrado's hand slid through Alessio's hair, threading

tight, while Ginevra's drifted lower to slip under his boxer-briefs.

Sex was always *just* sex to Alessio. He liked it, and so he did it. He needed that connection with Corrado, and he found it. Anyone else, though, and it was just a need he fulfilled.

Now, though, he couldn't get enough. This—them with her—would quickly become an addiction for him. A habit he couldn't kick.

Alessio didn't mind.

CHAPTER 14
GINEVRA

"We're taking you out. A date."

Those words of Corrado's, ones he'd spoke in her ear after she was drifting in and out of sleep between the two men in bed while her body hummed from one of the most erotic things she had ever experienced in her life, rang through her mind as she surveyed the items on the bed.

The silver boxes rested open on the bed as she eyed each item set out in front of her.

Black, patent leather, peep-toe stilettos with red soles rested in one box, and a black dress with a designer tag that made her blink rested in another. The layered necklace, glittering with red gems—were those real?—would hang low in the deep neckline of the dress.

And the matching earrings were just as beautiful.

Not to mention expensive.

"Miss?"

Ginevra glanced over her shoulder at the woman standing just behind her, full of styling tools, makeup, and whatever else the woman needed to pamper her. Because to Corrado and Alessio, a date could not be *just* a date.

It had to be a whole experience.

One Ginevra *needed*.

Or that's what they explained.

This was a lot.

Then again, so were those men.

"Would you like to begin?" the woman asked.

"Where do we even start?"

Cassidy—that was the woman's name—grinned. "Well, wherever you like? They told me this day was *your* day. So, it's all up to you."

Right.

"I'm not used to being spoiled," she admitted.

"That doesn't mean you don't deserve it, though."

Ginevra liked this woman.

And those men.

"I'll let you pick," she said, giving Cassidy a smile.

"You got it."

A low whistle cut through the penthouse as Ginevra turned the corner. The appreciative sound from Alessio had Ginevra grinning, and standing beside him at the door looking just as good in his suit as Alessio did in a blazer and black slacks, was a smirking Corrado.

"Look at you, huh?" Alessio said, his gaze drinking her in.

Corrado did the same—his deepening sexily. "I should send that boutique and their people a bonus, yeah?"

Alessio nodded. "Definitely."

"That's enough from the two of you," Ginevra said, unsure of how to handle their attention when it was on her like *this*. Some things just took time to get used to, she supposed. This was one of those for her. "And I think you went a little overboard today."

"We didn't do enough."

"Agreed," Alessio replied.

Ginevra sighed, coming to a stop in front. Brushing her fingers over the shoulder of Corrado's suit jacket, her gaze turned on Alessio. "I think this is the first time I have ever seen you wear something that isn't black jeans, a leather jacket, and a plain shirt. I like it."

"Don't get used to it."

"I like you as you are, too."

"You better."

"He cleans up well," Corrado murmured.

Alessio flashed his teeth in a tempting grin. "But only when I'm forced to."

"See," she said, "overboard."

"Not at all." Corrado's hand slipped around to her lower back, and with a gentle nudge, they headed out of the penthouse after Alessio opened the door. "Besides, this was just for *fun*. And you don't get enough of that here, do you?"

"I think I'm wearing about five thousand dollars between these clothes and the jewelry—"

"About fifteen, actually."

Ginevra balked. "How is that *fun*?"

Because now she was just worried that she might lose the goddamn necklace or earrings. That was before she thought to ask just how much of that fifteen thousand belonged to the dress, the lingerie she wore under it, or the shoes on her feet.

Damn.

"For a Guzzi," Alessio said behind her as he locked the door, "spending money *is* fun."

Corrado shrugged. "Yeah, mostly."

All Ginevra could do in response to that was laugh because it seemed *so* excessive. And yet, she wasn't at all surprised.

"Besides," Alessio said, coming up to her other side as they waited at the bank of elevators, "the best part of having a beautiful woman at your side is getting to show her off."

"And reminding everyone else that she is not theirs."

Alessio chuckled. "Exactly that."

Ginevra shook her head. "Terrible. Both of you."

"And yet, you like it," Alessio returned. "Does that say more about you, or us?"

Well …

"That's fair," Ginevra said softly.

Alessio pressed a quick kiss to her temple as the elevator doors opened. Corrado let his fingers dance up the low cut back of her dress. Both actions did different things to her body.

Tempting.

Both *lovely*.

This would be an interesting night.

Of that, Ginevra was most sure.

Ginevra learned that it was one thing to deal with Alessio or Corrado *individually*. The two of them were a handful when it was just them, smirks and cockiness included. But when someone had to handle these two men *at the same time*?

A woman didn't stand a chance.

Ginevra was not an exception to that rule. All it took was Corrado murmuring in her ear, leaning forward from the back seat to tell her the history of a building they passed, while Alessio's hand stayed curved around her thigh as he navigated the Mercedes-Benz into a parking spot.

They were two different men, and that's what enthralled her the most when both of their attentions focused in on her, even if they did it in different ways. Despite their uniqueness, she was very much present for *both*.

"It's a bar, restaurant, club … everything, really," Corrado said. "Depends on the day of the week, and what they've had planned."

"And private," Alessio added.

Corrado winked at Ginevra. "Members only, for those with deep enough pockets to be invited to join."

"And you two are members, hmm?"

"We are. They invited us through my oldest brother, Marcus, who likes to use this as a meeting hub when he doesn't want to have those in a more public place."

She didn't see a sign on the side of the old brick building they parked beside, and she hadn't noticed one at the front, either. "What's it called?"

"The Clubhouse."

Ginevra snickered. "That doesn't sound ... innocent."

"It's not meant to," Alessio teased with a grin. "That's why it's private."

"But today," Corrado added, giving Alessio a look that quieted him, "we're having dinner, getting out of the penthouse, and having fun. Nothing crazy."

"Right."

Because they made her crazy.

A little.

They were still close.

Still touching her.

That was enough to make *any* woman insane when her body was constantly ready ... hyperaware and finding a sinful temptation in every grin or word tossed her way.

She was the lucky one between Corrado and Alessio right now. And if she could help it, she would stay there. For now, her heart couldn't stand being apart from them, not now.

They broke the restaurant portion of The Clubhouse into several small rooms, which made it comfortable and caused the people eating to sit closer together than they might at the round table.

They weren't alone in the place—murmurings came from down the hall, and dishes clattered before laughter rang out, echoing to their spot. But with the four walls, and only a doorway to peek into their room, they had privacy.

And she appreciated that.

"I want that," Ginevra said, pointing her fork at the cheesecake Corrado had been teasing her with for ten minutes. She had her own, a different kind because she didn't want to order two, but he had to order the other kind for himself. "Let me have a bite."

"But you didn't want it when I ordered it a half hour ago."

"I do *now*. And you're not even eating it. It will go to waste, and *no one* wastes good cheesecake, Corrado. If it's not a crime, it should be."

"Like dog-earing books?" Alessio asked.

"Use a *bookmark*, Les."

"They're still not your books."

She gave him a look.

He winked and grinned back in a way that had her stomach clenching. Ginevra now understood the effect these two men had on each other, too. Oh, they were infuriating and amazing and *perfect*, yes. How they interacted, loved, and lived that made them so fascinating to her. Especially now that their attention and affection was also being put on her.

"I'm only saying to use a bookmark, that's all. It's not hard, but you seem to think it is."

"Or I keep doing it my way because you're terribly cute when you're worked up."

Ginevra scoffed. "That's—"

"Not a lie," Corrado interjected.

Ginevra let out a hard breath, knowing there were fights she would not win. Chances are, these would be some of those.

Alessio chuckled, nodding at the man across from him. "Corrado doesn't even like cheesecake—he's more of a pastry type."

Corrado glared across the table. "I'm having a teachable moment here, Les."

"Right, sure."

Ginevra grinned. "You just ordered it, so I would have it and not be guilty, didn't you?"

"Maybe … or not."

Alessio, leaning back in his chair so it balanced on only two legs while his foot propped itself on the edge, had his arm slung around the back of Ginevra's chair. It allowed him to play with the edge of the low neckline on her dress and drift his fingers through her hair at the same time. He seemed all too content with watching Corrado tease Ginevra, instead of finishing the dinner on his plate.

Well, it was mostly gone, anyway.

Corrado picked up the fork, swiped it through the top of the soft cheesecake, and offered it to her with a sly smile that showed off every ounce of his arrogance. "Bite?"

Alessio clicked his tongue, chiding and amused at the same time. Still, he stayed quiet and watched them.

Ginevra eyed the sweet on the fork. "Will you admit that you only ordered it for me?"

"I don't need to confirm things you already know, kitten. Take your bite."

She did.

And loved every second, too.

Corrado's thumb came up to wipe at Ginevra's lower lip while Alessio's fingertips danced along the column of her throat. Distracting and enticing. All of it—both. She didn't know which way to turn, so she settled herself on enjoying *both*.

Besides, wasn't that what they should do?

Sticking the tip of his thumb between his lips, Corrado sucked the bit of cheesecake off, and shrugged. "Tastes better coming off you, undoubtedly."

"Well, thanks." Ginevra took the fork from him and stabbed it into the cheesecake for another bite. "Now, what's the teachable lesson, again?"

Corrado laughed, tossing his head back as he did so. On the other side of her, Alessio hummed a low, sexy sound.

"Never *ever* feel guilty about doing something you enjoy," Corrado said, leaning in close enough for her to see those gold flakes in his irises. "Be it food, fucking, or living. You're only going to be on this earth once, Ginevra."

"Better enjoy it," Alessio agreed.

They had a point.

CHAPTER 15
CORRADO

"Here."

Corrado took the jacket Alessio held out, already turning to help Ginevra slip it on. September in Toronto was mild, but the sky had darkened, and he didn't want her getting cold between The Clubhouse, and the car.

Ginevra smiled sweetly back at him when he placed the blazer over her shoulders—Alessio didn't give a shit he had to give it up for her. God knew the man would much rather be in a leather jacket, anyway.

"Thank you," she said.

"Always, *mia cara.*"

Corrado pressed a kiss to the middle of her forehead, enjoying her fingertips drifting over his unshaven jawline with a tender touch. A few feet away, a couple waited with the girl who manned The Clubhouse's entrance, never allowing entrance to someone who didn't have the credentials to enter. Corrado didn't care who came in and out of these doors most of the time. Usually, he never noticed.

This time he did because the woman dressed in deep red continued to glance back at the three while they waited for their turn to take their leave. People stared at him and Alessio, anyway … maybe it was the vibes they gave off, or someone liked the way they looked. Either way, he didn't mind it.

Right now was not quite the same.

He didn't like someone staring at Ginevra *at all*. Especially not when she didn't notice they were doing it because she was far more concerned with him and Alessio.

Call it instinct …

Whatever.

He didn't like it.

Corrado arched a brow at the woman over Ginevra's shoulder where she couldn't see him do it. The woman saw it clear as day, however.

Which was the damn point?

At his stare, challenging her to continue watching them, she was quick to look away, but not before rolling her eyes.

Fuck it.

As long as she stopped staring.

"Do you want me to hold on to this, sweetheart?"

Alessio waved Ginevra's small clutch, and she shrugged, taking it from him when he offered it to her.

"Is Camden around?" the man at the podium asked the woman manning the entrance.

"He is," she said. "In his office."

"Does he have a minute to chat?"

"Let me call through."

Corrado passed Alessio a look who shook his head. The rules of this place was one of the few things Corrado disliked about it. Like needing to check in and out, which could take a while if there was someone ahead of them.

Like now.

The woman—Kasie, was it? He couldn't remember, and he didn't care to—spoke into the Bluetooth speaker in her ear, nodding once before smiling at the man on the other side of her podium, still waiting.

"He's got a few minutes, but your … guest will have to stay here," she said.

The man and the woman in red shared a quick word

before he passed by Corrado, Alessio, and Ginevra to head back into the main section of The Clubhouse. With the podium free so they could check out, retrieve their electronics that everyone was required to drop off upon entering, Corrado stepped up to finish their time here.

As soon as he left Ginevra's side, Alessio was quick to take his place, sliding an arm around her waist to keep her close to him. Corrado didn't miss the way the woman in red narrowed her eyes at that, or how her lips pursed when the two he left behind shared a quiet word, and Alessio kissed Ginevra's temple.

Not that he could say anything about her staring *again*. The chick at the podium was now pulling the phones out of a small drawer behind her and had the tablet on their information to remove them from the current patrons list.

"Camden wanted you to be aware that, should you bring your guest again," Kasie told him, "she will need to be made a member. You know the rules, Mr. Guzzi. Once is fine— twice, she'll need a card."

Corrado nodded.

He understood the specifics.

It was all about safety here.

"What is it, three members who need to vouch?"

"Correct."

Corrado tapped a finger against the podium, saying, "Me, Les, and Marcus … we'll add him to it, have Camden call him to get it done. Does that work for you?"

"Sign here."

He took the stylus the woman held out and scribbled his unintelligible signature to the bottom of a form she'd brought up on the tablet. There was one on him, and one on Alessio, too.

"And he must sign it, as well. I can email the one over for

Marcus after Camden calls first to make sure he's fine with it."

Corrado waved two fingers at Alessio, and his silent demand for the man to come over worked. Alessio left Ginevra's side, coming to stand next to Corrado so he, too, could sign the document. There were a few others things they had to fill out—standard information that The Clubhouse kept on file for all members.

It took five minutes.

It would allow them to bring Ginevra back, though, and she seemed to like it here. Or rather, the restaurant portion, anyway. There was a hell of a lot more to see.

"That's all," Kasie said.

"*Merci*," Corrado said.

Alessio handed the stylus over as he had been the last to initial a part of the document. "Are we good?"

"Perfect."

"Great."

The two of them turned, ready to take Ginevra home.

"I'm just saying, it's *interesting*," he heard a woman say.

The woman in *red*.

Somehow, with their backs turned, she stood next to Ginevra. Which wouldn't be such a big deal, or a problem at all, if not for the fact Ginevra looked like she was about to *cry*. She avoided the woman's stare next to her, her jaw tight, and her arms folded over her chest. If it wasn't clear, by the fact she wasn't talking, that she wasn't interested in a conversation, then her body language sure as hell should have done it.

Still, the woman in red continued, saying, "If you know what I mean."

"I don't, actually."

Ouch.

The venom in Ginevra's tone wasn't missed.

"Huh," the other woman said.

What the fuck?

"Ginny," Corrado said, stepping forward while shooting daggers at the woman next to her with his gaze, "are you good?"

He offered his hand.

She didn't take it.

Alessio cleared his throat, but stayed quiet.

"Are you ready to leave?" Corrado asked.

They could figure out the problem later. He wanted to get her away from the bitch beside her. Whatever the issue was, it started and ended right there.

"I am ready to leave," Ginevra said stiffly.

She still didn't take his hand.

And she sidestepped Alessio, too.

They followed her out.

What else could they do?

"Ginevra, will you talk now?"

"I would rather *not*."

"Ginny—"

"Leave me alone for a minute, okay?" She kicked those Louboutin shoes off in the hallway, the red-soled shoes smacking the wall hard. "I need five seconds to think."

"About *what*?"

"Corrado," Alessio murmured.

He ignored the man behind him.

Mostly, because he didn't understand what happened back at The Clubhouse in five minutes that turned their *fantastic* evening into ... whatever the fuck this was. She had been having fun—enjoying her time with them out of this goddamn penthouse, because fuck, she didn't get that enough.

And somehow, it was ruined.

Corrado wanted to understand why.

He needed to fix everything.

That was his *thing*.

"Give her a second," Alessio said when Corrado moved to follow Ginevra down the hall.

He shook off Alessio's hand that came to land on his arm. "Don't."

"Corrado—"

"What the hell happened, Les? Don't you care about what went wrong?"

Alessio shrugged, his face unreadable. "Sometimes, people need to work through shit."

Right.

Well …

"That doesn't work for me," Corrado said.

"That's half your problem. You don't let shit go, man."

"And we wouldn't be here if I did."

Alessio nodded. "All right, but don't say I didn't warn you."

"Noted."

Not that it made a fucking difference to him.

Corrado didn't bother to take the time to remove his jacket or shoes before following Ginevra. He stood in the doorway of her bedroom and watched as she struggled to pull the zipper down on the back of her dress.

She didn't ask for help, so he stayed back.

Finally, she got the dress down. Yanking the expensive fabric down her body, the dress fell to the floor in a heap, forgotten. Standing in black lace that hugged her curves in the best way, he had a view that showed all the parts of her that had his dick standing at attention in a breath. And yet, all he focused on was that anger written across her pretty features.

She let out a harsh noise, pulling the drop earrings from her ears, and shaking her head at the same time.

"Do you want help with the necklace?" he asked, staying put in the doorway.

"*No.*"

He straightened, her sharp tone taking him by surprise. Rarely did Ginevra get heated with her tone, even in her anger. She didn't need fury to get her point across, not when she wanted to.

"What is wrong with—"

"I said to give me a minute, didn't I?"

Corrado stayed put and shrugged as he tossed his hands in his pockets. "And yet, here I still am. Something clearly upset you back at The Clubhouse, and I want you to tell me what."

"You don't get to *know* everything because you want to, Corrado. That's not how life works, okay? People have feelings—*private* feelings."

"Right, but since, chances are, this has to do with me, or Les, or that chick who talked to you, I think you could at least tell me what happened."

"Or you should leave it the fuck alone."

Oh, cusses, now?

Yeah, she was *pissed*.

Leaning his shoulder against the doorjamb, Corrado settled himself on not moving unless she spoke up and told him what the hell was wrong now. "I'm not going anywhere unless you talk to—"

"*God.*"

Ginevra spun around fast, looking like an angry angel in her black lace, that ruby, white-gold necklace hanging low between her pert breasts covered *just enough* by the cups of the bra against her chest. At her sides, her hands balled into shaking fists.

But what hurt him the most?

The tears that formed in her eyes.

"You want to know what she asked me?" Ginevra asked.

Corrado swallowed hard. "I do. It upset you."

"How much you two paid for me."

What?

Corrado blinked. "I don't … what?"

"Yeah," she snapped, scoffing, too. "That's what she asked, Corrado. How much did you and Alessio pay for me —*hard enough for a woman to find* one *man that looks like that, let alone two? So, how much are they paying to fuck you tonight?*"

"Ginny—"

"Is that what will happen every time I step out in public now? The first thing someone thinks when they see me with you two is *oh, she's a whore*. Because that's hard for me to swallow, okay. Before Andino shoved me in your lap, I was able to count my partners on one hand. And now, I'm fucking two men. So, forgive me if I need five seconds to *breathe*. All right?"

He blinked *again*.

Like an idiot.

"You let her comment bother you *that* much?"

Okay, that might have been the wrong thing to say. Or even, a little cold of him. Still, this bothered Corrado that the first thing Ginevra felt when someone thought to place judgement on her choices or relationship with him and Alessio was something *bad*.

That she was a whore.

Or the suggestion she was a slut.

None of which was true.

It pissed him off.

"That's what it was?" he asked.

Ginevra stared back at him, unmoved. "Yes."

"Just that."

"It's not *just* that, Corrado. Think about what it *means*."

"To you," he intoned, "what this means to you, Ginevra."

"I don't get what you're trying to say here, but—"

"No, because you're stuck in your goddamn feelings about what *one* person said to you about your private relationship that has fuck all to do with them."

She stilled, her back straightening fast at his harsh tone.

Corrado didn't back down.

He wouldn't.

This needed to be clear.

"You need to figure out what you want here," he told her, pushing out of his lean to stand straight in the doorway. "Decide whether what makes you happy in private is worth the shit you might take in public, because *shocker,* this isn't only you here, Ginny. We're here, and we have to deal with it, too. Just because you have some complex about sex and relationships and monogamy, I suppose because society and religion and the rest of your life has spoon-fed what they consider to be appropriate and acceptable to you regarding our relationship or sex doesn't make this *wrong*."

Ginevra opened her mouth to speak, but he was quick to stop her with, "The way we love, or fuck, or *live* with each other behind closed doors, or out in the world, still will not be wrong just because someone else has a fucking problem with it. This is ours, and it doesn't have to be the way someone else does *theirs*. Figure whatever out. We can't do it for you."

He turned to leave, but a scoff left his lips before he added, "And guess what, the man you wanted to fuck and liked before you ever knew about Les, and the rest of our life, is the same man you're looking at right now. Just because none of that was staring you in the face before doesn't change the fact we still existed. We are who we are—you either want to be a part, too, or you don't. Simple."

Corrado didn't wait to hear what Ginevra had to say to that before he headed out into the hallway. He wasn't at all surprised to find Alessio at the end, waiting for him and listening to the argument. Alessio arched a brow before following Corrado to kitchen.

Fuck.

He needed a drink, now.

Pulling a beer from the fridge, not his first choice, he slammed the door shut harder than was necessary. A black card stock he hung on the front of the fridge with a magnet fluttered to the floor, the gold flake detailing on the corners and white font staring up at him from the floor. Alessio was quick to come up beside him, and pick it up, reading over the invitation to a club opening coming up soon for his brother, Marcus.

"When did you get this?"

"Yesterday."

"We should go. Get out of this penthouse again where we're all stir-crazy."

He wasn't lying.

"I told Marcus I would go," Corrado said, sighing.

Alessio gave him a look, leaning against the fridge. "Except, if this is an opening for Marcus, then there will be a handful of made men around, too, yeah?"

"Likely."

"So, I'll go, too."

Corrado sucked air between his teeth. "You don't have to."

"Yeah, but you get twitchy around some older fucks, so … I'm going."

"Which means she'll need to go, too, because she won't want to stay here alone."

Alessio didn't miss the heat in his tone if his frown was any sign. "Give her those few minutes she asked for from the jump, Corrado. People need time alone to work through their shit, and you need to accept that."

Right.

"And how long is that going to take?"

Alessio made a noise under his breath. Either he didn't have an answer, or he didn't want to give one. Corrado understood that all too well.

Until that night, apparently.

That's how long it took Ginevra to get out of her feelings and decide she didn't want to be without the two.

She darkened their bedroom door as Alessio drifted out of the bathroom with nothing but a towel wrapped around his waist. His footsteps hesitated, he made a noise in Corrado's direction, and that was how he realized Ginevra was standing there.

The girl looked smaller than ever with her gaze turned down, and her arms crossed over her chest, making the oversized T-shirt draped over her body tight around her trim waist. Still, Corrado said nothing as Alessio headed into the walk-in closet to pull something on for bed, and she stayed in the doorway, not coming an inch closer.

"I'm sorry," she whispered.

"For?"

Ginevra let out a steady stream of air and shrugged her delicate shoulders. "Letting someone else upset me about this."

"All right."

As long as she understood *that* was what happened. It wasn't her that did this—she let someone else affect her feelings. Someone who wasn't here doing this with them. Someone who understood nothing about this thing of theirs.

That was all.

Those people didn't matter.

If they weren't in their life, their bed, or their home, then they didn't get an opinion on what Ginevra, Corrado, and Alessio did together. Simple.

"The door is still open," Corrado said.

Ginevra smiled as she tipped her head up, her gaze landing on him across the room. "It always is anyway. Like I didn't listen to the two of you in the shower for—"

"Should have joined," Alessio returned as he came out of the closet, having pulled on a pair of boxer-briefs, and nothing else. "You get more that way, kitten."

Corrado chuckled. "I mean, *yeah*."

Ginevra shifted from foot to foot. "I'll keep it in mind."

He gestured at the bed, feeling the tips of Alessio's fingers drift over his lower back as the man passed him by. "Sleep?"

"If you want me in here."

Corrado smirked. "When do we *not*?"

CHAPTER 16
ALESSIO

Why, when things were going good in Alessio's life, something had to come around to fuck it up?

He didn't need to answer the ringing phone in his pocket to know whatever that call was about, it would fuck up the balance he had found with Corrado and Ginevra. Sure, it was touch and go after the whole *Clubhouse* incident, but after a couple of weeks, they found a comfortable routine he liked.

He didn't want to fuck it up.

"Are you going to answer that, or …?"

Alessio grunted under his breath. "I'd rather not."

"That's the ringtone you use for Cree."

"And?"

His sharp question drew in the gaze of several people inside the café, and even Ginevra who now waited closer to the cashier in line. Alessio and Corrado had opted to stand back to let the line weed itself out—she didn't need them standing beside her twenty-four seven even if that's what they both wanted to do more than anything.

The phone rang again.

Corrado sighed. "Stop ignoring him, Les."

"It's not about ignoring him."

And it wasn't. It would have little to do with Dare, or the fact Alessio still wasn't calling them to keep him and Cree updated like he did.

No, it wasn't for that.

The fucking Albania job.

Which meant as soon as Alessio picked up the call, there would be a timer ticking down. The job had been years in the making, and he would have a tiny window of time after being given the okay to begin before he would have to get on a plane, and travel to a different country.

Away from here.

Away from them.

After his last conversation with Cree, well, Alessio doubted the man would call just because. Cree wasn't the type to push Alessio's lines, and he'd certainly done that during their chat.

So, it could only be for one thing.

"If you don't pick up the damn call," Corrado warned when Alessio's phone continued ringing in his pocket, "I will call Cree back myself."

Jesus.

"Fine," Alessio grumbled.

He pulled the phone from his pocket, giving Corrado a look before turning his back to him and the rest of the café as he answered the call. He stepped over to the window, putting some distance between himself and Corrado, not to mention the others lingering in the café.

"Les here," he said into the speaker.

"Nice of you to *finally* pick up my call," Cree muttered.

Alessio sighed. "I was busy."

"But were you?"

"Listen, I picked up the call, Cree."

It was the best he could do right now.

Anything else, and they asked too much.

Alessio kept his eye on Ginevra who was now giving her order at the front of the line to the cashier. Her bright smile had his own growing, not to mention the way she kept glancing back to check on Corrado and Alessio.

The woman … was something else.

And Corrado had been right.

She fit *them*.

"What did you need?" Alessio asked.

Although, he had a good idea.

It was just a matter of saying it, now.

"The Albania job is a go," Cree said.

Alessio figured it would be pointless to ask, but he still had to try. "And we're sure there's no possibility of them allowing another member to do the hit?"

"I've told you no."

Right, right.

Alessio's gaze drifted to Corrado who looked his way with a sly grin, pleased he'd gotten his lover to answer the call from Cree. It was too bad Corrado didn't understand yet what Alessio picking up the call meant.

He needed to be *here*.

More than anything. He wanted to be here. They were still figuring this out, between them, and Ginevra. Yeah, shit was better … but they were all still walking a very thin line with one another. He wanted to believe it wouldn't take much for them to get to a better place, but right now …

Anything could happen.

It was all in the air.

"I just think it's ridiculous they wouldn't allow someone else to take it, if there's no reason *why not*," Alessio said under his breath.

"You want to tell me what that mood is about, or no?"

Alessio scrubbed a hand down his face and turned to stare out the window. Then, Corrado wouldn't be able to see the displeasure on his face if he was still watching Alessio on the phone. "It's nothing—me voicing my thoughts out loud."

"Right," Cree murmured, "but I think it's more."

"And we're still not discussing my personal business. That hasn't changed."

"Les, I get I crossed a line."

"So?"

"Cut the shit."

Alessio pulled in a lungful of air, wishing it helped to settle his nerves, but it didn't. Nothing helped with it anymore, it seemed. Not unless he was in bed with Corrado or Ginevra, because then, he only had to think about one thing, and none of this shit factored into that at all.

Another reason to be here.

"I want to take fewer jobs," Alessio said.

Cree made a soft noise. "Oh?"

"I used work and keeping busy as a way to run from my issues, and I don't want to do it anymore. So, I understand what I need to do to fix that."

"Take fewer jobs, stay home more."

"Exactly."

Something shuffled on the other end of the call before Cree replied, "There's no reason you *can't* do that, Les. And you always did well training the new prospects with the occasional job thrown in with the team. If you want to go back to that, you can."

"But not right now."

"No," Cree agreed, "you have to do the Albania job. Within seven days, you need to be on a plane to contact the client within the proper time frame we previously agreed upon. I will send his details over, and you'll have everything you need once you land in the country."

"Great."

Except it wasn't great.

Not at all.

"Within seven days," Cree repeated, "call me to confirm you're on the way, all right?"

"Yeah, sure. A week, I got it."

Without a goodbye, Alessio hung up the phone. Cree wouldn't give a damn, really. He'd only slid the phone back into his pocket when Corrado saddled up to his side, arms folded over his broad chest. He spoke to Alessio as he continued watching Ginevra.

"A week for what?"

Alessio's jaw clicked from how he clenched his teeth. "The Albania job—we were going to do it together, remember?"

"I backed out because of the favor for Andino, yeah."

"Well, guess who doesn't get to back out?"

Corrado stiffened beside him, but replied, "It's a job— what, a couple weeks at the most? You'll be back soon."

"Some things are more important than The League."

"Yeah."

"And stop glaring," Alessio added.

Corrado glanced his way, raising a single brow. "Pardon you?"

Smirking, Alessio nodded toward the front of the café where Ginevra chatted with the man behind the counter who now handed over her coffee, and donut. Alessio hadn't missed how if Corrado's glare could burn someone to the ground right where they stood, the man who had the nerve to talk to Ginevra would be a pile of fucking ashes.

"You know what I'm talking about."

Corrado grinned. "Hmm."

"Do you do that for me, too?"

"What?"

"Glare at people who get too close."

Corrado didn't reply.

Alessio didn't need him to.

Yes, he did.

Corrado was *very* good at hiding his possessiveness. At

least, to the people he was possessive over. He didn't have a problem with making people aware they stepped out of line.

Not at all.

"So, where to now?"

Corrado and Alessio broke their staring contest to find Ginevra had left the counter, and the chatty man behind, to come stand in front with a smile that reached her bright eyes. Honestly, she was probably happy to be out of the penthouse again.

"To get you a dress," Corrado said.

Ginevra sipped from the to-go cup of coffee. "I have dresses."

"No, a *new* dress."

"You have heard of reusing things, right?"

Alessio scoffed. "You have high hopes, woman."

Corrado scowled. "I can spend my money however I want to."

"Yes, you can," Alessio agreed, "but most people don't spend money like you do."

"Why do I need a new dress, though?"

"We have a club opening to go to in a couple of days," Corrado explained, "and because I want to. Also, something for dinner tonight with my parents, too."

"I miss Cara," Ginevra said absently.

"That's why we're having dinner. And because she demanded it."

Alessio reached out and snuck a piece off her donut … which ended up being a quarter. Well, she noticed.

Ginevra gave him a look.

He winked as he popped it into his mouth.

"Are we shopping, or no?" Corrado asked.

"Right after someone gets me another donut," Ginevra replied, not looking away from Alessio. "Since they don't know how to ask for their own."

Funny how she didn't share food well.

She shared them perfectly fine.

Win some, lose some.

"Well?" Ginevra asked him, looking entirely offended he dared to take a bite of her donut she now held out of his reach. "Because I'm not leaving until I get another."

Corrado chuckled. "You heard her."

Alessio groaned. "*Fine.*"

CHAPTER 17
CORRADO

"And," the older woman who handled the patrons of the upscale, private boutique said, "we're closed for the next two hours to make sure you find what you need, Ginevra."

Ginevra's wide eyes turned on Corrado and Alessio. Although, just him because Alessio was busy leaning over the glass counter to pull an item out from behind it. Something that was a no-no, but he didn't follow the rules. Or, how to act like he had any sense of decorum.

"Les," Corrado snapped, "leave it alone."

"But it's perf—"

"Would you like me to get that out for you, Mr. Sorrento?"

Alessio came back up with a sly grin. "The blue choker, if you wouldn't mind, yes."

The woman—Mandy—nodded. "I will do that for you."

She left Ginevra's side, who was still wide-eyed and taking in the large and modernly decorated boutique with high class designer names hanging from every tag, to slip behind the counter. Bending down, she found the particular blue-gem choker that Alessio had been admiring through the glass, and then decided he needed to touch because why not?

It was Les.

Sliding it across the counter, Mandy shrugged. "Sapphires imported from India, designed in Russia—seven thousand for the choker. It's not an accent piece, but a solitary. There is no matching designs, it's better—"

"On its own," Alessio said, picking the choker up from the black velvet where it was displayed. "Add this to the bill, yeah?"

"Absolutely."

"That's too much," Ginevra whispered at Corrado's back.

He chuckled, amused at how she lowered her voice so the other two wouldn't overhear. She was trying her best *not* to become overwhelmed by the boutique, and the items inside, but she was still wide-eyed and stunned.

He liked that look on her.

"It's a good price, actually," Corrado returned, turning to face her. "And it's going to hug your throat nicely."

Ginevra balked. "But—"

"We should look for something blue to match."

"You're … *impossible*."

Corrado arched a brow. "I didn't pick the jewelry, I'm just saying the rest should match."

"The more expensive things are, the worse it is to wear them."

"Why?"

"Because I worry it might break, or get ruined, or—"

"I don't want to tell you those feelings are nonsense, because Alessio likes to tell me that all too often, I dismiss others' experiences and emotions, and I shouldn't do that."

Ginevra glared at him. "*But?*"

"But this is ridiculous. Last year, I pulled in four million doing jobs for The League, but that's only spending money," Corrado murmured stepping closer to her, so she had to look up at him with those big, brown eyes. Her lips fell open in surprise, but Corrado continued on with, "It was spending money because my trust fund, for being born a Guzzi, which is spread between four investment portfolios, made me two times that in profits and interest last year. That's before I talk about the money that is just sitting there *working* to earn that profit and interest. A *trusted* money manager handles things like taxes, my major donations to several charities, and whatever else, but those cards in my wallet I swipe every time we go out?"

Ginevra's throat jumped when she swallowed. "What about them?"

"They have no limit." Corrado bopped her on the tip of her nose with the tip of his finger, adding, "And that's before we talk about the money Les has. So, can we shop, wear beautiful things, and be happy that we're lucky enough to do this?"

"That's a lot of money, Corrado."

"I can't be buried with it, Ginevra."

Her gaze flashed with an understanding. "You have a point."

"I understand that my wealth, to others, can seem excessive, and a little overwhelming."

"It is."

"So, I won't dismiss what you think, but I won't change how I live, either. I would rather you learn to be comfortable with wealth than afraid of it."

Ginevra let out a light laugh. "Well …"

"Hmm?"

"As long as it's not *my* money that's being thrown around, I guess."

Corrado grinned. "Compromise. Now you're talking my language, kitten."

Her cheeks pinked, but she didn't hide it.

"Now, what are we shopping for again? What kind of event?"

Mandy's voice had Corrado turning to face the woman. She was still standing behind the counter, and Alessio was already looking their way with a lazy smile.

"A club opening for the Guzzis," Corrado said, "but we can handle finding something on our own, if you wouldn't mind."

Mandy waved a hand. "The shop is yours for the next two hours. If you wouldn't mind, I might take my lunch. You won't need me hanging around, and I can pop over to the café across the street."

"We'll be fine," Alessio assured.

He left the counter to join Ginevra and Corrado, his hand sliding around her lower back while Corrado turned to check out a rack of large church hats. His mother liked those, and she might like to find a gift here waiting for her when she came to shop the next time.

"Oh, and that royal purple hat," Corrado said, "box it up for my mother, would you?"

"First thing when I get back, Mr. Guzzi."

"*Merci*."

"That was sweet of you," Ginevra said as Mandy picked up her coat and purse, readying to leave. "Does your mother shop here often?"

"A few times a month."

By the time Mandy had locked the shop's door as she left, the three of them were already closer to the back of the store. Corrado remained closer to Alessio's side as Ginevra reached up to admire a glittering blue clutch hanging on the wall.

"So, which Guzzi is opening the club?"

"My oldest brother—Marcus."

Ginevra peeked back at them, her nose crinkling in *that way*. It only did that when she had something on her mind. "Huh."

"What?"

"Your family … they're Cosa Nostra, right?"

Alessio cleared his throat and gave Corrado a look from the side. One he did his best to ignore because Alessio was quite aware this was a goddamn touchy topic for him.

"The majority are," Corrado replied tightly. "I expect there'll be a handful of important made men there considering Marcus is my father's current right-hand, and while it's never been explicitly said, the next Guzzi to take over the *famiglia*."

Ginevra turned to face him. "What was that about?"

"What? Nothing."

Her gaze darted to Alessio and then back to Corrado. "No, there was *something*. In your tone, like it annoyed you."

"It was—"

"Something," Alessio put in.

"Don't," Corrado warned the man beside him.

Ginevra nodded. "Okay, now I *really* want to know."

God.

Why couldn't people leave him to stew about his issues alone? Not every piece of baggage he carried around needed unpacked.

"Some people in the Guzzi organization," Alessio said.

"Could you *not*?"

"No," the man murmured to Ginevra, "some of them take issue with the fact Corrado didn't join the family business and went outside of the organization instead. And this is before we deal with the fact that Cosa Nostra isn't kind to boys who like boys."

Ginevra blinked.

Corrado sucked on his teeth, annoyed again.

"Thank you," he told Alessio.

The man shrugged. "Better to just handle it, I guess."

Right, that's what it was.

"And they understand you two are …?" Ginevra asked, leaving the rest of her question unsaid as she raised her brow.

"For the most part, no," Corrado said. "We're always very careful about how we present ourselves outside of our private space, and not *just* because of the opinions of people who might not like we're together, but also because emotional attachments in this business can sometimes be a target for those who would think to use it. I never wanted someone to use Alessio against me, or vice versa."

Alessio cleared his throat. "You never explained this to me like that."

"Yeah, well …"

Shit left unsaid, *again*.

"But yes," Corrado added, shrugging one shoulder, "I didn't care what people from my father's *famiglia* thought about the fact I sleep in bed with a man, either. They're not the ones living my life, so their voice counts for very little."

"Oh."

Corrado smiled at Ginevra's soft reply. "It doesn't matter, anyway. If most of them aren't already aware, they suspect, anyway. I am at a point where I don't say, and they don't ask. I no longer care what they think though."

"Was that another rule?"

Alessio grinned. "Pardon?"

"Like the not sleeping with other men thing, or that women were okay as long as one told the other," Ginevra said. "Was the whole not talking about your relationship another rule?"

"No, more like an unspoken agreement."

Ginevra nodded. "Are there still rules?"

Alessio tipped his head to the side. "That kind of got blown out of the water when Corrado broke the important one."

Yeah.

Ginevra frowned.

Corrado sighed. "We handled that, right?"

"Mostly," Alessio agreed.

"Well," Ginevra said, picking a blue dress from a rack she passed before heading toward the back of the shop, tossing her words over her shoulder, "while I'm here, nobody better be fucking *anybody* else but the people standing right here. Got it?"

The heat in her tone couldn't be missed.

That possessive glint in her eye?

Clear as day.

Corrado appreciated that.

Alessio chuckled beside him.

"Yeah, we got it," Corrado said.

"Absolutely," Alessio agreed as Ginevra disappeared into the back hallway where the large changing rooms were situated. "But that means we get what we want, too, right? And *when* we want it, yeah?"

Ginevra peeked back around the corner, an eyebrow cocked in curiosity. "What does that mean?"

"How long do we have?" Alessio asked him.

Corrado glanced over his shoulder, his gaze finding the café across the street where Mandy had gone to be full with people lined up close to the door. "A safe while, I'd say."

"*Good.*"

"What does that mean?"

Ginevra's voice was a little higher, now.

Anticipation, Corrado thought.

"You know what it means," he said.

She disappeared into the hallway again, and they were quick to chase after the sound of her laughter. Alessio darted past Corrado by *jumping* over a rack. Not that Corrado minded as Alessio had always had the benefit of speed between them. He could outrun Corrado on his *worst* days, and that was saying something because he sure as fuck wasn't *slow*.

They turned the back hallway corner into the section of changing rooms in just enough time to see Ginevra drop the dress she had worn out that day to the floor. Then, she slipped into one of the six-by-six changing rooms with a wink over her shoulder, and that fucking blue dress from the wall in her hands.

"Too slow," she called out.

Corrado made a thick noise in the back of his throat. Alessio, at his side, tipped his head to the side with a cunning smile growing.

"She thinks we're teasing her, doesn't she?"

"Yes," Corrado murmured.

"She doesn't think we're at all serious, huh?"

"Nope."

Alessio laughed darkly, a sound that had Corrado's cock perking, and his chest tightening in the best fucking way. "She's in for a surprise."

Fuck yeah.

"I'm gonna need someone to help me zip the back of this up," Ginevra said, her words muffled behind the door. She didn't seem to have heard them—*good*. "But just a second, I might be able to do it myself."

"You got it," Corrado replied, his gaze settling on Alessio at his left.

"I want that woman between us," Alessio said under his breath.

"Here isn't the best place for that, Les."

"I know, but it needs to happen *soon*."

Corrado agreed.

Entirely.

"But that doesn't mean we can't show her a little," Alessio said, looking Corrado's way. "Just a little, yeah?"

God.

Corrado nodded. "A little, then."

"See what happens, yeah?"

A groan fell out of Corrado's throat without his permission. "Killing me."

"Not quite," Alessio returned, winking.

Prick.

He knew his words turned Corrado on as much as they would Ginevra. That was, if she could hear them.

"Okay," Ginevra called out, the door to the changing room door opening. "I got it."

Alessio drifted past Corrado, but he was right behind him. Ginevra's sweet gasp rang out when Alessio slipped into the changing room before she could even come out. By the time he got past the door, Alessio already had Ginevra backed against the wall. Corrado took a second to take in that sight—oh, he'd seen it a couple of times over the last two weeks … they tempted and loved her as much as she wanted, and yet, it still *stunned* him.

The way Alessio handled her.

How he *kissed* her.

The way the man just seemed like he couldn't get enough, and God knew Corrado understood that far too well where Ginevra was concerned. Everything about her, from the way her skin heated under their hands, to the way she sounded, and even the sensitivity of her skin was addicting.

And that was before he mentioned how he ached to fuck her, or to get her flavor coating his tongue while she shook and called out his name.

Or Alessio's.

Fuck.

"Yes, then?" Alessio asked. "Tell me yes, and we'll make it so fucking good, Ginny."

Corrado moved in beside them to tilt Alessio's head back

by tangling his fingers into the hair at the nape of the man's neck. His lips crashed down on Alessio's, tongue slashing against his that was already waiting to war in their familiar way. He reached for Ginevra, his fingers drifting down the fabric of the dress covering her chest, hearing her soft whimper.

Something about that did it for her.

He learned that, too, over these weeks. They could find her soaking fucking wet after she watched them do anything —fuck, kiss, *touch*. It didn't matter, for her it was hot as hell, and he fucking loved that.

Les, too.

Alessio's teeth caught Corrado's lower lip as he moved to pull back, that sting hardening his cock to a painful point as Ginevra whispered, "*Yes.*"

The stormy blue of Alessio's gaze locked on his for a brief second, he took that connection for what it was, those silent promises of *yours is coming too.*

He wanted that.

As much as he wanted Ginevra.

But her first.

Alessio kneeled down, his hands shoving the blue satin of Ginevra's dress higher as Corrado focused on her lips, and getting her kiss, too. The shuffle of fabric, thin lace being yanked away, sounded over her hard breaths. She shifted against Corrado's side, and how he was leaning over her, her legs widening for Alessio down below. He knew the *second* Alessio had his face buried between Ginevra's thighs, because even if the man's hard moan wouldn't have been enough to tell him he found heaven, the broken cry Ginevra echoed against his kiss would have done it.

Shivers raced through her body. His hands chased after them, yanking the straps of that dress down her arms, and past her chest, making her lace-covered tits spill out to his waiting palms. He dragged those lace cups down, too, still lashing his tongue against hers as she whined into his kiss.

Corrado pulled back, thumbs tweaking her nipples as he peered down. Alessio stared up, their eyes locking again as he worked between her thighs, his tongue beating a fast rhythm against her clit as the sounds of his fingers sinking into her wet pussy filled the surrounding space.

"Come, and he'll fill you," Corrado told her. "Stretch you out nice, Ginny, while I get a taste of you both, and show you how good it will be when we're both filling you full, kitten."

"Oh, my God," she breathed.

"That works, too."

She choked on her next cry.

Corrado watched as Alessio bared his teeth, giving him a silent warning, not that he needed it. He could sense how close Ginevra was to coming, and the right move on Alessio's part would throw her right over the edge. All it took was the scrape of Alessio's teeth against the hood of her clit before he sucked it between his lips, and she flew.

His hands ghosted up from her chest, her racing heat thrumming into her throat, as his fingers wrapped around the column of her neck. He took in all those sounds of hers with kisses dotting across her trembling lips, over her jaw, and back to her mouth again.

"I … I …" Ginevra couldn't get words out, the air of her voice pulsing along Corrado's mouth as she tried. "*Please*."

"Easy, easy, *breathe*," Alessio murmured as he lifted, and Corrado moved aside for him. "Fuck, doesn't she look good like that?"

"She does," Corrado agreed. "So fucking good, Les."

"You hear that, Ginny? How much we love watching you come for us, huh?"

Her darkened brown eyes, hooded with lust, focused in

on Alessio. His hands were already working to undo his pants, and shuffle them down. He took the condom Corrado handed over as he held out two fingers to Corrado, wet with Ginevra. *Fucking hell.* Corrado took that offering *happily*, getting her hot and tart arousal on his tongue as he watched Alessio give Ginevra a taste with a kiss.

Alessio took his hand back, but only to get his cock sheathed in latex. Ginevra, though, reached for Corrado with one hand, and Alessio with the other. Her fingers drifted through his hair, fingernails dragging over his scalp to pull him in for a burning kiss while she laid her palm flat against Alessio's chest.

What came next was fast—a blur to Corrado's eye because he felt like they moved out of need, and nothing more. In a blink, Alessio had pulled Ginevra away from the wall, and Corrado's hands skipped up her back as he followed behind, making sure she didn't fall from the rushed movements.

She sat down in Alessio's lap when he fell onto the plush white leather chair in the corner facing the mirror.

"You got a nice fucking view," Corrado said as he keeled down behind Ginevra, between Alessio's widened stance, his hands palming her ass. "You can watch it all, Les."

"And you," his lover murmured.

Yeah.

Corrado did. The perfect view of Ginevra's wet, pink cunt hovering above Alessio's cock. He got his fingers wet with her arousal, letting the digits slide through the lips of her sex, and teasing the entrance of her slit before sliding further back.

Alessio wasn't the only one who liked to watch.

"*Now,*" Ginevra said, her body vibrating. "Fuck me *now.*"

"Whatever you want, kitten."

Corrado pressed a single finger into the tight ring of

Ginevra's ass as Alessio brought her down on his cock. Her loud cry echoed, but Corrado focused, now. Watching the way Alessio's cock slid in and out of Ginevra's pussy, stretching those sensitive tissues of hers open as his dick came out coated in her with each thrust.

And then his fingers.

One, at first, working her ass. And then a second, making her feel a little more full. He went slow, using her body's natural cues and the wetness he'd been able to gather from her sex to make it easy. He didn't want it to hurt.

Sex *shouldn't* hurt.

Not unless someone wanted it to.

"Like this, Ginny," Corrado murmured, his tongue sliding along the curve of her ass as he spoke. Her noises climbed higher as Alessio continued pulling her up and down on him with a brutal pace, something he *loved*. Sex was always better for Alessio when he could let go of his control. "It's going to be like this when we're *both* fucking you—but better. You'll be so full, kitten, *too fucking full*. And then it will drive you crazy, make you fucking high, baby. Imagine, huh?"

"*God*," she whimpered.

Alessio chuckled, and Corrado peered up to see him pull her in for a deep kiss. At the same time, he added a third finger, and let his teeth drag against the curve of her supple ass. She tensed, just a split second, before a low moan crawled out of her throat.

So raw.

And loud.

Jesus.

"It'll ache so goddamn deep," Alessio told her. "But it'll be so fucking good, too. Do you want that—both of us fucking you?"

"I do."

"Oh, you'll get that." Even Corrado heard the promise in Alessio's tone—*soon* was coming far sooner than Ginevra thought. If they got this woman through dinner tonight before they said fuck it and took her home to bed, it would be a fucking miracle. "Are you going to come like this?"

"Y-yes."

"Give it to us, then. *Give it.*"

It took Corrado widening his fingers on the withdraw, and Alessio pulling her in for another kiss before Ginevra fell over that cliff into her second orgasm. She stilled on Alessio, sitting down on him entirely as her shoulders shook violently.

Corrado took that chance to lean in, his lips finding the base of Alessio's cock where the condom didn't quite reach all the way down, but where Ginevra was still stretched around him. Her pussy, and his cock against Corrado's mouth, their tastes blooming across his tongue, was enough to make him think he was about to blow.

"*Shit*," Alessio muttered.

A familiar pulse thudded in the base of Alessio's cock, and the way Ginevra's muscles at the same time around him, her sex still flexing from the remnants of her orgasm.

Alessio's next words came out in a groan, his hands slipping down around Ginevra's ass to widen her for Corrado as he licked them both again. "Holy fuck, Corrado, you made me—"

He pulled back, grinning as he countered, "Come, yeah."

Ginevra's voice was airless as she whispered, "Did we even have time to do this?"

"Oh, we had time—still do," Alessio replied.

"*Still?*"

His gaze darted to Corrado as he stood, and then drifted lower to the outline of his erection pressing against the leg of his pants, the lower portion of the zipper biting into him.

"Yeah, Ginny, now we get to see how much Corrado can take."

She peeked back at him, a demure smile playing at the edges of her lips. "We do."

Fuck, yeah.

Corrado was up for that.

CHAPTER 18
ALESSIO

The thing Alessio wanted to be doing?

Well, it certainly wasn't what he was doing.

"You're quiet down there," Cara said, drawing Alessio out of his thoughts.

The loud chatter at the table continued like she hadn't called him out on the fact he wasn't feeling the conversation tonight. To his benefit, Alessio turned his attention away from Corrado and Ginevra sitting across from him. He wanted to be over *there*—or rather, get both home, and in his bed.

That's what he wanted.

Instead, he smiled at Cara, tipping his wine glass up for a quick drink. "Things on my mind, that's all."

Corrado's mother returned his smile, her gaze drifting across the table from where he was sitting to the other two, but came back to him. "So, what you're saying is I should thank you for making time to leave the penthouse for us, hmm?"

Alessio laughed. "Anything for you."

He loved Corrado's mother. There was something warm and inviting about the woman. She comforted without trying at all, and he never felt unwelcome here. And, through watching her with her small army of sons, he had learned how a mother should love their children. He respected her for that, more than anything else.

"Well, I'm glad you're all getting it figured out," Cara said, winking.

Alessio shrugged. "Getting there."

"Figuring out what, now?"

Corrado's voice drew Alessio's attention back across the table. He would have sat over there, on the other side of Ginevra, but he didn't trust his control to do that right now. Corrado had a *far* better handle on his needs and keeping them tampered down until it was an appropriate time.

No doubt, his hand was on Ginevra's thigh under the table. He'd have the soft skin of her thigh against his palm, warm and shivering. Despite having ate dinner here, he bet Corrado could still taste the woman on his tongue, too, because Alessio sure as hell could.

And he wanted *more*.

If he was over there, like Corrado, they would have already left. So, he took the seat across from them, and settled himself with his fucking imagination. Which frankly, was just about as bad as *having* them.

Alessio shifted in his seat, ignoring a raging erection because *now was not the goddamn time*, and his body didn't care.

"Figuring out what?" Corrado asked again, grinning.

Alessio gave him a look as Ginevra turned into the conversation, her conversation with Bene over. He gestured between them with a flick of his wrist. "This."

He wondered how Corrado would take him outright saying that at his family's dinner table. Sure, they'd come here a lot over the years. Both had sat at this table, ate meals with his parents and siblings, and were together through it all. Yet, never once had they said those words.

Oh, sure, he told Corrado's father when Gian asked.

That wasn't the same.

Corrado nodded, unbothered at the silence stretching

over the table, and glanced his mother's way. "Yeah, that's about right."

"How?"

Both Alessio and Corrado's attention snapped to the youngest of the second set of Guzzi twins. Bene, who Ginevra had just been conversing with moments ago. At the lift of Corrado's brow, a silent order for his brother to clarify, Bene did just that.

"How does that work?" he asked.

Corrado cleared his throat. "Bene."

The warning was clear.

Don't ask.

"I get how *that* works," Bene muttered, "I'm not a fucking idiot, Corrado."

"Then don't ask."

Bene looked only to Ginevra. "No, how does that work? Because Corrado was like a sixteen-year-old girl with her heartbroken throughout high school—in a fucking mood, and you just wanted to punch him in the throat and tell him to suck it up. And Les? *Yeah*, in case you didn't get the memo, he's a fucking asshole on his good days, too. How does she put up with it all the time? Because I had to live with one for a long while, and that was enough for me."

Ginevra's mouth popped open, but she said nothing. Maybe she didn't know what to say. Light laughter drifted down the table, from the other twins, Marcus at the end near his father, and the heads of the household, too. Not nervous laughter, either, but genuine. Because well, none of what Bene said was a lie, and he always had the biggest fucking mouth at the table.

Alessio wasn't even offended.

Corrado grunted under his breath. "I am not *that* bad."

"I am," Alessio said, nodding in his seat, "and Corrado is … well, Bene isn't wrong."

"See," Bene said. "I wanna know *how*."

All eyes turned on Ginevra again. Alessio was sure this was not what she had planned for the dinner, but hell, one had to expect anything with the Guzzis. Well, everything except judgement or problems. As long as they gave a shit about you, then that's what mattered. They would be the first to jump in and support whatever someone needed or wanted even if it meant everyone else would back away.

Her cheeks tinted with pink as she said, "Well, I learned to like it, I guess."

"But *how*?"

Ginevra's stare drifted between Corrado at her side, and Alessio across the table. "Kind of hard not to with those two, that's all."

Bene opened his mouth to speak again, but it was Gian who spoke up to stop him at the other end of the table. "That's enough, Bene, you understand the rules. Unless someone offers, you mind your own."

The youngest twin scowled. "I can't help I'm curious."

"Be curious privately and allow others the same respect."

"*Fine.*" Bene muttered to Ginevra out of the corner of his mouth, "But they're still moody as fuck, and I'm not sure how you do it."

Alessio smirked at Corrado's mother, shrugging as he took the final drink from his wine glass. "So yeah, it's good."

She laughed. "That's all I care about."

Right.

Him, too.

～

Alessio whistled low, admiring the twin Ducati super bikes parked in front of the large garage. "Damn, I will need to get me one of those."

Matte black.

Chrome detailing.

Speed like nothing else.

"Yeah, I need one," Alessio said.

Beside him, Chris chuckled and shook his head. "Ma saw them, and the first thing she said was it was just another way for Bene and Beni to kill themselves."

"Well …"

"She had a point," Chris muttered. "They have no concept of fucking danger, and if anything, they chase that shit. Usually together."

"You're aware I like you, right?"

"Mostly, yeah."

Alessio nodded and gave Corrado's twin a smirk. "But I'm also grateful you're not as close to Corrado as those two are with each other. I couldn't handle your ass in front of me every single day."

Chris chewed on the piece of gum in his mouth before muttering, "You know what? Same."

Yep.

He respected Chris a great deal, like the rest of Corrado's family, but he also wasn't lying. He wouldn't appreciate and like Chris as much as he did if he was around twenty-four-seven.

Facts were facts.

"And what are you two doing out here, hmm?"

Chris and Alessio spun around to see Gian crossing the driveway, coming their way with a knowing smile. The man tossed his hands in his pockets, looking unconcerned that they had snuck out of the house, and away from the noise.

Mostly, Alessio just needed to breathe. Corrado should enjoy dinner with his family—they had tonight planned for a week, now. Ginevra was having a good time, too. It didn't matter that Alessio wanted to take them home, and move onto *far* better things.

His needs could wait.

So, he needed distance.

A *breather*.

"Admiring your sons' bikes," Alessio said, spinning back around to look over the Ducatis again. "I hear your wife doesn't appreciate their beauty."

"No, she doesn't appreciate that they stunt on them, and regularly break two-hundred kilometers an hour on the highway. Because she knows, when they hit the pavement, there will be nothing left."

"And yet, here they still are."

Gian chuckled darkly. "Only because Cara has not gotten mad enough to tell me to get rid of them, yet."

"They're not kids anymore, Papa," Chris said. "They're adults, with their own money, and they can do what they want with it."

"Except you all will always be *my* kids, regardless of your ages. And you keep thinking you can do what you want, Christopher, we'll see how that works out for you."

Chris sighed.

Gian smiled as he came to stand in between the two. He gave Chris a nod and then tipped his head back toward the house. "Give us a minute, would you?"

"Sure. Later, Les."

Alessio tipped his chin in Chris's direction, his silent goodbye. It was only once the front door of the mansion slammed shut that Gian turned his focus on Alessio next to him.

"I'm glad to see things are better for you three, but I didn't think you—or him—wanted me to mention it in there," Gian said.

"We're getting there. Still complicated, but—"

"There's three people," Gian interjected, chuckling, "the complications can't be helped."

"It's good complications, though."

"I bet." Gian rocked on his heels, surveying the bikes in front of him, and then staring up at the dark sky overhead. "On another note, I had a phone call with Dare earlier."

Alessio made a noise under his breath, bitter and annoyed. "Right, well, I should go find Corrado and Ginny."

"Or you can accept that when people care about someone else, sometimes they make bad decisions or say things without thinking them through *because* their feelings sometimes get in the way. All things considered, Alessio, I think you should be able to understand that better than anyone else. Stop ignoring his calls—he's the only father you've ever had, blood or not. Attempt to keep what you have, regardless of what your pride thinks about it."

Jesus.

Alessio let out a harsh sigh. "I have a job I need to do— sometime over the next week, I need to be on a plane for it. I planned on seeing him before I left, or when I came back, considering I have to make a stop at The League before I head out."

"Good."

"And he doesn't need to use you as his messenger. He has Cree for that."

"Right," Gian said, turning to face the house with a knowing grin, "but sometimes, it's better to go to someone who can make more of an impact when it counts, you understand?"

"Not really."

Gian patted him on the back. "You don't have to."

CHAPTER 19
GINEVRA

"Where did Alessio go?" Ginevra asked, peeking up at Corrado over her shoulder where he stood close to her back. "I didn't see him sneak out."

All Corrado had to do was tip his head down, and as he spoke, his lips whispered over her skin. It was enough to get her body *humming* again. From that moment in the changing room earlier that day, she had been on a high. Her mind knowing where this would lead, and she wanted it more than anything. That anticipation had curled around her nerves; she felt like she might snap.

"Careful," she said quietly enough that the people laughing a few feet away wouldn't hear them or notice their distraction. "You will start something we can't finish here."

Corrado's dark chuckles pulsed against the back of her shoulder. "Patience is a beautiful thing to learn, but you get me best when I have none, Ginevra."

God.

Well, he wasn't wrong.

"And he snuck out with Chris a while ago," Corrado murmured. "I suspect he needed a second to relax … get his mind off things. He's another one, you know? Alessio doesn't have a fucking ounce of patience in him."

That dark, suggestive tone of his had her stomach clenching. All husky, and deep. Like he already had the taste of her on his mouth, and he was ready for more. It was enough to make her wish they were anywhere but here, and that Alessio was with them.

As though he could read her mind, Corrado's hands tightened on her hips. Those fingers of his pressed firm enough to make her breath catch, reminding Ginevra how good it was to have his fingers filling her ass while Alessio had been fucking her on that chair.

It also reminded her they were not at all in an appropriate place for her to be having those kinds of thoughts.

"We should go," she whispered.

Corrado's lips curved into a smirk as his mouth drifted along the line of her shoulder to the junction at her throat. "We should. Let's say goodbye, and go find Les, huh?"

"Please."

A thick noise fell from his throat, and those fingers of his flexed at her hips harder, promising the best of their night was yet to come. She couldn't wait.

"Leaving, are we?"

Ginevra smiled, tipping her chin down to hide the reddening of her cheeks at the familiar, sexy voice behind them. Why wasn't she surprised that Alessio had sneaked up on them in the family room while they were distracted together and then stayed quiet, so he could watch them.

He loved that.

It made Ginevra hotter.

"Well?" Alessio asked, stepping up beside Ginevra. "Are we leaving?"

She heard the other question in his statement he didn't outright ask. That simple *yes* or *no* they always waited for her to give. It was their reminder, even when their movements were rough, and she felt like she was spiraling down to crash between them, that … she still had the control here.

Even when it didn't seem like it.

"Yes," Ginevra said. "Yes, we're leaving."

~

They knew *her* so well.

They knew each other so well.

And maybe that was what captured Ginevra the most when she was between Corrado and Alessio. That even in the simple things, as they undressed her, they were so aware what the other did that in their rushed movements, they didn't clash. Their hands *knowing* and sure, like they had mapped these paths out on her in their minds a million times before they had ever gotten her on her knees on the bed.

It was how they moved with each other, how they *worked* that took her breath away first. Even as their attention focused in on her, she stared up in enough time to watch Corrado lean over her from the front, reaching for Alessio. His thumb caught the other man's lip while Alessio drew soft circles against Ginevra's clit.

Corrado's other thumb slipped past Ginevra's lips for her to suck on the tip even as he kissed Alessio.

Still, her body hummed.

Still, she had to watch.

She barely remembered the drive home. Not when Alessio had settled into the backseat with her while Corrado drove *far too fast* down the highway. She didn't think about the blur outside their windows from the speed when Alessio was between her thighs, his hands holding her down against soft leather while his tongue found a spot on her body *no man's* mouth had ever been. And his fingers were there, too, pressing into her ass to stretch her open.

In the front seat, Corrado told Alessio, "But don't let her come."

Yeah.

Alessio followed the direction, too. Throughout the drive, on the way up to the penthouse, and now she was in their bed, one standing on the right of the mattress as he worked her pussy and clit with his mouth and his fingers, and the other in front of her ...

She still hadn't come.

Oh, they brought her *so fucking close*.

To that edge where blissed numbness came in, the seconds right before they would push her into the abyss of an orgasm ... and they stopped. Corrado would kiss her, his hands driving over her spine, and under to her chest where he tweaked at her nipples. Alessio would back off from behind her enough to let her shaking subside.

And then they would begin again.

Like *now*.

And Ginevra?

Fucking *crazy*.

If there was a raw, pure version of her, this was it. She didn't recognize the sounds climbing her throat every time they denied her another orgasm. Her begging had started three denials ago.

"*Please, please,*" she mumbled.

Corrado's hand curved her cheek, the tender touch about the only thing that didn't make her ache in the best way from the rest of their roughness. "Not yet, kitten. See, you're almost there ... he will edge you again and again, until you want to scream. And then it's going to feel like *nothing* will sate you except everything."

"And don't you want that, Ginny?" Alessio asked behind her.

Why did their voices sound so *hot*?

Throaty.

It drove her crazy, too.

"Almost," Alessio murmured. "She's shaking good."

Corrado peered down at her, a glint staring back at her. "You can see it in her eyes, too. They darken when they widen."

She didn't understand their words, not when another orgasm was so fucking close as Alessio continued circling her clit at a much faster speed than before. And yet, she was scared they would take it away from her, too.

Deny her *again*.

Corrado kept his touch at her cheek, his thumb roving over her trembling lips as he freed his cock from the confines of his boxer-briefs. A grunt escaped from his mouth when she leaned forward, her mouth encasing the head of his cock even as he stroked the base made her wetter.

It seemed like it.

Then again, it might have been when Alessio's mouth found her pussy as his fingers kept working her clit, his tongue lapping at her sensitive tissues and flicking at her entrance for more sensation added to the rest.

Or it might have been all.

"Fuck, *Ginny*." Corrado's words sounded like they ached coming out. "*Les*, at this one, yeah?"

Alessio's hand at her ass flexed roughly against her muscles, and he pulled away from her sex, making her whine low. "You s—"

"*Yes*."

Ginevra sucked in a loud breath as the numbness came, the orgasm *right there*. She was sure Alessio would pull his hand away from her clit like he had so many fucking times before, but he didn't.

He didn't.

"Oh, my—"

Ginevra didn't get to finish the cry before she slipped into the beginnings of her orgasm. Further than they had allowed her to go before. *Edging*, Corrado had called it. She didn't know whether to hate it, or love it.

And then, Alessio pulled away.

His hands, his mouth, and his body. All of him drifted away from her, taking every bit of sensation with him. Corrado kneeled down, pulling his cock away from her as the disbelieving yell left her mouth.

"*No*," Ginevra gasped, "*no, no, no … why?*"

The orgasm of hers, with no sensation to aid her through it, was ruined. A waste, really. Weak as fuck, and it left her almost empty inside, somehow. Her vision blurred as Corrado got close, tipping her head back to drop hot kisses to the seam of her trembling lips.

"What do you want *now?*" he asked.

"*Why?*"

Why hadn't they given her that?

Why had they stopped?

She couldn't breathe or *think*.

"Why?" she mumbled.

"*Kitten.*"

Ginevra's gaze snapped to Corrado's, her entire body acting like a live wire because *goddammit*, if she didn't come, and soon, then she might lose her mind. She hungered for the release like they would never understand.

It was the basest urge she'd ever experienced in her life.

Deep in her gut.

Thick in her blood.

Harsh in her heart.

Hot in her mind.

Something cold slipped against her ass, but it relieved Ginevra. Something to help her overheated body. The sting of Alessio's two fingers pushing into her ass only made her shake and want more. Because even the pain seemed too fucking good to be true.

Corrado swallowed thickly, his nose skimming hers as he murmured, "Now you get it, kitten. And it's about to get *so fucking good* for you."

The only thing Ginevra could say was, "It fucking *better*."

Corrado's rich laughter drifted over her skin with hot intent, a lot like the way Alessio's behind her added to the hard slap he leveled down on her ass.

Christ.

These men would kill her.

Surely.

It would be worth it.

A rustle sounded, and Corrado's hand flew up to catch the condom tossed across the bed. Alessio added a third finger to her ass, making Ginevra fist the bedsheets harder as she whined from the lovely sensations.

Except she needed more.

Now, after everything, that would not be enough to make her come.

Corrado slid the condom down his length, stroking his cock as his free hand caught her under her jaw. He tipped her head back and then drifted lower. Behind her, Alessio stepped back, withdrawing from her body as she found herself drawn up to her knees.

They were back to those rushed, but *knowing* movements again. Warm, rough palms sliding down her sides, and two more down her back. Corrado settled her onto his lap as he came to rest on his knees on the bed. It allowed her to straddle over his body as he filled her pussy full of his cock, lips attacking hers.

Shaking all over, Ginevra was hyperaware of Alessio fitting in behind her. How his knees tucked in under her ass, and his hands came lower to spread her ass as the lube still soaking her ass and pussy met the head of his cock.

"Easy," Corrado murmured.

Behind her, she heard, "*Breathe*."

Wasn't she?

Ginevra had no clue.

Still wild.

Still out of control.

And yet, in the back of her mind, she understood all she needed to do was say *one* thing to stop this, if it's what she wanted. She had the power here, and they had given it to her time and time again to prove it.

One of her hands landed on Corrado's shoulder as he filled her, seated deep on his cock while the head of Alessio's dick pressed at the tight ring of her muscles. Her other reached back, grabbing to Alessio's hand at her hip, while his other kept her ass spread wide for him.

The pain she thought would come was there, too, but brief … and diluted. Because still the pain was something *good*.

Something to get her there, *finally*.

"Fucking *beautiful*," Alessio muttered, his kiss grazing the back of her damp neck.

"Perfect," Corrado said, his gaze locking onto hers. "Good, kitten?"

Alessio had started slow, short strokes at her back. His cock entering her just enough to stretch her out while Corrado stayed still inside her pussy. Not that it mattered because both filling her made her tighter.

"So good," she breathed.

Alessio's teeth found her shoulder.

Corrado's found her jaw.

Ginevra's fingernails scored red lines across Corrado's shoulder, and Alessio's hand as they worked her body against theirs. Corrado used his hands to move her against his cock, while behind her, Alessio flexed his hips against her ass while he worked his way in.

Her body burned.

Hummed again.

"How good is he in your ass, Ginevra?"

Her cry came out raw.

Broken.

"So fucking good, yeah?" Corrado grinned wickedly. "You're gonna want it so much now—getting your ass filled while one of us is eating your pussy or fucking it the way you like. Do you want to come?"

Her throat clenched with words wanting to spill out.

Alessio gave one more hard flex of his hips and settled all the way inside her ass as Corrado seated her down entirely on his cock, too.

That forced the words out.

"*Corrado* ... please, I have to ... come. Les ... *please.*"

Stilted, fractured, and rushed.

"*Yeah,*" Alessio said hoarsely, "I fucking need that."

Corrado groaned. "Me, too."

Their pace turned into a rhythm that matched the other one would fill her as the other pulled away. Every single one of her nerve endings snapped and twisted as their cocks worked her body to the peak.

Because even if it was too much, she needed it.

Ginevra came *screaming*. Shocked the orgasm came at all because she hadn't felt it until it slammed on her at once. More than fucking relief, if heaven existed, she saw it—sensed it deep in her bones. She wanted nothing more than *that* ... and when they gave it to her, it was surreal.

Blinding.

Impossible.

But it was possible.

It was real.

Like them.

That final peak, so high and unbelievable to her, reminded Ginevra of the men who had given it to her. They'd been out of her reach, and almost unreal to her before.

And she didn't know if she could ever let them go.

CHAPTER 20
CORRADO

"You got her?"

"Mmm."

Corrado peeked over his shoulder as he yanked a pair of cotton sleep pants up—enough to keep him decent for now. That's all he needed. Behind him, he found Alessio had picked Ginevra up from the bed in a cradle hold as he waited for Corrado to finish getting dressed.

Ginevra smiled sweetly when Alessio winked down at her. "Oh, do I get special treatment now? Because I thought the sex was it."

"Not even close," Alessio returned.

"The big bath, yeah?"

Alessio nodded his way. "Sure."

Corrado led the way out of the bedroom, and Alessio followed behind without a word. He couldn't help but to check behind him as he headed for the penthouse's main bathroom where a large clawfoot tub waited.

Alessio's head tipped down, and he nuzzled his nose and mouth along the line of Ginevra's hair, murmuring words too quietly for Corrado to discern a few steps ahead of them. Ginevra's soft smile and hooded eyes were more than enough to tell him that she liked whatever he said, though.

It wasn't lost on Corrado the affection Alessio showed to Ginevra without even thinking about it, really. Sure, they *always* took care of a woman after she allowed them to share her between them. It was only right, after all. Alessio never, however, showed affection very much while doing it. Always kind, but he wasn't *loving*.

Not like right now with Ginevra.

For a brief second, Corrado wondered why he experienced no jealousy at the sight of two people he loved showing ... well, love to one another. Because that's the thing, wasn't it? It had been inevitable, something he expected would happen with enough time, but he still only realized was a reality now.

Alessio loved Ginevra.

He might not say it.

He didn't have to.

Not when he showed it.

As for her ...

Corrado didn't have to wonder if Ginevra loved them. She did. Otherwise, she wouldn't be still doing this with them at all. He had thrown her in this mess between him and Alessio, but she didn't have to continue to indulge it.

And yet, she did.

She *wanted* to.

More than anyone else ever had—including the two of them—she helped them. Probably more than she would ever know.

In the bathroom, Alessio set Ginevra down on the toilet with a raised brow when her cheeks pinked. "I don't have to p—"

"Yes, you do. UTIs are a *bitch*."

He wasn't wrong.

Ginevra sighed when Alessio left her to come stand next to Corrado as he leaned over the claw tub and turned the levers on the rose-gold tap to start the water running. They worked together at the tub, keeping their backs turned to Ginevra while she did her business, and the running water masked their quiet conversation.

"You should tell her," Corrado murmured.

Alessio glanced his way. "Pardon?"

"That you love her, Les."

"I—"

"You should tell her."

"Have *you*?"

Corrado hesitated when he reached for the bath salts Alessio handed out to him. "No."

Not because he hadn't wanted to, but rather … the time never seemed right. Maybe a part of him still felt like, after all this time of him not saying those words to Alessio, it might be a betrayal, too. Didn't he at least owe that to Les, or did it even matter anymore?

He didn't know.

Alessio never defined the lines, either.

Corrado wasn't sure where to go from here.

Alessio shrugged. "It'll happen when it happens."

Right.

Ginevra made a quiet noise, making both men straighten to their full height at the tub, their attention going to her where she stood next to the sink. Her stance was careful, and when she stepped closer to the sink, her walk was measured.

Because *yeah*, he didn't doubt she was tender.

Sore.

"It's time to relax," Alessio told her.

"I have to wash my hands, don't I?"

"Fine." Alessio left Corrado's side, so he could slip in behind Ginevra at the sink. His chin rested on her naked shoulder as she washed her hands. As soon as she finished, not that her hands were dried because it wouldn't matter, he picked her up in that same cradle hold and carried her to the bath. "It'll help the muscles, Ginny."

"Is someone getting in with me?"

Corrado chuckled as he placed her in the hot water. "Better that we *not*."

"You should rest," Alessio agreed.

Ginevra sunk lower under the water, all of her curves and lines available for them to admire as some of her tension drifted away. "This is nice."

Corrado kneeled down, resting an arm along the edge of the clawfoot tub while he tucked stray strands of her hair behind her ear with his fingers. She turned her head into his touch, tucking her cheek into his palm, and smiling.

"It's your turn to be taken care of, huh?" he asked in a murmur. "You're always so busy worrying about *us*, Ginevra. We're fine … we've been driving each other up the wall for years."

"Not a lie," Alessio said behind him.

"Point is," Corrado continued, "it's our turn to take care of you. Whatever you want, you ask."

Her gaze drifted between him, and then to Alessio.

"I have what I want *here*," she whispered.

Right.

Corrado heard what she didn't say.

It was outside of this place where she was missing the important parts of her life.

"I miss my sisters," she said, shrugging. "But I know—"

"I might be able to help with that."

Now.

It was a risk, and Chris had been quick to refuse the first time Corrado asked for help with his plan a couple of weeks back. Corrado was done trying to get something from Andino Marcello for Ginevra related to her sisters.

The man wasn't giving anything.

So, fine.

Corrado would go elsewhere.

Ginevra's gaze lit up. "Really?"

He smiled. "It might not be *everything* you want, but it is something. Will that help?"

"*Yes.*"

"All right."

Good enough for him.

Corrado stood straight and turned to Alessio with a shrug. "You good for a minute?"

"Of course."

Alessio was quick to take Corrado's previous place at the side of the tub. Although while Corrado had been fine to let Ginevra rest in the water for as long as she wanted with no interference from him, Alessio was more practical.

He pulled a folded up wash cloth sitting on a stand next to the tub and dipped it into the water before dragging the soft terry fabric along the column of Ginevra's throat. Her sweet smile turned on Alessio, and Corrado decided to slip out while he distracted her, and he wouldn't be missed by either of them.

Unlikely, but whatever.

He missed them constantly—whether they were five feet away, or five miles. It didn't matter, a part of him felt their loss. Which, if he were being honest, was one of the most terrifying parts of this thing they all shared.

And not something he wanted to think about.

Corrado headed for where he'd dropped his coat, earlier. He found it draped over the back of the couch, and funnily enough, couldn't even remember putting it there. They focused on getting into bed and clothes went wherever the fuck they went.

Like Alessio's jeans in the hallway.

Corrado's shoes at the end of the entrance.

Yeah.

He found what he needed in his coat—a small scrap of paper that Chris had written a phone number, and a name on.

Siena Calabrese, it read in his twin's familiar scrawl. Apparently, Siena, the full-blood sister to Kev and Darren, and half-sister to Ginevra and her siblings … was tasked with looking after Ginevra's younger sisters. Oh, and from Ginevra, Corrado knew Siena had been the person to help her get away that day of her arranged marriage, alongside Andino's plans.

Not to mention, it seemed Siena had a taste for a certain Marcello herself. A very *important* Marcello, considering the man she was messing with, Johnathan, happened to be the nephew to Dante Marcello, the organization's Don. It was no wonder Siena had helped Ginevra, and was now taking care of her sisters when, she had her own secrets to keep hidden.

She had things she wanted, too.

Chris figured, if anyone might be able to help Ginevra's worries, it would be Siena. Was it a risk? *Yeah.* That's also why Corrado picked up a burner cell phone—which he also pulled from his jacket—on their way to the dinner at his parents' mansion as a *just in case*. It wouldn't be traceable, and he could dispose of it when Ginevra finished her call.

Simple.

Mostly.

Or fuck, he hoped, anyway.

Corrado made his way back to the bathroom, but instead of going all the way in, he lingered in the doorway to watch Alessio and Ginevra chat. Alessio had sat down on the floor next to the tub, resting his chin on his arm sitting along the edge. Their quiet words, and soft laughter, had Corrado smiling to himself.

It didn't take long for Ginevra to see him standing there though. And once her attention shifted to him, Alessio's did as well.

"Find what you were looking for?" Alessio asked.

Corrado nodded and waved the paper and phone in his hand. "I did."

Ginevra tipped her head to the side, considering the items he flashed at them. "What is it?"

"Something you've been asking for."

Corrado crossed the space in the bathroom keeping a distance between them. Kneeling down beside Alessio, he took his time turning the phone on for the first time and getting it ready to use with the card that was attached to the back with a set number of minutes. Anymore, and he would have to buy another card.

Not that it mattered.

He'd grab a second phone instead.

Swiping his thumb along the screen to unlock it, he brought up the call icon, and typed in the phone number written on the paper. Instead of hitting the bottom to make it call through, he held the phone out for Ginevra to take after Alessio had dried her hands with a small towel.

She took the phone, glanced at the number on the screen, and froze. Her breath caught in her throat, and Corrado dragged in his own, anxiety slipping through his veins for reasons he didn't understand.

Well, that was a lie.

He knew.

Perfectly well.

What happened when this was over here? When Ginevra had to go back to New York, and they left this penthouse behind? Where would that leave the three of them?

Corrado didn't like to think about those things.

He wasn't sure what she wanted.

And he'd learned, with Alessio and all of this, that he shouldn't influence their choices. In order for them to be happy in this thing they had together, everyone had to make their own decisions, and be sure about them. *Pleased* about them. What he wanted didn't always factor into their wants, too. They were all different people.

So, he said nothing.

Especially not on this.

If Ginevra wanted something, then she would have to speak up and tell him, or Alessio. It was as simple as that.

Even if it killed him.

"Siena?" she asked.

Corrado nodded. "Supposedly, she would be someone we could trust to talk to, yes?"

"Yeah, of course. She only ever helped me."

"Call her," Alessio murmured. "I'm sure she'd be willing to chat about your sisters and fill you in on what she can."

"Right, yeah."

Still, Ginevra hesitated.

Her hands trembled.

"Call," Corrado told her. "It's safe."

Or as safe as it would get.

Ginevra nodded and pressed the call button before putting the device to her ear. Alessio and Corrado were quick to give her privacy but not much. They drifted just outside of the bathroom, their backs turned to the door.

Not that it mattered.

They could still *listen*.

"Siena?"

Her voice ached.

So close to tears.

Corrado stared at the floor.

Alessio leaned against his side.

"Yeah, it's me," Ginevra whispered. "How are my sisters?"

"Who takes care of her?" Alessio asked.

Corrado glanced at him. "Hmm?"

"She takes care of everyone else, but who takes care of her?"

"I think it's supposed to be us."

CHAPTER 21
GINEVRA

"Ah, they let you out of the penthouse again to spend time with the rest of the world, did they?"

Ginevra grinned at Marcus's teasing. He ignored Alessio and Corrado behind her, who no doubt, were glowering at Marcus for his comment. Not that it was a lie.

"I came to dinner last night, too," she pointed out.

Marcus nodded. "Right, but does a dinner really count?"

"They're working on it."

"Well, that's what counts." Corrado's oldest brother laughed, and stepped in close enough to press a quick kiss to each of Ginevra's cheeks. "Thank you for coming—drinks are on the house, yeah? Have fun, Ginny, I am sure you deserve it with those two."

She smiled. "They're not so bad, actually."

"I'm sure." Marcus kept an arm around Ginevra's waist as he turned them both, so he could greet Corrado and Alessio behind her. "Behave tonight, huh?"

Corrado smirked. "When do we not?"

Marcus arched a brow. "You want a rundown?"

Alessio tapped his temple with one finger. "No need."

"Listen," Marcus said, his gaze drifting over the people lingering near the bar, "I'd like for this opening to go off well, if you wouldn't mind. So, if someone opens their mouth about something the two of you don't like, let me handle it."

"I'll try," Corrado murmured.

Marcus looked to Alessio displeased with Corrado's answer. Alessio only shrugged like he didn't have an opinion one way or the other, saying, "It's a sore topic."

Right.

Ginevra understood now.

Made men.

The *famiglia*.

Corrado joining The League.

Him and Alessio.

Yeah.

"You would think the two of you would try to keep each other *out* of trouble more often than you do," Marcus muttered.

Alessio made a dismissive noise under his breath as he rocked back on his heels. "You *would* think that, but no."

"Marcus!"

His arm slipped away from Ginevra as he turned to see who was shouting his name behind them. Quickly, he found whoever he was looking for, raised a hand, and then shot a look over his shoulder at the rest.

"Business calls," Marcus said. "We'll be in the VIP section upstairs when you're ready to join us."

Corrado reached for Ginevra as he replied to his brother, "Got it, Marcus."

Ginevra found herself tucked into Corrado's side with Alessio on her other side as Marcus walked away from them.

"He's just like your father, you know?" Alessio asked.

Corrado sighed. "Too much, sometimes."

"Just enough, maybe."

"Yet to be determined," Corrado muttered.

"I'd like to dance," Ginevra said, peeking up at him.

Corrado made a face.

She laughed.

"What?"

Alessio chuckled. "Someone doesn't *dance*."

"Not unless it's a waltz," Corrado said under his breath.

"Why not?"

"Never cared to bother, *but* …"

Ginevra pouted. "But what?"

"Alessio loves to dance."

"*Yes.*"

Corrado's heady laughter drifted all around them, over the music in the club and the loud people, as he stepped aside so Alessio could take his place at her other side.

"Ah, see, now she's happy," Corrado told Alessio. And then to her, "And he likes to make those he loves happy, Ginny."

The words were said almost *carelessly*. Just tossed out like they shouldn't have meant very much at all, and she shouldn't take them too seriously. It didn't matter. Their weight upon impact still took her breath away as the word *loves* kept ringing around in the back of her mind. Not that she could think about it or dwell for too long. Alessio was already pulling her out to the floor.

Later, she thought. She would deal with that word, what it meant, and her own feelings later. Surely, they would have enough time for that. Besides, she thought they should be aware.

They *needed* to know how she felt, too. That nothing in her life would ever be the same because of these two men, and she didn't want it to be. There wasn't a single part of her that wanted to be without Corrado and Alessio. She wasn't sure how that happened, but she understood *why* it did.

Them.

Simply put—because of them.

How could someone not love those men?

Yeah, she suspected things would be tricky when she had to go back home, but shouldn't they at least *try*? She winked back at Corrado while Alessio pulled her further away, waving two fingers as her silent goodbye.

He grinned back.

Turning her attention on Alessio, she said, "They won't bother him, right?"

"Who?"

"His father's people."

Alessio's hand at her waist tightened at her words. "Corrado is grown—he knows how to handle that nonsense."

"Yeah, but *still.*"

Their walk came to a stop on the dance floor after they had weaved in and out of the moving people, so they were closer to the DJ booth on the other side rather than the tables and bar at the opposite end. Alessio spun around on her, a faint smile playing at the edges of his mouth, although she could still see the wariness in his gaze.

"No, they rarely make it a point to say anything directly," Alessio explained, shrugging his shoulders under his leather jacket. "Mostly, it's underhanded comments that people overlook because nobody wants to cause shit for something like that. And *never* when his father is around to hear it."

Ginevra swallowed the lump forming in her throat. "Gian isn't here tonight, though."

"No, he isn't."

"So, a quick dance, we get drinks, and then we go back to Corrado. Right?"

Alessio's gaze drifted to somewhere behind her, searching the crowd. Probably for where Corrado had gone after they left him. He didn't bother to mask the concern flashing in his gaze. Oh, sure, he *acted* like he wasn't worried, but he was.

Because it was Corrado.

Otherwise, he didn't give a shit.

That was his line.

"Sounds good," Alessio murmured, his attention coming

back to her with a sly smile. "Now, someone wants to dance, huh?"

Ginevra laughed. "Very much."

"Two fingers of whiskey," Ginevra told the bartender—for Corrado—before adding, "spiced rum on ice, and—"

"Try the house drink," Alessio said in her ear, "it's the same one across all the Guzzi clubs. Like a signature drink, it's how you can tell when you're in one of their spaces."

He winked over her shoulder.

"Fine," she said. He leaned in and kissed her lips, but backed away so she turned to the bartender and add, "and one of the Gold Dreams."

"Coming up."

"Thanks."

"Turn around," she heard Alessio murmur along the shell of her ear.

Ginevra grinned, but didn't move. "Many people are watching, Les."

"*And?*"

"And we're supposed to get drinks, and find Corrado again, remember? You're a bad influence, and a distraction."

Not a single bit of that was a lie, either.

"We're *waiting* for drinks. And I don't see what the problem is."

Of course, he didn't.

Under the urging of his strong hands, Ginevra found herself turned around to face him. He had her pinned against the bar, his fingers tightening deliciously around the curve of her waist, so she was unable to move.

Not that she wanted to.

Not when he was looking at her like *that*.

Alessio tipped his head down, and caught her mouth with a slow, searing kiss. He was soft at first, his tongue teasing the seam of her lips until she parted them to allow him entrance. Then, at the taste of her, that kiss turned a hell of a lot hotter. All the while, he kept her steady against the edge of the bar, unbothered by the people around them or the noise.

His focus was on her.

That's all that mattered.

All too soon for Ginevra's liking, Alessio pulled away. Sure, he didn't go far, only enough that his lips grazed hers as he spoke, but it was enough for her to sense his loss, and wish he was kissing her again.

"I have to tell you something," he said.

Ginevra tensed, knowing nothing good *ever* came from those words. "Oh?"

"Relax."

"What do you have to tell me?" she asked.

Alessio sighed, his tongue snaking out to drift along his lower lip before he muttered, "I have to leave soon—The League business, and whatnot. A job that has been in the works for quite a while now, and they have the okay for it. I was the contractor put up for it, and we're not able to change those details."

Ginevra blinked, taking in those words. "How soon?"

"Likely within two or three days, we'll see how long I can stretch it. I got the call yesterday when you were ordering at the café; that gave me seven days to get my shit in order before I have to head out."

"Oh."

Alessio made a dark noise. "Don't do that."

She peered up at him. "Do what?"

"Sound so fucking sad, it kills me."

"Should I be happy?"

"Well … no."

Ginevra gave him a teasing glower. "I can't feel *nothing*, either, so you get one or the other. And sad was the one you got."

Alessio chuckled, his hands flexing against her waist again. "I get it, sweetheart. I need to go to Vegas first and grab things I need there. And if I play my cards right—or rather, work the flights right—I'll have a daylong layover in Toronto before I head out on the assignment, but still, it'll be soon."

"Soon," she echoed. "What kind of job?"

"Better not say for that."

Ginevra shivered.

"But that wasn't why I wanted to tell you," Alessio said.

She met his gaze again. "No?"

"No, more like … if where you want me to return to is wherever you are, and him, too, that's where I will be. Is that where you want me, Ginevra?"

Didn't he already know?

"Yes, this is where I want you."

CHAPTER 22
ALESSIO

A bouncer for the club led Alessio and Ginevra upstairs to the VIP section. He suspected that's where they would find Corrado, considering he no longer lingered on the lower floor of the club.

"Aren't you hot in that?" Ginevra asked, fingering the neckline of his leather jacket.

"Yes."

"Why not take it off, then?"

"Discomfort doesn't bother me that much."

He thanked The League for that.

And training.

Ginevra looked like she would say more, but he pointed across the room to distract her instead. Her gaze followed Alessio's movements, and a playful smile curved her cheeks at the sight of Corrado sitting beside Marcus in a booth.

"Better take the *principe* his drink, yeah?"

"What does that mean?"

"Hmm?"

"*Principe*," she said as they crossed the floor.

"Oh, don't call him that, it makes him pissy."

Ginevra arched a brow at Alessio.

He shrugged.

"They like to call sons and daughters of mafia Dons *principes* or *principessas*," Alessio said, shrugging one shoulder. "And I only say it when I want to get a reaction out of Corrado."

"Because he doesn't like it."

"Exactly."

"That's terrible."

Alessio made a noise. "Well, it's not terrible when it ends with him fucking you."

Ginevra shivered.

He laughed.

"Now you get it," Alessio told her.

"What are you two grinning about?"

Corrado's question had Alessio turning to wink at his lover, forgetting for a moment about the people around them, and *who*. Although, as soon as that thought drifted through Alessio's mind, it left with one look at Corrado.

He was unbothered.

He grinned back, in fact.

Ginevra had changed more than she realized for the two. Things that had once been a source of discontent for Alessio between him and Corrado now became a background thought because it didn't factor into what they shared, not when everything they had together proved it unimportant.

He probably should tell Corrado that.

There was never a good time.

"Well?" Corrado asked.

Alessio ignored the other people milling about—the ones at the booth with Corrado and his brother, and the others around surrounding booths. "I told her there will be a lot of *principes* in this club tonight, yeah?"

Corrado's features flashed with darkness.

A *warning*.

Alessio smirked. "All the Guzzi *principes*, in fact."

Ginevra smacked Alessio with the back of her hand, but he didn't even flinch. "That's enough of that."

Corrado chuckled and waved two fingers at her. "Come here, you."

He didn't mind that Ginevra left his side to slip in the booth beside Corrado because Alessio quickly slid in after her. There, she was between them. He had his hand on her bare thigh, just under the skirt of that short dress of hers, while Corrado slung an arm behind her on the booth.

Conversation turned on the club, and Marcus. An easy, *safe* topic. It allowed Corrado to join in without having to bring *himself* into it, which Alessio figured the man appreciated. With Guzzi mafioso, it could go either way.

For now, Corrado relaxed, but Alessio kept an eye on him because that could change in a blink. An offhanded comment from one of the many men who just wanted to point out *again* that Corrado didn't wear the Guzzi legacy the same way his brother did, or his other brothers who hadn't arrived yet. Or perhaps someone who wanted to share their opinion about what they believed about Corrado and Alessio's relationship.

Although, now, it was different.

A woman stood between them.

Alessio *highly* suspected a comment would come because of that if nothing else. And if he could shut it down before it turned into something that might cause a problem, then that would be far better for all of them.

He'd become used to this game with these people. They were careful when their boss happened to be around, but other than that … Corrado became fair game. Like he had been for most of his life.

Alessio wouldn't stand for it.

For the most part, Corrado ignored the shit they threw at him from people who, as far as it concerned Alessio, didn't deserve to breathe the same air as either of them. He didn't want to cause issues for his brothers, or father. God knew

Alessio could understand that, but it left Corrado as the proverbial punching bag.

Which he was *not*.

Anyone else, and he'd cut their throats.

Just not these people.

It irritated Les to no end.

"He's not wrong, though," Ginevra said.

It didn't take Alessio and Corrado long to figure out what she was referring to. Across the VIP section, the rest of the other Guzzi brothers had arrived in a trio. Chris, and the other twins didn't waste time greeting the people closer to the stairs before crossing the floor, and joining the rest of their family.

Bene and Beni busied themselves with Marcus, congratulating him on the club before turning their attention on Ginevra just long enough to greet her the same way their older brother had earlier. Chris laughed as he leaned over the booth to give his twin a one-armed hug.

"Got them both out tonight, huh?" Chris asked.

Corrado flashed his teeth in a grin. "Careful."

"I'm just saying you're in a far better mood when one of them happens to be around. That's good for all of us, Corrado."

Alessio glanced at Corrado from behind Ginevra, nodding as he did so. "He's right, though."

"Fuck off, all of you."

Someone had to tease Corrado, but they did it in such a way that didn't make him the lesser man in the room because his choices didn't match their own. All in good fun, and Corrado knew, too.

There was no malice here.

Only respect.

And of course, love.

They were simply careful about how they showed it.

Alessio doubted they would change that about their relationship. He didn't *want* people to see the depth of this thing between them. Oh, he believed Ginevra understood, but that was different.

She should.

She was in it, too.

Everyone else?

Fuck them.

Corrado caught Alessio's stare again, but he didn't find playfulness reflecting back. Instead, he found the same silent intensity that had accompanied their relationship from the beginning. A conversation that wasn't had with words because they never needed to say things to make sure the other heard what they wanted said.

Alessio gave Corrado a half smile. In response, Corrado's hand lifted from Ginevra's shoulder, and two of his fingers ghosted along the side of Alessio's neck. Barely there at all, and yet he still somehow felt it all over.

Fuck.

He needed to get this goddamn Albania job done, come back home, and settle out all the shit they had left to work on. Which wasn't that much, but more ... things left unsaid.

They needed to be *out*.

Tonight, however, wasn't the right time.

When would it ever be?

Or there wasn't a right time for this. Timing didn't matter when something should be said, full stop. As long as they put it out there, wasn't that all that mattered?

Alessio didn't get the chance to think on that for too long. A sound behind him—someone's disgust at *something* coming out as a harsh noise. Like a cross between a scoff, and a grunt, he thought.

Turning his head, his gaze landed on an older man. With a middle as wide as his shoulders, and his gray hair thinned on the top. Still, the fitted suit he wore, the lit cigar dangling from his fingertips, and the smug look of utter arrogance on his face told Alessio all he needed about the man.

Likely a Capo.

His choice in dress, and the attitude wafting from him gave it away. They all acted the same fucking way, but especially the older generation.

Alessio's gaze darted to Corrado when he turned to look for the sound behind them, too. He hadn't recognized the man, but clearly Corrado did what with the way his jaw tightened at the sight of the prick staring at them. Apparently, their chat and Corrado's touch wasn't missed by that fuck.

He didn't even try to hide his disgust.

"Do you have something you want to say, George?" Corrado asked, his hand coming to rest along the side of Ginevra's shoulder when she thought to turn around to join the conversation, too. His hand kept her facing the rest of their booth which had now gone silent. Alessio's attention went back to the Capo in the booth behind them. "How long has it been, anyway? Three years since I last saw you? Could have done with another three, to be honest."

George smirked, flashing yellowing teeth. "I feel the same way, Corrado. I prefer it when your father keeps you out of sight, if I'm being honest."

Alessio tensed at that.

Where the fuck did this guy get—

"And why is that?" Corrado asked, stopping Alessio's train of thought.

What was he doing?

Purposely trying to bait the asshole?

Why?

"Fucking *queers*," George uttered, his gaze darting away from Corrado and Alessio. "Gian Guzzi ought to be fucking ashamed of what he's allowed to happen with you, Corrado. Had you been my son, I would have beat your ass until you understood what I expected from you."

Yep.

This time, the comment hadn't even been underhanded, but right fucking out there. Alessio drifted away from Ginevra in the booth.

Alessio didn't get offended at being called a queer, frankly. He was bisexual—he fit the bill of queer perfectly fine, even if he didn't use the label. Some people needed labels because it gave them a sense of belonging.

Words were important.

People forgot.

"What did you fucking say?" Alessio asked, straightening to his full height as he exited the booth. George looked his way, gaze narrowing and still looking too fucking arrogant for Alessio's liking. The man likely figured nothing would happen to him because of who he was, and his position. "Say it again … *go on.*"

George sneered. "I said *fucking qu*—"

"*Les,*" Ginevra whispered, her hand reaching out to grab him.

Her, and those words, had him glancing her way. Not that it mattered, his attention flew back to the Capo behind their booth when Corrado turned, and launched himself over the back of the seat.

Nobody saw it coming.

Nobody planned for *this.*

Not when Corrado had always been the one with the calmer head between the two. He'd resigned himself for years to turn his cheek, and ignore the shit people liked to say about him, or them.

Not this time.

And nobody had time to react.

By the time Marcus decided to climb over the table at their booth, and head for Corrado, it was already too late. Someone else tried to jump in, too, but nothing helped.

Alessio stood *stunned.*

He heard every fucking punch.

Smack, smack, smack.

Bone hitting bone.

He saw the blood.

Spewing to the checkered floor. Spraying across Corrado's silk shirt. Dotting his busted knuckles every time his fists slammed into the face of the Capo again and again. Marcus tried to pull his brother back by grabbing onto the back of his shirt, but Corrado would not move.

"*Fucking help me here!*"

"Corrado, stop! *Stop it!*"

Marcus's shout echoed.

Ginevra's *ached.*

Alessio cared nothing for Marcus's demand, but Ginevra's had him moving. And only because she looked like she would get out of the booth any fucking second, and Alessio couldn't have that. She didn't need to get in the middle of this mess.

Already a whole group tried.

And failed.

It was chaos. Men shouting. Corrado's brothers holding back those trying to get to him to save the man on the ground. Pointless. In the background, Alessio seemed removed, somehow.

As though this had been inevitable.

Why were they surprised?

Alessio shoved between the semi-circle of people trying to yank Corrado from the man on the floor—who was no longer moving. He would have been fine to let Corrado get out *years* of frustration, hurt, and anger on the face of the asshole, but it only took one peek at a *terrified* Ginevra for Alessio to realize this wasn't good.

"*Corrado.*"

His first shout did nothing, not that he expected it to. Alessio got down, wrapped his arms around Corrado's chest, and pulled back hard enough to send them both tumbling to the floor.

"That's enough," Alessio muttered, forcing them over so he had Corrado pinned under him to the floor. The daze hadn't left—*fury* stared back at him, written in heavy lines all over Corrado's strong features, and exhaling in every hard breath he let out. "*Fucking stop.* That's enough, Corrado."

He didn't fight him, though.

Didn't shove him off.

No, he *stared* at him.

So goddamn angry.

And yeah, Alessio got it.

"*Fuck*," someone—Marcus—hissed behind them. "He's dead; someone call in the cleaner, this mess needs to *go.*"

Someone else cried.

Ginevra.

Alessio looked her way.

Corrado did the same.

That, more than even Alessio dragging Corrado from the dead man on the floor, brought him back to reality. Alessio sensed the change in Corrado's body, how all the fight and tension and anger bled away when his gaze landed on where she stood just five feet away.

Shaking.

Crying.

Scared.

She could be frightened of them, or of Corrado, or just what he had done. Alessio wasn't sure, but when Corrado reached out a hand to her, a *sorry* already falling off his tongue, she took a step back.

A whole step.

Away.

"Get him out of here," Marcus said, blocking Ginevra from Alessio's view when he came to kneel beside them. "Calm him the fuck down, I need to handle this and fast."

Right, right.

Mafia business.

Can't kill made men.

All *trash*.

"Ginevra," Corrado said.

Marcus gave his brother a glance from the side. "She's fine for now."

Except she wasn't.

Even Alessio understood that.

CHAPTER 23
CORRADO

Alessio shoved Corrado through the exit door, making him stumble into a back alley that was cold, and yet still somehow smelled of garbage and piss. *Fucking perfect.*

Not that it mattered.

The cold air helped to soothe some of that rage inside his soul—that bitterness making the beats of his heart faster. And not in a good way, either.

It barely helped, though.

Alessio stayed back by the door, sticking a rock in the track to keep it from closing before he turned to face Corrado. He didn't need to look at Alessio's face to see the disappointment staring back from him.

Corrado wasn't the hothead here.

He didn't *freak out*.

Over the years, he had become rather good at pretending like people's bullshit didn't bother him, and … tonight had been more than enough to make him fucking snap.

Oh, sure, Alessio would have taught the guy a lesson, too, but just differently than Corrado. Like taking him outside and beating the piss out of him where people couldn't stand there and watch.

People like *Ginevra*.

Corrado let out a heavy breath, his back hitting the brick wall opposite to Alessio. Still, his companion said nothing as he snarled under his breath, dragged his palms down his face, and stared up at the inky sky with bright stars dotting its surface.

He still missed the stars.

They didn't see them enough in Vegas.

"Corrado—"

"Just don't," he muttered.

Alessio sighed. "That was bad."

"I don't need the memo."

"No, I mean … that was a mess, and what the fuck?"

What was it?

A lot of things.

Nothing, too.

Everything.

Five fucking years of comments under people's breath about what they thought with Alessio and Corrado, like they had any fucking business opening their mouths to say anything at all.

It was *more years* of him always being told *famiglia* should be the only thing Corrado did—he would only ever be useful as a man, if he was his father's clone.

The frustration.

His anger.

A *reaction*.

Corrado finally reacted, and surprise, it came out badly. Why on earth was anyone surprised? Because he wasn't.

This felt like a long fucking time coming.

"He didn't give a fuck, you know?" Corrado asked.

"Who?"

"That *fuck*—George."

He still stared at the sky and willing that hatred in his heart to disappear, loathing the emotion—it had no place in his life. He felt a lot of ways about a lot of different things, but *hate* terrified him.

Hate made people do awful things to one another. Fear bred in hate, and people had killed for nothing more than their hate of someone else, or for their hate of *something*.

Be it differences, sexualities, religion, or skin color … hate caused pain. That's all it was good for, and he proved that tonight, hadn't he?

His hate came out in *violence*. How did that make him any worse or better than the man who was dead on the floor upstairs?

Corrado didn't think he was better.

"I don't understand," Alessio said quietly.

Of course, not.

Because Corrado hadn't explained.

All that shit unsaid.

"He didn't give a fuck," Corrado repeated, "because he didn't know anything about us, and that's what pissed me off, okay. All he sees are two men who are affectionate, and that made him uncomfortable enough to say something about it. Not because it hurts him, or affects his fucking life, but just because he *didn't like us*."

"There are millions of people like him, Corrado."

Yeah, he understood.

Clearly.

"Does that mean they should open their stupid fucking mouths and spew their bullshit, though?" Corrado asked, lowering his gaze from the sky to stare at the man across the alley from him. Alessio stared back with his face an expressionless mask, not that Corrado took offense to that. They *all* needed a few seconds to deal with this, and what it meant. "When they know nothing—not what we are, what it's been like for us *together*, or what you mean to me. And they sure as fuck don't have a clue how much I fucking love you because they're too worried about the fact two men might kiss where they can *see*."

Silence echoed between the two in the alley.

Finally, Alessio cleared his throat and muttered, "You drop that bomb, huh?"

"What?"

"The *love* bit."

Corrado gave him a look. "*Cette partie de mon cœur est à toi*—this part of my heart, it's *yours*. I have been telling you this for years, but you only wanted to hear it in the way you wanted me to say it, Les."

Alessio's throat jumped, and his cheek twitched. Corrado waited him out because now, he didn't have a choice. He did what he did—it'd been *said*. The rest would be determined by the man across from him.

"I figured out something over the last while," Alessio murmured.

"Do tell."

"You don't have to be an asshole."

Corrado checked his attitude. "Sorry."

Alessio shrugged, stuffing his hands in his pockets as he looked up at the sky above them while he spoke. "I figured out I clung to that—to *words*, Corrado, putting too much faith and weight in what words meant, and not what's true. I thought, if you said those words, then it would mean this was *real*. I held onto a need for words when literally everything else about us and what we are is the definition of what I wanted. It's love, and I'm sorry I didn't tell you this sooner."

Corrado blinked, quiet again.

This *thing* that had been such a fucking problem … now wasn't one. Like that, it was done, and he wasn't sure if he understood what it meant.

"And you know I love you, so," Alessio added. "I've always loved—"

Corrado crossed the alleyway before Alessio could even

finish his sentence because *no* … no, that could not be an afterthought. Not when he was aware, regardless of what Alessio decided he had figured out about all of this, that those three little words had meant a lot to him when he felt like they weren't freely given.

Alessio might have understood *now* Corrado wasn't like him, and he didn't show his affection and love in the same ways. That didn't mean he couldn't do it, anyway.

Because that was love.

Corrado crashed into Alessio hard enough to send them both into the wall beside the propped open door. Alessio's fingers threaded into Corrado's hair when their lips met, moving to a fast, familiar rhythm as his frustration and anger started to bleed away.

All the hatred?

Gone when he got a taste of Les on his tongue.

Because that was the thing about hate, too.

Love always won.

Corrado flexed his hands, the pads of his fingers scraping against the brick wall as his mouth ghosted over Alessio's when he whispered, "I fucked up tonight."

"You had a moment. We all have them. He's a prick, and so fucking what if he was made, they'll handle it, Corrado."

Right.

But no.

"I meant with Ginevra, not *la famiglia*."

Alessio let out a slow stream of air. "It scared her."

"Of course, she was."

"She comes from violent men. She's sensitive to this kind of thing. Give her a second to come back. We're not them, and it might take a bit for her to figure that out."

Corrado looked away, the reality a little too sharp for his liking. It stung. "I—"

"We're not *saints*, Corrado. This is our life; we are who we are."

No exceptions.

No apologies.

He heard what Alessio didn't say. This had always been their way.

"And what if it's not the life she wants?"

"You always want what you love, even when you're not supposed to."

The door beside them swung open before Marcus stepped out into the alley. Corrado didn't bother to step away from Alessio at the sight of his oldest brother—he no longer cared to make others comfortable by hiding the best parts of himself.

Because that was another thing.

Alessio?

Ginevra?

They were the better parts of him.

His better *pieces*.

"What?" Corrado asked.

"The cleaners have arrived. They will take the body out the back here." Marcus fixed his suit jacket and shook his head. "You made a mess—I have to call Papa and make him aware."

"Whatever Gian wants," Alessio blurted before Corrado was able reply, "we'll be happy to do for him."

Marcus nodded, turning to head back into the club. "And Ginevra ... she asked to leave, and so I had someone take her home."

"Home as in our pent—"

"Home as in *my* home," Marcus said. "She asked for some time, Corrado. Let her have a moment."

Right.

Yeah, he expected that.

It still fucking *hurt*.

Corrado went cold all over.

Alessio's hand tightened on his shirt. "It's *fine*."

No. Not at all.

CHAPTER 24
GINEVRA

Knowing something was different from it being *your* reality. Out of everything Ginevra learned since being put in the lives of Corrado and Alessio, that seemed to be the most important lesson to stick with her.

She'd known about *many* things before them. For life, about herself, and even the bad parts forced upon her. And then she met them—one by one, everything changed into something else.

About life.

Herself.

And even the bad parts.

Still, a piece of Ginevra had been hiding one aspect of who those men were and what it would mean to her. She understood what Alessio and Corrado did for a living—they were *connected*. They were more like the people who hurt her, and less like the boy who sat next to her during her first class of the morning at the community college.

She understood it, but knowing those things different from seeing it. However, being shoved in her face, a man capable of violence that scared her and did it *without* retribution, reminded her she was not like these people.

Her life had been different.

She hadn't seen their version of life through their eyes and experiences, and she'd been shaped differently because of it. And yet, she chose to turn her cheek.

That wasn't right.

Even she got that.

And yet, that other part of her was clear, so much so it became impossible to ignore. Knowing might not be the same as seeing, sure, but she had still known and still stayed.

In fact, she *wanted* to stay.

Ginevra realized far too late, as she sat staring out the bay window of Marcus Guzzi's beautiful townhome the morning after the night at the club, that she was not having an internal dilemma about Corrado and Alessio.

Of them, she was *most* sure.

Them, she wanted.

It stuck her in this dark place because of her own complex about who she thought she was, and how much changed. Ginevra never said she was a saint, but she had *some* morals. That in the end, she was the person who understood where right and wrong fit in her life.

The mafia came for her when she barely knew it existed.

She'd almost been forced into an arranged marriage.

Her mother had been murdered.

All those things meant Ginevra should have made the easy choice—with freedom at her fingertips, she should run from these people, and those like them, that had done to her what they did without as much as a blink about it.

Because they were made differently.

And somehow, Ginevra found herself inexplicably and irrevocably in love with men who, while they'd not done bad things to her, had done them to others. She overlooked it before, but not so much now. The man they killed, she bet like others in their business, said awful things—he was not a good man, and to some, he deserved to die for it, and for other reasons.

But to someone?

That man had probably been a father—maybe a good

one. A husband. He'd been a son, perhaps a brother, a grandson, and more. He was a *person*.

Her dilemma in a nutshell

For herself—just her.

After knowing what they could do … what had been done to her … After everything, Ginevra still found that need deep in her bones that she wanted to be with Corrado and Alessio more than she had wanted anything in her life.

Ginevra was not who she assumed she was before them. And she would never be the same after, either.

That terrified her.

And changed nothing.

"Ginny."

Turning on the bench seat in front of the window, Ginevra found a *very* familiar face in the living room's entryway room. Chris smiled, but the sight didn't quite reach his eyes.

"How're you doing?" Chris asked.

Ginevra shrugged under the oversized sweater that Marcus found for her. "I'm not sure."

Chris cleared his throat. "Hmm. Corrado called—Les, too."

She swallowed the ache in her throat. It only became even more painful with every beat of her heart, making it impossible to ignore. Somehow, she talked through it. "I just … need a bit of time."

To keep thinking, and to realize, *this* was the life she wanted. To get over herself, in a way.

After the time she had spent with either one, or both men in the past months, they should at least give her a day to herself.

"Let them explain," Chris said.

Ginevra's brow furrowed. "What is there to explain?"

She understood perfectly well what happened. The mess

in her heart and soul needed dealt with now, and they couldn't help with that. This was on *her*.

Right?

Chris's features went stony, leaving Ginevra confused. "I will let them know, then."

"A lot was taken from me," Ginevra tried to explain, "and I've shoved it aside while I was here … so it's catching up in different ways."

This was one.

Chris nodded. "I understand."

It didn't sound like he did, though.

Then, he asked, "Anything else you want me to tell them? I'm about to meet up with them at the mansion in a couple of hours, so I can pass it along face to face."

All over again, she considered the conversation with Cara in the restaurant. How she told her, in so many words, to always make the best of this life.

She didn't have to *make the best* of anything.

Not when she had Corrado and Alessio.

"Ginevra?" Chris asked again. "Anything?"

"Yeah. Tell them I lo—"

Marcus stepped into the entryway beside his brother, making her words stop short as he held out a phone with a small smile. "Someone would like to speak to you from New York, Ginevra."

Her gaze darted to Chris, but he stepped back to let Marcus offer the phone still outstretched for her to take. She did but didn't look down at the screen right away to see if she might recognize the number.

She wanted to thank Marcus first.

He had been kind to her.

Even if he didn't have to be.

"Thank you for everything," she said.

Marcus shrugged. "No worries, this is what I was taught to do."

She looked past him to finish her conversation with Chris, but she found the entryway empty. He already left.

Damn.

Ginevra would have time.

Later.

She would go back to Alessio and Corrado and say what she wanted to say face to face. They would get it from her mouth, and not from someone else's.

She loved them.

They deserved to hear it from her.

"Take your call," Marcus said, bringing Ginevra back to reality.

She laughed under her breath, and nodded, pulling the phone up to her ear as she said, "Hello?"

"Are you ready to come back?"

Ginevra stiffened all over. "Andino?"

The man on the other end of the line chuckled darkly. "That would be me, yes."

"Why are you calling—"

"I am the one who sent you away," Andino said fast, "and I should have access to call you if I need, even if I am in jail, right?"

He really was an asshole.

And … "*What?*"

"I'm sorry?"

"You're in jail?"

"Semantics, and I have access to a private cell, so my business, like you, is still being handled."

Ginevra moved onto another topic, then. "What did you mean—about home?"

"Exactly what I said."

"You mean—"

"I heard you spoke to Siena," he noted, a slight hum in the background of his call lowering to nothing at all as a door shut on his end. "But what she didn't tell you was just how close we were to the end the night you called. A few days before you spoke to Siena, Darren got caught in an unfortunate situation—a bomb that did quite a bit of damage."

Ginevra dragged in a breath, surprising herself when she cared nothing for a man who shared at least half of her blood.

"And a while ago," Andino added quieter, "they buried Kev—did they tell you?"

"No. Is Darren alive?"

"Barely. Life support most of the way. He won't come out of it, and Siena only has to sign paperwork after filing to take over his next of kin as their mother is missing, and can't do the job of pulling the proverbial plug. No one is left who will give a fuck, or can change the fact, that you didn't marry me, and ran off instead. Not anymore."

Jesus Christ.

"It's over, Ginny," Andino said, "and you can come home. Siena said your sisters have been told the truth about you recently, and they ask for you every chance they possibly can. I will be emailing Marcus with the name and contact of a pilot who is willing to overlook a hidden passenger on his private jet when he makes the trip across the border today, where he will land in a safe, private strip to drop the passenger off. *You*, I mean."

It was over.

She didn't know how to feel.

"But we are running on a short timeline," Andino said, "because I was barely able to call in that favor and contact today. Just my luck that my old friend is making the trip this morning. So, otherwise, we'll have to wait and pull strings to get you back home soon. It's up to you."

Ginevra didn't have to think about it.

She wanted to be here.

Should be here.

But she missed her sisters. She needed to go back to them.

The boys would understand.

Surely.

"Well?" Andino demanded.

"I'll be on that plane if it's waiting for me."

CHAPTER 25
CORRADO

"Stop obsessing."

"I'm not."

"Corrado."

He glowered at the phone in his hand. "What, Les?"

"It doesn't help to sit there and—"

"Or you could leave me the hell alone?"

Alessio sighed.

Corrado shrugged.

"Fine," Alessio muttered, "I need to pack up my shit, anyway. I got the new flight set for this afternoon, so we can head over to your parents together, and I'll leave for Vegas after."

Great.

Just perfect.

Corrado said none of that out loud because his pride kept him quiet. That stupid bitch of a thing seemed to follow him no matter how hard he tried to forget about it. He didn't want to speak up and tell Alessio he couldn't leave—right now, he was the *only* person here that Corrado wanted besides Ginevra, and she wasn't calling.

All she had to do was use Marcus's phone.

Except she didn't.

And his phone was still in his hands, no calls or texts.

The very last thing he needed was for Alessio to leave. But they didn't get a choice because of that fucking Albania job, and Corrado's pride kept him quiet. Instead of saying what he needed and wanted in those moments, he kept his mouth shut.

It wasn't easier.

It made sense.

"Give her some time," Alessio said, "to process whatever it is she's got going on in her head, and then we'll go from there. That's all you can do—she asked for it, Corrado."

"*I get it.*"

All too fucking well.

And it killed him.

"All right," Alessio muttered, stepping out into the hallway out of sight.

Just like that, Corrado was alone again. He was all too aware that soon, he would be far more alone than he was right now. Alessio would be gone—for a week, maybe two, who fucking knew? Ginevra was ... out of reach.

Not taking his messages, or calling back.

He'd not told her how he loved her. That, more than the rest, he regretted the most. The time had never been right to say that, but he realized now, far too late ... there shouldn't be a right time for love.

Too little, too late.

His mind was hell.

Far too dark.

Frustrated, Corrado glared at that phone in his hand, and before he could think the action though, tossed it to the hardwood floor harder than he should have. Was it smart? Not particularly, but it felt better than feeding the hot fury flooding his veins in another way.

Too bad he hadn't figured that out the night before.

Getting off the side of the bed, he scooped the phone up in one hand, popping the broken back into place before turning it over to see a large crack across the screen. The battery hadn't come out, and the screen blinked black and white.

Shit.

The screen wouldn't react to his touch, and it wouldn't bring up the home screen. Turning it on and off did nothing for him, and neither did restarting the device.

It was good and fucked.

A lot like him.

Fuck it.

Corrado tossed the ruined phone to the comforter on the bed, settling himself with the fact he would have to get a new one. Right then, though, he didn't want to do *anything*. He was feeling entirely too much, and that never worked out well for him.

Shit was out of control.

Things he wanted, gone from his grasp.

His heart hurt.

Corrado never did well like this. He wasn't weak, and he didn't want something like *love* to make him that way, either. That might have been his pride talking again, but it was the only goddamn way he protected himself.

Heading to the bathroom, he stripped down and turned on the shower. Stepping under the spray, a hiss left his lips as the hot water stung when it beat down on Corrado's back. He should turn the water temp down, but at least like this … he focused on the pain of that, and not the fact that he was losing something important.

He didn't want to lose anything.

"Hey."

Corrado heard Alessio's voice outside the shower, but he didn't reply. Alessio continued talking like that didn't bother him.

"Your father called the penthouse—he's ready to see you whenever you are."

"Great."

Except it wasn't.

Not at all.

"What happened to your phone?" Alessio asked, the shuffle of clothes following his question.

"Les, just leave—"

Corrado didn't get the chance to finish his statement before Alessio had opened the shower and was stepping inside with him. *Naked*, too. One second, he had been alone with his thoughts and fears, and in the next, he wasn't. It only hurt him, though, even if he loved the way Alessio backed him into the wall with a rough, demanding kiss ... because this distraction wouldn't last forever.

He was leaving soon, too.

And what would Corrado do then?

Not that he was able to think about that for too long with Alessio's kiss demanding attention from him, the clashes of his tongue against Corrado's hardening him. He found the friction he wanted for his erection along the hard lines of Alessio's form shoving his into the wall, and the ridges of firm muscle that somehow fit perfectly alongside his own.

Alessio's mouth left his to skim along the line of his jaw, lips dragging over Corrado's stubble as words drifted over his skin. "You want to feel good, then—not think?"

"Yeah. Just for a bit, Les."

"Whatever you want."

And Alessio was so fucking good at *that*—at just giving Corrado what he wanted.

That knowledge was written in the way his hands ghosted confidently over the slopes of his body. How he found Corrado's cock with a rough palm to stroke fast while his teeth dragged across his lower lip to leave a sharp sting behind. Alessio worked him high, and as fast as possible, so that Corrado was aching by the time he was done, when his strokes slowed, and his legs were shaking from the intensity …

Corrado had never been more grateful. Just like that, Alessio had taken his mind from a bad place, to somewhere else. He pulled him from the edge of one insanity to take him right to the cliff of another one.

He could handle this one, though.

Corrado reached for the small bottle of lube they always kept in the shower—one of their favorite places to fuck because it made clean up *easy*. Alessio took it from him as he kneeled down, making quick work of popping it open to get what he wanted from it before he was back to making Corrado think he was going insane again.

This time, it was Alessio's mouth sucking down his length, and the fingers that worked into his ass with the help of that lube. There was always something about the sight of Alessio sucking him off that did it for Corrado—maybe it was the way he always looked so fucking contrary and cocky at the same time staring up at him with something akin to a smirk dancing in his gaze.

Like he was *daring* Corrado not to come because Alessio was all too aware how goddamn hard it was for him like this. And like when he jerked Corrado off, he used his fingers to stretch him open, and his mouth on his cock to get him ready to blow in barely anytime at all. It was Alessio's teeth dragging gently down his length when he sucked him in again that about had his knees fucking buckling as the sensation of an orgasm drew near.

His balls tightened with his.

Shoulders tensing.

Corrado's groan threatened to bubble out of his chest, and Alessio let him go all at once. *Everywhere*, he was hands-off, letting hot water and cold air beat down on Corrado instead of allowing him to come.

Fuck.

But it was always so much better when Alessio did that, and Corrado was well aware what would come next because of it, too. Alessio lifted to his full height, lips crashing down on Corrado's for just long enough to have his cock jerking between them before he was spun around to face the shower wall.

One of his hands hit the tile, the other went back to grab onto Alessio's side as the man's hand came down to smack Corrado hard on his ass before he grabbed hard to the same spot. Heat flooded to the bits of his skin where Alessio's fingers dug in, holding him still while the head of his cock pressed against the tight ring of muscles at his ass.

"Jesus Christ," Corrado grunted against the wall.

Alessio's teeth found the junction between Corrado's shoulder and his neck. His gaze pinned onto Corrado's, lips curling upward. That ringing pain from the sharp bite took away the bit of sting from Alessio working his way into Corrado's ass with quick flexes of his hips.

They had been doing this for years.

Working each other to their limits.

Alessio knew what to do, and how to do it without Corrado needing to stop, or even wanting to.

"Fucking *yeah*."

Alessio's words murmured along Corrado's shoulder as he *finally* worked his cock to the hilt. His hand wrapped around Corrado's front, his fingers snaking along his length to stroke him in time with his next thrusts.

They came *hard*—fucking deep, fast, and brutal.

It was exactly what Corrado had needed.

He couldn't breathe, but he didn't think he needed to. Not when it was far better to focus on the way Alessio felt fucking him, and the ache spreading through his muscles.

From the bites and rough kisses Alessio kept peppering

over his neck and shoulders. To the way he stroked him faster with his hand, tightening enough at the head of Corrado's dick to make a moan fall between his clenched teeth. And even his fingers digging into Corrado's hip while his hips met Corrado's ass again and again at a pace that made it impossible to hold back the orgasm.

Not that Alessio seemed to want him to hold it back. "*Come on*, fucking give it over."

Corrado did, coming fast and painting the shower wall as a thick moan followed, every part of him growing hot and tense from the relief that swept through his system. Alessio wasn't very far behind, those pumps of his hips working faster for a moment before they stilled all together, and his hands tightened on Corrado again.

Alessio's groan echoed.

Corrado still had trouble breathing because the pain flooded back in, so air came second. It was worse, too, taunting him for daring to forget it.

Alessio held him tighter.

Somehow, that helped.

~

"You good?"

Alessio nodded at Corrado's question and took the cigarette Bene offered him next to the bright red Lambo his brother loved. "Yeah, I'm fine out here. This asshole will keep me company."

"Nice," Bene muttered around his own cigarette as he attempted to light it. "Papa's waiting in the kitchen, Corrado, don't fuck around."

Right.

"I'm running low on time," Alessio said as he turned to

head for the mansion entrance, "I have to be on the road in twenty minutes to make my flight."

Loneliness stabbed at Corrado's back.

He didn't turn around, though.

"Yeah, I got it."

Inside the mansion, Corrado navigated the familiar halls until he stood in the kitchen entryway. It wasn't only his father waiting. Cara sat on a stool at the island, flipping through a home décor magazine while she sipped from her tea. On the other side of the island, his father stared his way.

Gian cleared his throat. "Cara."

Glancing up from the magazine, Cara peered at her husband, who nodded in Corrado's direction. His mother didn't smile at him, but in her stare, he still found love. The same as his father. That was the thing about his parents—he might fuck up, and he had, but they still loved him.

Unconditionally.

Wasn't that love?

"Where is Marcus and Chris?" Corrado asked.

He'd thought his twin, and oldest brother would be around. Or, that's what he had been told about this quick meeting.

Gian set his coffee down. "Chris got stuck in traffic—an accident, apparently. Marcus had to handle something else. He'll come later, but I assume you'll be gone by then."

"All right."

"Care to tell me about last night, and why I now have a dead man—a *made* man—to bury, and explain to the rest of my organization what happened that caused his death, Corrado?"

No.

He still did.

Corrado talked through the events of the night before in a monotone, not bothering to justify his actions, or where they led them to now. He'd done wrong—crossed a line. Oh, sure, he wasn't the least bit fucking *sorry* for it. But yes, he had gone too far.

So, he was here.

He expected to be punished for it.

"I apologize for putting you in a bad position," Corrado finished.

Gian sighed, his fingers drumming against the countertop. "That's a careful choice of words, yeah?"

"He deserved what he got, Papa."

"Perhaps, or he might have been another old fool with an opinion to share because of his raising, Corrado."

He scoffed hard. "People don't get to use age or their raising as a reason for their bigotry or homophobia—they just *are* those things, and they don't want to change. Don't excuse him, or people like him, thanks."

"I didn't mean it like that, but … point taken."

Cara made a noise under her breath and peered at Corrado over her shoulder with a sharp stare that pinned him in place. *All* mother's had that one look. That stare that put the fear of God into her children, even if she had never raised a hand to them, let alone her voice. When his mother turned that look on him, Corrado wouldn't be stupid enough to open his mouth and make it worse.

"And what about others?" she asked.

"What?"

"He is—was—not the only person in this world who will have an opinion and something to say about your life, the choices you make, or the way you love, not to mention … the *people* you choose to love, Corrado."

"I'm aware."

"So, what about them?" Cara demanded. "Are you going to beat the life out of every person who dares to say something you don't like? Because that's the thing, son. He's one of many, and the next comment that hurts is right around the corner. You cannot *kill* every person who has something to say about you, or them."

"Why, because you agree with them?"

Cara's expression didn't change. "You know *far* better than that."

He did.

"Sorry, Ma."

Cara turned more on the stool, resting her hands in her lap as she spoke to say, "The world is full of close-minded people who will have no problem opening their mouths. It's up to you whether what they say or think matters to your life or choices. It's up to you to decide if what they say *matters.* You have been fine to stick your head in the sand and hide your activities before now … but that can't continue, and it's not going to work after last night."

Corrado's chest ached from the tightness. Nothing his mother said was untrue. That didn't mean he liked it pointed out to him like this, not that he was being given a choice. Hell, perhaps that was it.

Someone needed to say it.

And he needed to hear it.

"Figure out a better way to deal with people like that, and your issues," his mother finished quieter, "and a way that doesn't involve your hands taking their life."

Right.

Easier said than done.

"I will handle my people," Gian said, "because there isn't much someone can do when you're not made, and you don't belong to this organization, Corrado. Being a member of The League saved you retribution for this, and I hope you know that."

"I didn't. I still expected something."

"And you're ready for it."

Corrado lifted his shoulders. "I did what I did."

"Be careful when you come home to visit," Gian said, waving a hand. "Respectful, and mindful of your words and actions. They will watch to make sure you're not stepping out of line against them after this. Do you understand me?"

Everything about the mafia came down to semantics.

Theatrics.

"I got it," he replied.

Gian tipped his chin in Corrado's direction. "Then, that's all I have to say. I know Alessio is catching a flight soon, yes?"

"Too soon."

That's all he offered.

Corrado tried not to think about it.

"Better spend the time you have with him, then."

Yeah.

Cara pushed off the stool before Corrado turned to leave, and he waited as his mother joined his side.

"I'll walk you out."

"You don't have to."

"But I want to."

Corrado *almost* smiled. His mother wanted something, and so, she would get it.

Cara grabbed a shawl hanging from a hook in the entry hallway and took her time wrapping her shoulders. She smiled over at her son, a familiar softness coming back into her eyes as she murmured, "I would ask you to stay for lunch, but ..."

"Les has to leave, and I'm not in the mood, Ma."

"I bet. Your father didn't want to mention it because he didn't want to upset you more but I'm sorry. I'm sure this'll work out, Corrado."

His brow dipped. "Sorry for what?"

"Ginevra—Marcus told us she's on her way to a private

airstrip to catch a flight to New York today. I assumed that would upset you."

Sure did.

A lot.

He hadn't known until now. He couldn't call Marcus to ask anything because he ruined his phone. He could use *anybody's* phone to do it, but he didn't want to.

If Ginevra needed to leave, why should they stop her?

Yeah, it fucking hurt.

Life took from him again.

"Corrado?"

His mother's hand came up to rest on his arm, letting him know how stiff and quiet he had gone after she delivered her news. He forced a smile on his face, not wanting to worry his mother, and shook his head.

"I'm fine, Ma," he said softly.

Cara frowned. "Are you?"

No.

Still, if Ginevra wanted time and space, well, it was hers to have.

"It will be."

She sighed. "Let me see you out, then."

"Sure, Ma."

Outside, on the front steps of the mansion entrance, Corrado kissed his mother on the cheek to say goodbye before leaving her to approach Alessio standing under the maple tree with Bene. One look from Corrado, and Bene gave Alessio a shrug before he darted off to join their mother.

"What's wrong?" Alessio asked.

He just knew.

Because of course, he did.

Corrado's life took a nosedive.

Fast.

"Nothing," he lied.

Alessio arched a brow. "Really?"

"Yeah, just some news."

"And?"

"Ginevra is on her way back to New York today."

Alessio stiffened all over, but returned with, "So, you catch a flight, and meet her."

"Why?"

The two of them stared at one another, saying nothing.

"If that's where she wants to be, Les," Corrado said.

"You know nothing she wants. You didn't *ask*. Neither did I, Corrado, not really. She asked for *time*, not for us to fuck off."

"You have a flight to catch, don't you?"

"Corrado." Alessio's phone buzzed in his pocket, and he scowled. "She's supposed to be with *us*."

"Answer your phone."

Alessio continued ignoring it.

"Cor—"

"If she wants to be with us, she will, but I will not force her," Corrado said, letting that be his final word on the topic. "And answer your phone."

"It's Cree. Or *Dare*. I'm supposed to be on a flight this morning, but changed to one this afternoon instead. They got a notification for the change, I imagine—doesn't matter."

"The world doesn't stop for me, Les. I learned that a while ago. You still have a job to do, people are still waiting on you, and I have to figure shit out on my own."

"Don't start."

"Start *what*?"

"This," Alessio snapped. "*Run* because you don't like to deal. You've been doing this for years, and I've chased after you the entire time. Stop, Corrado."

"I'm not running."

For once, he came to a standstill, and he didn't have the

first clue how to fix it. He was one of three people here—he couldn't help if Alessio couldn't understand that, not to mention, that he didn't think he wanted more pain from this.

Because she left.

Ginevra *left*.

And that's all leaving meant to Corrado.

CHAPTER 26
ALESSIO

The phone continued to ring in his ear; the call went unanswered. Alessio didn't want to let that bother him, except it did. It wasn't like Corrado to ignore his calls. For another, he could tell Corrado was in a bad headspace before he left, and wanted to check in last minute before he headed out of The League's complex to catch his second flight of the damn day.

That night-long layover he was supposed to have after leaving Vegas in Toronto before flying off the continent had changed to *two* hours. People didn't complain when a long layover was shortened, but Alessio was the first to do exactly that. Not that he understood why the flight schedules had changed, but it meant he would barely have enough time to get to the penthouse and back to the airport in enough time to catch his flight.

But fuck him if he wouldn't *try*.

The ringing in his ear clicked before Corrado's standard message came on for him to leave a message. Cussing under his breath, Alessio ripped the phone away, and hit the end call button. His calls hadn't been going straight to voicemail, but rather, ringing through to it. Which meant Corrado didn't have his phone shut off, at least.

He was just ignoring calls.

Including Alessio's.

Great.

The one thing that Corrado was ridiculously good at which Alessio couldn't stand? *Wallowing*.

"No phones on the job—hand it over to Cree, or leave it on my desk before you head out, all right?"

Alessio stiffened in front of the safe he had been opening in Dare's office. Not that he had been avoiding the man since he arrived back at The League, but his flights and the shit he had to do didn't allow him time to seek Dare out.

Dare hadn't been in his office after Alessio came over from the Vegas penthouse he shared with Corrado, and so he figured the man was giving him some space to get his shit done before he headed out. Apparently, he had been wrong.

Nodding over his shoulder, Alessio muttered, "Yeah, I know. Just some last-minute shit."

He tried dialing Corrado again, but once more, the call rang through to the voicemail. *Jesus Christ, this is the hill you wanna die on, huh?*

Corrado was a shit.

So stubborn.

"Les?"

"Yeah?"

He pulled documentation he needed from the safe. A file with a plain silver stripe across the front, color-coded to him so he knew which one was his. Inside, he would find identification to get him through customs regardless of which country he was traveling to. A whole set of IDs that would be destroyed once he was back on American soil, and the job was done just in case he attracted attention in Albania.

Not that he should do that.

It wasn't the job.

He also pulled out a stack of cash—ten-thousand, nothing more, and nothing less. All in small, unmarked bills. He could take ten thousand in cash through customs, and they wouldn't say shit about it. One dollar more, and they would confiscate it, and arrest him for attempting to smuggle money.

Because right, *that's* what he would do.

Fun times.

"Are you listening at all?"

"No," Alessio said.

Dare sighed. "Listen, I understand you're still pissed at me and everything. I know I overstepped my bounds, Alessio. You don't need to continue giving me the silent treatment as a way to punish me, okay?"

Standing straight, and closing the safe, Alessio kept a tight grip on that folder, and the stack of cash as he turned to face Dare in the doorway. "First, anger doesn't work that way —I can be mad for as long as I fucking want, and you don't get to decide when that changes. Not that it matters because I'm *not* pissed anymore, I'm just *busy*. I have a solid two hours to make it back and catch my flight."

Dare nodded, shoving his hands in his pockets as he did so. A sign of his nerves. Growing up under this man's feet from age ten allowed him to recognize all of Dare's *tells*.

"Sorry, yeah, you're right. And I noticed all those flight changes."

Alessio shrugged. "I tried to work something out, that's all. It didn't … well, work."

"I see."

"Second," Alessio continued, because he wasn't done yet, and now seemed like the best time to get it out because he wouldn't have time when he got back from this job, "you're right, you overstepped your bounds."

"And I'm sorry for that," Dare added.

Right.

Alessio was aware.

That didn't change a lot, though. At least, it didn't change what he thought or had to say about all of this, anyway. He wanted his line to be clear between him and Dare, and in case the man hadn't got the memo, that line was *way* before Corrado. Someone getting too close to Corrado, or the life Alessio shared with him, and his walls would go way up again.

Simple as that.

"If you have an opinion, *and* I care to hear it, then I will tell you. About Corrado and me, though? You could at least give me the same respect for him I've given you about Cree for the last decade. I never asked because it was not on the table. This is the same thing—or when you wanna stick your nosy ass into our issues, anyway. Just stay way the fuck back. Got it?"

"Understood."

"And I get it's because you *care*," Alessio added quieter, softening his stance, "and I love you for that, but please stay out of it."

Dare shifted on his feet, glancing away from Alessio as he did so. "That's the first time you've said that—the love thing."

"I'm doing a lot of new shit."

"Huh."

"I need to get going. Can you do me a favor?"

"I can try."

If what Alessio thought about Corrado was true, then the man had shut himself off. He was powering down and putting a distance between himself and everything that might penetrate his *very* high walls.

That's how he protected himself.

Not that there was anything Alessio could do about it right now. Not only did he need to get rid of his phone in the next minute, and he likely *wouldn't* get to the Toronto penthouse when he got back for that two-hour layover because traffic was a bitch in the city. He would have no contact with him for the next week or two … depending on how long this job lasted.

To Alessio, that all said one thing.

Corrado wouldn't fix this mess—not the one made of himself, or the one he made with Ginevra because she had gone back to New York. Alessio would fix it because that's just what he did.

They were all human.

They all made mistakes.

Alessio would let Corrado make his.

And he would fix them.

"Ginevra Calabrese, lives in New York, and she's the illegitimate daughter of a dead Cosa Nostra boss," Alessio said to Dare. "She has two full-blood sisters, if that helps to narrow it down. And her half-brothers were recently killed. Her half-sister, Siena, is still alive, same last name. You'll find her somewhere around the Marcello family now, I think. I need as much information on her as you can pull for me by the time I get back. *No one* can be aware you're pulling it and leave it in one of my folders for me to grab when I come back."

Dare cocked a single brow. "That's a woman."

"*And?*"

"Why are you doing a check on a woman?"

"Because she's ours," Alessio explained, "and I don't like waiting for other people to figure shit out that should be obvious."

Dare didn't reply.

Alessio was fine with that.

He had a fucking plane to catch, now.

～

Somehow—by the grace of God—traffic in Toronto hadn't been bad. He went twenty over the speed limit to make it back to the penthouse with lots of time to still catch his flight on the way back, though. Not that it left him very much breathing room for minutes to stay ... because it didn't.

Alessio had a whole ...

He checked the dashboard, the digital clock spelling out the time for him as he pulled the car he'd left at the airport when he first left the city to a stop in front of the building. Right in a *No-Parking* zone, too.

Fuck it.

Tow it, motherfuckers.

Ten minutes.

It's all Alessio had to spare right now. If in that time he wasn't able to convince Corrado to pull his motherfucking head out of his ridiculous ass, well, he would go to plan B. Which unfortunately, would have to wait until he got back on the continent.

Perfect.

Life loved him.

Sarcasm was Alessio's best friend.

He left the car running at the curb, knowing he would be back down here and speeding through the city in no time to get back to the goddamn airport. Ignoring the look the doorman passed him when he didn't even wait for the older gentleman to open the door, Alessio headed into the building.

He didn't bother with the front desk—rarely did, anyway—instead opting to head for the bank of elevators at the other side of the entrance. A lady behind the desk calling his first name made Alessio hesitate in his steps.

He shot the redhead a look over his shoulder. "What?"

She smiled, waving a white envelope for him. "I'm supposed to give this to you, if I saw you come through."

What?

He felt like a parrot.

Even inside his head.

Alessio glanced back and forth between the elevators, and the waiting woman. He didn't have time to fuck around here —it would take him a few minutes to get upstairs, and inside the penthouse anyway.

"I'll grab it on my way out," he told her, going for the elevators.

"The penthouse is empty, sir. That's why I have this."

Alessio's back stiffened.

Of course.

Fucking Corrado.

He loved the man.

Loved him stupid.

But he did dumb things.

And this was probably one of those.

Alessio spun on his heel and crossed the space to the front desk in six long strides. He took the envelope from the woman with a tight smile and turned his back to her as he ripped it open. Pulling the piece of white stationary from it, he found familiar handwriting staring back at him.

Something else people didn't have a clue about Corrado?

He didn't like to *talk*. Communication wasn't his thing because he'd never been good at it when he was in a mood, and he would avoid it at all costs.

Corrado had known Alessio was coming back. It didn't surprise him all that much that the man had done this—left him a small note—instead of sending him a message or answering one of his many texts.

I need a couple of days, it read. *Sorry, Les. I'll see you when you get back. Love you.—Corrado*

Alessio tapped the paper against the palm of his hand, aware he had to get back to the airport soon.

Fuck it.

Plan B, then.

As soon as he got back.

CHAPTER 27
GINEVRA

Andino had lied.

Sort of.

Ginevra could not immediately see her sisters when she arrived back in New York. *Details*, someone thought to explain. Yes, the girls knew she was coming back, and yes, she could see them soon, but first they had to finish out a few things.

Just in case.

Those *things*?

Pulling the plug on Darren's life support. Apparently, with her half-brother still technically alive, though no one believed he would make it through considering the doctor's prognosis on his condition, people on the Calabrese side of things were still holding out hope. Like that would make a difference.

Ginevra didn't pretend to understand the way Andino Marcello's mind worked, or why the man seemed to enjoy pulling the strings of the people around him in a way that showed he was the only person who was in control, but here they all were.

Because of him.

Instead of being granted access to her sisters, Ginevra was tucked away in a fancy room at the Waldorf in Manhattan for the better portion of three days. *Without* a phone, or any other way to communicate with someone outside of the hotel.

There had even been two men who worked in twelve-hour shifts that guarded the hotel door. They were also the ones who took the phones from the Waldorf suite and only allowed room service in when she let them know ahead of time, so they could order it.

They're not for you, she was told, *but for someone who might want to hurt you.*

Right.

Ginevra wasn't sure if she would accept that shit, or not, but she hadn't been given much of a choice. If she wanted access to her sisters, then she had to follow the rules. Hadn't the last several months proved she was more than willing and capable of staying in line when it meant getting something she wanted?

Still …

Ginevra could have stayed in Toronto for just a couple of more days if this was what Andino had planned for her when she arrived back in New York. Then, she might have fixed the mistake she made by leaving the club that night. No doubt, Corrado and Alessio assumed her leaving was about them when she hadn't given them a reason to think otherwise.

Sure, Marcus could have told them she had gone home for her sisters, but if they had been told … wouldn't they come to her?

Ginevra thought so.

Hoped so.

And yet, here she was.

Alone in this goddamn room.

"Miss?"

Ginevra looked away from the bay window positioned across from the large seating area. She found one of the two men tasked with guarding her room standing just beyond the entry that led between the kitchen section, and the sitting room. He gave her a tight smile when she stared at him, waiting.

She had nothing to say.

What did they want from her?

"The boss just called—"

Ginevra frowned. "Who?"

"Andino, Miss."

Oh, right.

So many things had changed in her time away, and that was only *one*. Not that she had understood the mafia, or how it worked before Andino sent her to Toronto, but since she came back, things she didn't understand were different again.

Andino now controlled the Marcellos. Johnathan, Andino's cousin, headed the family that used to belong to her half-brothers.

They acted like she was supposed to already be aware of these things, and she was still trying to catch up with what happened before she left, let alone what was going on now. Ginevra would not apologize for needing a minute to get herself together.

"And what did he want?" she asked.

The man—Tim, was it?—nodded once. "He wanted me to let you know your sisters are on their way here … or they're almost here. About ten minutes away, now."

Her heart stopped.

She was sure it did.

"Yeah?"

"Yep. I will let them in when they get here."

So that must mean …

"Darren is—"

"They shut his life support off days ago," Tim said, shrugging. "I assume Siena will get the information together for his burial."

"Huh."

"You okay?"

She gave the man a second look. He hadn't bothered to care before if she was fine, or not. He was there to do his job, and she respected that. They all had roles to play in this life, and she was all too aware of that fact.

"Fine," she blurted. "I'm fine."

"Good. Your sisters will be here shortly."

"Thank you."

Tim left her to resume his post outside the room, and Ginevra *paced*. Next to wishing Corrado and Alessio were there with her, she wanted nothing more than to be back with her sisters.

But would they be resentful because she had left them here alone? Would they be angry that she run off without them? Might they feel like she fed them to the wolves to save her own skin?

Those were things Ginevra wasn't sure.

And it hurt her heart.

Ginevra continued to pace, unaware of the minutes ticking by, until the hotel door's knob jiggled. All at once, she turned into stone, her gaze darting to the opened doorway, and there they stood.

Greta.

Giulia.

Looking too much like younger versions of their mother, with water in their eyes as though they feared what would be waiting on the other side for them, too, and yet, still searching for *her*.

"Ginevra?" Greta asked first.

Ginevra sucked in a ragged breath. "*Hey.*"

And yet, she didn't give a fucking damn, either.

Giulia smiled widely, the first tears making lines down

her cheeks when Ginevra took a step toward them. "I missed you so much. I tho—"

"*No, no, no.*"

She didn't want to hear those fears. She wanted to take these teenagers, not quite women yet, away from those that wanted to take her from them. No one would ever take her from them.

She decided that.

Not again.

Ginevra quickly crossed the floor then, her arms already opened to hug her younger sisters. Greta stepped forward first, slamming into Ginevra at full speed, but Giulia came right after. She kissed the tops of their heads, trying to search them at the same time for any changes.

It was just a couple of months.

There shouldn't *be* changes.

Still, she wanted to check. Were they taller? Greta changed her hair to a stark red that looked beautiful against her olive-toned skin. A change from brown, and their mother once *loved* the color red.

"God, look at you," Ginevra said quietly, her hands skimming over both her sisters' faces to wipe away their tears. "Don't cry, okay? It's all going to be better now—I'm not going away again."

"Promise?" Greta asked.

Almost eighteen, but right then, Greta sounded *small*. Childlike, even, and it killed Ginevra a little. They'd all been nothing more than pawns to a bigger game played by people who didn't give a single shit about them at the end of the day.

"I promise," Ginevra whispered.

Giulia hugged Ginevra again, and Greta followed her lead. She let them, and the hotel door closed by Tim when the tears fell once more. Was this the reunion her sisters expected? It was still good.

They loved her.

She loved them.

That's all that mattered.

She wished two other people were here, too.

～

"Here we are."

The car rolled to a stop in front of an apartment complex that was decent, considering the area and location.

"And what am I here for?" she asked.

In the driver's seat, Andino chuckled. "Well, you need a place to live, and your old apartment is gone."

"Gone *how*?"

"Kev and Darren forced the girls' into Siena's care—not that she minded," he added when Ginevra gave him a sharp look from the side. "But she has things to take care of with John, and starting their life, so I figured you would want the girls with you. The apartment is furnished, and ready for you to use."

He leaned over and opened the glove compartment. There, he pulled out a manila envelope that looked to be two inches thick, or more. "Here—*cash*. It'll take care of whatever else you and your sisters need for a time while we wait for Siena to settle out your brothers' estates, which she has decided will be divided between you, and the girls."

Ginevra swallowed hard, trying to take all that information in. "And how much is their estates worth?"

"A lot."

Huh.

Did that mean she would go back to college? Buy a

house? Could she pay for Greta's college next year, or put Giulia into a private school? What did it mean?

Ginevra didn't have the first clue, and she didn't care to ask. She took the envelope, nodding as she said, "Thanks."

"No worries. Least I can do."

"No, you didn't need to let me think I would have to marry you right until the last second, Andino."

He made a noise under his breath, amused. "Everyone needed to believe the ploy. Even you, and I won't apologize for it, either."

"People aren't pawns on a chessboard for you to move as you deem fit."

"They are if it gives me what I want."

Ginevra had the strangest urge to hit the man beside her because that *might* make her feel better if only for a second. "And what's that, Andino? What you wanted, I mean."

"A woman."

His frank answered stunned her.

"A woman," she echoed.

"And I got her," Andino said, offering nothing else. "So, I care very little about what you or anyone else says about how I did this when I get to spend the rest of my life apologizing to her for the things I did ... and trust she is the *only* person in this world I will apologize to, and mean it. As for you, the girls will be brought over by Siena later, and then you are free to do whatever."

Go back to normal.

That's what she would do.

Make sure her sisters were able to resume their normal life before *all of this* happened. It would be hard without their mother, and nothing would ever be the same, but that's what she planned on doing. And somehow, amid that, try to get back to the men she left behind in Toronto.

Speaking of which ...

"Has anyone tried to get in contact with you to speak with me?" she asked.

Andino passed her a glance. "I don't understand."

"From Toronto, I mean." Ginevra didn't want to *out* her relationship with Corrado and Alessio because that wasn't anyone's business, but she still had to ask. "Corrado, maybe, because he watched after me. Or … Alessio?"

It took Andino a second.

Then, two.

He gave her a curious glance when he said, "I heard rumors about those two, but I didn't know if they're accurate. People say they're *together*, but they share women, too. How true is that?"

Nope.

She wouldn't do that.

Not with this man.

"Has anyone tried to contact me?"

Andino shook his head. "Anyone in Toronto has been quiet since you left. That's all I can tell you."

Why did that sound like a door closing? Like an *end*—an answer she didn't want, but one she now had. What should she do with it?

CHAPTER 28
CORRADO

It was almost strange how when Corrado needed something to relax him, or pull him out of the hell that was his mind, he often found himself back at a place that *rarely* allowed him those things in the past. The League, that was.

There was little about the complex that allowed Corrado happy memories. In fact, his training had been some of the worst months of his life. Demanding, intense, and often mind-breaking. Although, that had been the point. They had to break all the pieces of him to put him back together better.

Maybe that was why, now, his mind didn't work the same way. He didn't find *normal* things relaxing—not the shit other people liked to use to chill them out, anyway. Now, he needed the familiarity of a space that had humbled him in more ways than one, and gave him something he hadn't known was possible in Alessio.

Love, that was.

Even if love wasn't here now.

Corrado spent a few days at his family's lodge in Quebec, hiding away from the world, focusing his attention on taking care of himself, and doing what *he* needed. He didn't have a phone to answer, and he didn't use the landline at the lodge to call out except once to let his father know where he was, if needed. He hadn't stayed on the call long enough for his father to ask questions, and he informed no one else about his whereabouts, either.

Should anyone at The League need him, Dare could use Corrado's tracker. His brothers had their own life and business to handle, so they didn't need to worry about Corrado.

Alessio left—the fucking *job*.

Ginevra …

Well, she made her choice.

Didn't she?

Corrado was letting her make it.

Simple as that.

Except it wasn't that simple.

The one thing he never experienced with Alessio in all their years together was heartbreak. Not because there hadn't been opportunity or things that came up between them that might separate them. They always chose each other first, and everything else second.

Usually.

For the first time, Corrado learned about having his heart broken by someone he loved, and he realized that, no, he did not react well to it. In fact, he took it so badly that he wanted to hide away from the world.

That was the problem, though.

It wouldn't be over.

He would not be okay.

And that's why, when the trip to Quebec didn't work, he made his way back to Vegas, to sleep in a familiar bed that still smelled like one of the people who still held a piece of his soul and heart in their hands. To walk familiar halls he once walked with Alessio; to focus on *anything* except the ache in his heart.

Not that it helped.

His mood became worse.

Hence, Cree inviting him for a sparring round in the ring

that morning. Had Corrado been a smarter man—apparently, he wasn't today—he would have refused the offer. Anyone with any brains understood sparring with Cree was pointless because he either beat the shit out of someone, or he nearly did so. Besides, this was him substituting one pain for another.

"*Fuck*," he hissed, ducking back to miss a punch Cree threw his way. "If you don't break one of my bones, that would be great."

"Or get quicker." Cree bounced on the balls of his feet as he said that, fists already up and ready to go with Corrado again. He carefully measured every single move he made, and never without an intentional impact when he fought. It made Cree one of the more difficult opponents in a match. "Besides, if you didn't want this, you wouldn't have gotten up here today, right?"

Well, he had a point.

Not that Corrado would admit it.

"Fuck you," he muttered.

Cree raised a brow. "Your mood is about as bad as Alessio's this morning when I saw him."

What?

The word rang so loudly in his mind that everything else around him came to a standstill, including his desire to defend himself against Cree's oncoming attack. Corrado froze —like a fucking *cafone*.

Cree, never one to miss out on an opportunity, used the chance to swing back with a roundhouse. The kick landed hard against Corrado's ribcage and sent him flying back to the mat with enough force to take the air right out of his lungs.

Pain bloomed in three of his ribs as he sucked in a gulp of air, and stared at the ceiling of the complex's gym, trying to let his mind catch up to what he learned. Cree said *when I saw him* and *this morning*. Meaning, Alessio had to be back in the country, but not just *back* … no, *here*. In Vegas.

And he hadn't told him? Didn't come to the penthouse?

"What?" Corrado asked, still looking like an idiot on his back.

Cree's figure came into his view when he moved to stand next to Corrado's prone form. "He got back this morning—job finished two days ago."

"Well, where the fuck is he now?"

"Doing something he wants to do, I imagine. You know how he is."

Very well.

And whenever Alessio came home, he came back to Corrado. So, what was different this time? Hadn't the last week, and a half been bad enough for him dealing with the Ginevra thing alone while Alessio had to go out of the country?

"You look confused," Cree murmured.

"I'm fine."

Corrado wouldn't let them see his pain.

Cree kneeled down next to Corrado on the mat and rested his arms along his bent knees as he spoke. He didn't look at Corrado, and yet it still seemed like the man stared into his mind even so. "There was a time, and I still think it's possible—if I cared to try, which I don't—when I believed I would *beat* the pride out of you. It's something you couldn't get rid of, and it still holds you back in your life when it shouldn't. Alessio has accepted it is a flaw in your character he has to love like the rest of you. So, where I want to fix it, he will work around it."

Corrado's brow dipped. "What?"

And *damn*, his ribs ached now.

Fucking Cree.

The man reached over and *patted* Corrado's head like he

might for a goddamn puppy. "I'm sure you'll figure it out. You're a smart man."

Annoyed, Corrado waved his arm to knock Cree's hand away from his body, lest the fool pet him again. "Knock it the fuck off. Either tell me where Alessio is, or—"

"Or *what*?" Cree cocked his head with a slight smirk that rivaled the devil's. "Because one of us can make threats and demands, and one of us cannot. Guess which one you are, Corrado? Go ahead, I'll wait."

Fucking asshole.

"I'll go speak with Dare," he muttered, pushing up from the mat to stand. "And see what he can tell me."

"Wise choice," Cree replied, "not that he will tell you anything, either."

Right.

Well, Corrado would try.

Cree lounged at the edge of the ring, resting his arms over the ropes as he eyed Corrado while he gathered his things. All the while, he said nothing, but he didn't wipe that amusement off his damn face.

Corrado headed out of the gym with his phone in one hand, and his discarded cross-body bag in the other. The bag wasn't his style, but neither were the jeans and faded T-shirt he'd thrown on that day to go with his runners, either.

He didn't come to The League to look like he walked out of his parents' mansion, though. He came here because he needed to work out some of his frustration, and there was only one person who might help with that in a short amount of time.

Cree.

Or rather, he *usually* helped with that. Today, he only pissed Corrado off and left him with more questions than answers.

Speaking of which …

Swiping his thumb over the screen of his phone, Corrado woke the device up, and typed his pin in. Pulling up the call icon, he selected the top contact highest on his list.

Alessio.

He hadn't bothered to call the man for the last week and a half because he assumed it would be pointless. Being on a job meant Alessio needed to leave his phone behind, and when he was back, *then* he would call Corrado, or show up at home.

This time, Alessio did neither.

He was *back.*

But where?

Despite being back in Vegas for the last week, Corrado had a flight to catch tomorrow that would take him back to Toronto for the weekend. His parents annual Halloween party, something they threw every year for all the kids who lived in their gated community, was on Sunday evening, and if he didn't show up …

He'd never hear the fucking end.

Which meant if he didn't get ahold of Alessio, and let him know where he would be, if the man wanted to see him, it was going to be several more days before they got together. Corrado didn't like that at all.

The past while had been hell on him. He didn't like being alone, and if he couldn't have both people he loved, then he needed one.

Where the fuck was Les?

In his head, the phone rang and rang. By the fourth ring, Alessio's voicemail would pick up because the man wasn't answering his calls. Or maybe it was just Corrado's number he didn't want to pick up.

But *why?*

That heaviness came back in his chest.

Hard.

Thick.

And *aching*.

Actually, it hadn't left him since he got the news Ginevra headed back to New York, but he got better at ignoring it. Now, it was back with a vengeance.

Fuck his whole life.

The call clicked, and Alessio's standard message to leave a message came through the speaker. Corrado gritted his teeth, yet still left a simple message that said, "Les, call me."

Stuffing the phone back into his pocket, Corrado navigated the halls of The League's complex until he stood in the doorway of Dare's office. He never understood why the man rarely closed his door, but he didn't.

Not unless Cree was in there.

"What can I do for you, Corrado?"

Dare, with his back facing Corrado as he watched a screen on the wall showcasing a news reel, hadn't even twitched a finger to let him know he was aware of his presence.

"Alessio arrived back from his assignment today?"

"Apparently."

"What does that mean? Either he did, or he fucking didn't."

"It means yes, he was here, and no, I didn't see him."

"Well, where is he?"

"I'm not sure, but if he's not picking up your calls, and he didn't let you—"

"Try not being an asshole for five minutes."

Dare shook his head. "*Eh.*"

Corrado clenched his teeth so hard his molars ached. "Dare—"

"I made a promise to Les—I would stay out of his business for you, and other personal issues. That's what he asked, and that's what I will do. But understand, Corrado, that if he's taken off again because of something you did, I will cut your heart out and mail it to your father with blood still in the chambers. Do you hear me?"

He blinked.

Dare continued to watch the screen, unbothered.

Well ...

"I'm not even sure if it's about me, or not," he muttered.

"Yes, well, that happens when you choose selfishness over selflessness."

Right.

Dare made a good point.

And Corrado *hated* it.

CHAPTER 29
GINEVRA

"Thank you."

Siena's head popped above the island counter, so she could see Ginevra on the other side. Slowly, she stood, a casserole dish in her hands she planned on using to cook their dinner. "For what, Ginny?"

"Everything you did, I guess. For me, but also for the girls when I couldn't."

"But …"

"Yeah?"

"That's what a family *should* do," Siena said quietly.

Ginevra nodded. "You're right, they should. I think because me and the girls were so used to depending on each other, and our mom, that we got used to it. We learned not to expect kindness from others because if we ever needed something, we could just go to each other for it."

Siena set the dish down to the counter and offered a smile. "You probably don't see me as your *real* sister, even if we are, but I hope you can someday, and that you'll come too. I didn't have a close family unit growing up, either. Dad preferred the boys, too."

"Well …"

"What?"

"I wanted life to go back to normal for Greta and Giulia. Before all this happened, when the mafia hadn't touched us, and we were just … *normal*."

Siena let out a soft laugh. "Doesn't work that way, huh?"

Not at all.

Ginevra tried to put as much distance between their life, and the people affiliated to the mafia as she could, and yet they still kept drawing her in. And while she understood people like Siena—or the woman's boyfriend, John—were safe, she knew that didn't matter.

All it took was one connection to become a target, and she never wanted her sisters to be that for anyone ever again.

"I just want them to be safe," Ginevra whispered.

"And they will be. We made sure."

Right.

For now.

Ginevra didn't say that out loud. "And you love them, don't you?"

"The girls?"

She nodded.

Siena smiled. "I do. And I never had sisters growing up—just a pair of asshole brothers that only cared about me when I was doing something for them. I was always the one expected to look after everyone else, and I do that with the girls, too. Except now, I don't mind it. They don't *demand* that of me, they need someone who gives a shit."

"Yeah, they do."

"And now they have you home, too."

Greta and Giulia flew into the kitchen, their laughter high and breathless as they watched whatever loud video was playing on the tablet they were using. They had been the first ones to jump at the chance to have dinner at Siena's place when she called earlier to ask. The girls fell into the chairs at the table, unaware or uncaring about Siena and Ginevra's conversation. Not that she minded all that much.

She preferred them close.

She needed her family.

It had more people now.

"I had been so settled on what I wanted to happen when I came back for them that change scares me," Ginevra admitted. "And I might seem a little too protective, but after everything, how should I be? So, I apologize in advance if I come off strong."

Siena shrugged. "I get it."

"Do you?"

"Of course, but you should know it's easier to be open to change than to live with an ache in your heart because you'd rather things stay the same, Ginevra. That's all."

Ginevra had to laugh at that.

Heartache.

"I can't find more heartache and trouble than I already did in Toronto."

The words slipped from her lips before she could stop them. Maybe it was because Ginevra didn't have anyone to talk to about the craziness going on in her life—things she hadn't shared with her younger sisters because for one, she didn't think it was appropriate, and for two … because she didn't want to worry them. Without Corrado and Alessio, she became hollow.

Instead, she handled it alone.

Lonely.

Siena cleared her throat, and her gaze drifted to the girls at the table behind them, distracted with a tablet. "Andino had hinted to John that you found someone in Toronto that you became close to."

Close.

Right, that was a good way to put falling in love.

And *someone*?

"More like two *someones*," Ginevra replied.

She had to be mindful of those younger ears behind them. She wasn't sure how to appropriately explain the relationship she found herself in with two men when in general, all society showed as respectable couples were a pair of *two* people. Not that society was right—love came in many forms, she had learned.

It wasn't easy to explain.

"Huh," Siena said. "Really?"

"They were together before I came into it with them, but I fit there ... with them, between them, and with each of them. It wasn't easy, but it was right—somehow, it was right, and now everything seems wrong."

Siena let out a slow breath, her gaze reflecting only sympathy. She opened her mouth to say something, but one of their sisters at the table spoke up first.

"What does that mean, that they were together before you?" Giulia asked.

Apparently, those young ears had been listening.

Great.

"What do you think?" Greta asked. "Guys can like other guys, Giuls."

"Yeah, but—"

"No *buts*. It's true."

Greta wasn't wrong.

"That's kind of like cheating, isn't it?" Giulia asked, not knowing Ginevra's face was heating from their conversation as they pondered her private life. "If they were with someone else—even if it was Ginny, right?"

"Poly, Giulia," Greta said, like it should have been obvious.

"What?"

"*Poly.* Polyamorous. There are lots of people in committed relationships who go outside to sleep with other people."

Ginevra sighed. "Could we not talk about this right now?"

"Well," Greta asked, "how is she ever going to know about that kind of stuff if no one takes the time to explain?"

She had forgotten that although Greta was younger than her, and she had helped to raise the girl, she was still almost eighteen. The world was not so rose-tinted to her anymore, and she had noticed boys and things like sex a while ago.

Siena giggled, but popped a hand over her mouth when Ginevra shot her a look. "Sorry," she mumbled.

"So, it's not cheat—"

"Look at it like a triple Venn diagram," Ginevra said, not wanting to keep letting them *assume* what they wanted about her relationship with the men. It would be better if they understood what it was, and that was it. "We are all individual people, but there are parts of me that overlap with one, and then another part that overlaps with the other. And there are parts of them that only overlap with each other, too, but there is a piece of all of us that overlap together. *That* is how it works, for us. Not everyone is the same, and no, it is not about sleeping with anyone you want."

Or she assumed she had made that clear to Corrado and Alessio.

Now, nothing was clear.

That's what killed her.

"Okay, so I was kind of right," Greta said.

Giulia made a noise under her breath. "Sounds complicated."

"Funny," Ginevra replied.

Siena gave her a look across the island. "What is?"

"It never seemed complicated at all. Easy, really."

More like … it was where she was meant to be.

And now, she wasn't there at all.

Where were they?

Siena whistled. "Props to you, though, because I have a hard enough time keeping up with one man let alone *two*."

Ginevra grinned at that, her cheeks heating all over again. "They … made it worth it."

Giggles echoed from the table behind her.

Damn.

Young ears, again.

Because even if she had been *very* careful to explain the relationship without making it seem tawdry with sexual innuendo and details, those girls were still fifteen, and seventeen. They were still teenage girls.

"What's their names?" Greta asked.

"Are they cute?" Giulia put in right after.

To Siena, Ginevra mouthed, "*Help me.*"

Siena shook her head. "Nope—on your own here."

Perfect.

"Thanks."

"Well?" Greta demanded.

"I'm not sure it matters. I kind of left them high and dry, and—"

"That doesn't tell me their names."

"Or if they're cute," Giulia added.

Ginevra turned around to eye both her sisters with a curious eye. "Corrado and Alessio."

"*And*," Giulia said, eyes wide.

"They're both … very handsome."

That was putting it mildly.

Giggles lit up the table again.

Ginevra figured, this would be a long night.

"Not that it matters," Ginevra said, "because I am here, and they're not."

"But is that how you want it to be?" Siena asked behind her.

That question was easy to answer.

No.

She wanted both with her. That didn't mean she would

get what she wanted, though. As far as she understood, neither of the men had tried to contact her, and she didn't have a way to get ahold of them, either.

It was what it was.

Even if she hated it.

~

"Okay, but like how does it work, does one get mad when you don't spend enough time with them, or—"

"Could you save some of your questions for another day?" Ginevra grumbled as her sisters followed behind her in the hallway of their apartment building. "Because that would be great, Greta."

"I'm just curious."

"You have asked me a lot of questions in the last three hours."

Too many questions.

Their dinner with Siena turned into a game of twenty-one questions with Ginevra. All focused around things she didn't want to explain to her younger sisters, but also a topic that made her heart ache.

She couldn't win.

"And," Ginevra said, coming to a stop in front of their apartment door to pull the keys from her bag before sticking it in the lock, "while I get you want to understand how it works, it's also none of your business. Some things are private unless I offer the information to you, Greta. Respect that."

Greta leaned against the wall and rolled her eyes. "Fine."

"Thank you."

"Still think it's complicated," Giulia muttered next to Greta.

Well …

"I guess that means it's probably not for you, huh?"

Greta considered that for a second before she nodded. "That's fair."

Ginevra waited just long enough to decide that the girls had finished with their questions for the evening—thank God—before she twisted the key in the lock and opened their apartment door. The first thing she noticed was the lights. They were on when she had shut them off before leaving.

The second thing she noticed? A leather jacket hanging over the arm of the couch just beyond the hallway.

The third?

His scent.

Leather, smoke, and man.

Distinct to Alessio, and Ginevra swore every nerve in her body lit up when she dragged in another lungful of the smell. There wasn't enough, and she might never taste it on her tongue again.

The girls, seemingly unaware of their sister's frozen stance, pushed past her to enter the apartment. They didn't notice the familiar cologne Alessio preferred lingering in the air, or his jacket tossed over the back of the couch.

She might have spoken up …

Might have told them to wait …

Her words wouldn't come.

The girls didn't even reach the end of the hallway before Alessio stepped around the corner, directly in their path. Giulia, with her head down to watch whatever she found interesting on her phone, rammed into the back of her sister when Greta came to a full stop in front of Alessio.

He tipped his head to the side, amusement lighting up his gaze when the two teenagers lifted their heads to meet his stare. His lips quirked into a wicked grin, too, almost making Ginevra laugh at the sight.

"Hello," he told them.

Giulia squeaked.

Greta said and did *nothing*.

"Do they not speak?" he asked, his gaze lifting to find Ginevra at the end of the hall. She found affection staring back.

Her heart beat again.

"They do, you shocked them, Les."

"Les—*Alessio*?" Greta asked.

Giulia made another one of those *squeaky* sounds.

"That is my name," Alessio told her sister.

"Oh, wow," Greta mumbled.

Alessio cocked his head to the side again. "Uh, what?"

Ginevra pressed her lips together and decided the wall was a far more interesting thing to stare at because it would not make her laugh out loud.

"Greta, Giulia," she said, still keeping her attention on the wall, "this is Alessio. Les, these are my little sisters."

"They don't talk well," he noted.

Ginevra let out a sigh.

Greta huffed. "How did you even get in here?"

"Picked the lock."

"*What?*"

Ginevra looked their way again only to find Alessio had arched a brow when he drawled, "I picked the lock with a tool in my pocket—I'll show you sometime."

Greta glanced back at Ginevra and pursed her lips before she nodded. "Okay."

Okay.

Just like that.

Giulia giggled under her breath, likely because she wasn't sure how to handle this situation.

"Would you two give us a few minutes alone? Close your bedroom doors, too, please."

Giulia looked like she would argue, but Greta pulled her

away from Alessio as they slipped past him in the hallway. Once they had left around the corner, and the sounds of a bedroom door slamming shut—they each had their own room, but must have gone into just one—Alessio's attention came back to Ginevra.

And *shit*.

She felt that.

"You left," he said, "and you didn't even say goodbye. You *left* ... and you haven't even tried to call, or anything."

She swallowed hard, and he took one step closer. "Andino called—he said I could come back. My sisters needed me. I figured you and Corrado would understand ... I didn't have a way to contact either of you. I don't have your phone numbers; neither of you gave me them and I never needed them before now. Who am I supposed to ask to help me? The same people who sent me away, who didn't give a shit about what happened to me? Who?"

Alessio tipped his head back.

Ginevra held firm.

"You left," he repeated.

"Where were you?"

"Albania."

All at once, the air left Ginevra's lungs.

Right.

The job.

He'd told her the night at the club.

"What about Corrado?" she asked.

Alessio smiled, but *damn*, it was bitter all over. It made her heart go crazy when he took another step closer to her, leaving only a few feet between them now.

"Corrado is the ..." Alessio considered his words, adding lower, "... well, he's the difficult one here. See me, I'm used to being abandoned, Ginny. I can take it."

"I didn't abandon either of you."

"You left," he returned, "and when you leave, this is what it feels like when no one explains anything to us, and we're all just … *stuck*. Wondering."

Alessio shrugged. "Corrado … he's not like me. When something seems like it will hurt, he shuts all the way down. Almost everyone in my life has left me, so I can handle this, but not him. I don't like to see things hurt him, either."

"I didn't *leave* like that, Les."

"But he thinks you did. It's a pride thing for him, Ginny … because that's who Corrado has always been. Despite how much it pisses me off sometimes, it's also one part of him I love the most. You can't fault him for his flaws, just like he didn't want to fault you for yours, either."

Ginevra hid her shaking hands at her sides, balling them into tight fists when Alessio took yet another step toward her. *Careful.* Holding himself back because that's what he thought *she* wanted.

He had to know …

She wanted him so fucking close.

"I missed you," she whispered, "and I miss him. All the time. Every single day. I wasn't sure what to do, and I'm sorry."

Alessio dragged in a hard breath. "Yeah, me too."

"I'm still not sure what to do."

All at once, Alessio closed the distance between them, and Ginevra had never been more grateful. She found herself wrapped up in his strong, familiar embrace. She pulled in lungful after lungful of his heady scent, letting the comfort take her back to a happier place.

Alessio's hands slipped under her jaw, and he tipped her head back. First, he kissed her soft, and tentative. So unlike him though she loved the gentle press of his lips against hers. But then, the kiss turned into something else when his tongue snaked out to tease the seam of her lips, seeking more.

God.

She gave him that.

And took what she wanted, too.

Nothing was like kissing someone you loved. Everything was … perfect. Her world almost tilted back on its proper axis. Except she missed someone else, now. *They* missed someone else.

Alessio pulled away, but his thumbs stroked her cheeks, taking away the tears that had escaped from her eyes. "Don't cry, sweetheart."

"I … this has been a lot."

"We'll fix it."

"How?"

Alessio chuckled, and pressed another quick kiss to her mouth before saying, "By not giving him a choice—making a *statement.*"

Ginevra gave him a raised brow. "What, like a grand gesture? Cliché, yeah?"

"Maybe, but it *is* Corrado. And as much as he figures he's hard to understand, he really isn't. Sometimes, show him where he's wrong while you also admit to your own. Those flaws of his again, and you have to love them, too. Not just *parts* of him."

"I do, and you, too."

Alessio's throat jumped when he asked, "Do you?"

"What?"

"Love me?"

Ginevra reached up and stroked the underside of his jaw. "*Too much.* I love you too much."

"How else would this work, huh?"

Exactly.

Now, she had to let Corrado know, too.

CHAPTER 30
CORRADO

I'll see you there.

Corrado stared at Alessio's last text after he'd cut the engine to the Porsche in the driveway of his parents' mansion. He hadn't wanted to come to this goddamn Halloween party at all, but he wasn't able to come up with an acceptable excuse to get him out.

He couldn't even use *Les*.

Not considering Alessio was here, or if not, was on his way, if his last text to Corrado was any sign. He had no idea where Alessio had been for the last couple of days. He hadn't come back to Vegas, he wouldn't pick up Corrado's calls, and he only answered back one of his texts.

The one about the Halloween party in Toronto.

That was it.

Corrado wasn't sure what in the hell was going on, but he didn't like it. At all. It felt like Alessio was hiding something from him, and he needed to find out what that was. Which was what he planned on doing tonight.

He couldn't do that if he continued to sit in this damn car, so he shoved his phone into his pocket, and stepped out of the vehicle onto the driveway. He took in the fake strings of a spider web hanging from the trees lining the driveway, and the pumpkins decorating the cobblestone. He didn't know what it was, or *why*, but his mother never went half-assed for decorating.

Cara didn't understand the meaning of *subtle*.

When he was younger, Corrado used to love that, he thought as he headed for the mansion. Every single holiday had been a memorable experience with his family because his mother and father made sure of that, no exceptions.

Given the time of night, closer to nine, he suspected all the neighborhood kids had come and were long gone. The damn bylaws in the gated community made sure all the parents knew their kids had to be home by eight-thirty, sharp.

Now, given the cars in the driveway, and the music filtering out of the mansion, it was time for the adults—and older teens—to have their fun. The invitation went out to anyone who was a friend of the Guzzi family, and anyone in *la famiglia*.

Corrado tried not to miss it—or any big party his parents threw. This one hadn't been quite the same, though, because the last thing he was in the mood for was to entertain other people when he could barely stand to look at himself in the mirror.

Yet, here he was.

Doing that.

And why?

Corrado wasn't sure. Maybe because he was trying to be a little less selfish for one—God knew it had been pointed out more than enough to him over the last while that he could be a self-serving prick when he wanted to be, and this party was about his parents and family. So, he could show up for them, right? Put on a suit, because he was not wearing a costume, a smile, and be the good son for an hour or two.

Or maybe it was because this was the only place Alessio seemed to be willing to meet him, and so Corrado had to do what he had to do.

End of.

At least, tonight, he would get *one* person he wanted. The other? Well, Corrado was refusing to even let himself think about Ginevra at this point.

It was easier.

"You look *really* pleased to be here, yeah?"

Corrado's walk came to an abrupt start, and his fucking heart was ready to explode in his goddamn chest at the same time. *That voice.* All calm, cool, and unbothered. Like it didn't bother him at all he hadn't seen Corrado in two weeks, and nothing had changed at all.

He turned his head, finding Alessio standing under a canopy of fake spider web hanging from the largest maple tree on the property. He wasn't sure what it was about those specific trees, but they were Les's favorite.

"Waiting for me?" Corrado asked.

"Or I stepped out for a smoke—it doesn't have to be about *you.*"

Yeah.

Right back to normal.

Corrado smirked, giving a pointed look at Alessio's hand. "Except there's no cigarette, and we both know you only smoke here with Bene or Beni."

"You can't ever just let me *have* a moment, can you?"

"Where's the fun in that, Les?"

Alessio shrugged, stuffing his hands in the pockets of his black jeans. The leather jacket he'd thrown on was new— different from the last one Corrado saw him wearing. This one had a dozen buckles, and small, silver spikes on the shoulders.

Very … *Alessio.*

And he looked good.

Too good, really.

"Why are you smiling like that?" Corrado asked.

Alessio's sly grin drifted away. "Like what?"

"Where have you been the last couple of days? I knew when you got back, and you just … fucking *took off*. You couldn't call me, or—"

"I had things to handle."

"Oh?"

"Yeah, shit to take care of that you wouldn't."

Corrado stiffened, his throat growing tight. "And what does that mean?"

"This," Alessio said, pointing between the two as he met Corrado's gaze, "it's not all about you. It's about *me*, too. And someone else because *you* brought her into it. You keep thinking you're also the only person here that gets to decide about it—like the choice to say fuck it, hide away, and pretend like nothing is wrong. The rest of us here aren't always going to just fall in line with you, Corrado. That's not how love works."

That ache was back in his heart.

"You don't get—"

"Yeah, I get you don't like shit that hurts. Don't worry."

"I needed a minute to figure out what I was doing, Les."

"Well, you got two weeks, and I'm fucking tired of waiting."

"*What?*"

Alessio grinned and gestured at the mansion. "Do you know why I didn't call you or come back home the last couple of days since I got back?"

"Because you wanted to punish me?"

"*Really*, that's what you think it was?"

"That's what it seemed like."

Alessio's smile drifted away. "I'm sorry."

"You're all I have, Les."

"No, I'm not. I am *one* of two people for you, Corrado. And I'm fucking sorry that life gets in the way, and you're not sure how to deal, but you gotta learn. Like the rest of us did, okay? You can't run when shit gets rough. You *can't*."

Corrado nodded. "Yeah."

"I didn't call or come home because I didn't want to lie to you. I *don't* lie to you, no matter what. And so, if I didn't see you or speak to you, then I wouldn't have to do that, not even by omission."

He stared at Alessio as still as stone.

Alessio stared back, *waiting*.

"What did you do?" Corrado asked.

"I brought her back for us. Ginevra is here tonight."

He hadn't been ready for that.

He also wasn't *at all* surprised.

"She *left*."

"Yes, because not everything in her life will always be about *us*, Corrado. We had a spread of time with her *away* from her life—without her responsibilities, and the things she left at home. She didn't have to worry about that during *our* time, but that time ended. And she needed to get back to reality, but that doesn't mean she didn't want to stay."

"If she wanted to stay—"

"It is possible she both wanted to leave and stay but with only those two choices … someone will always get hurt."

"I don't understand what you're talking about."

Alessio gave him a look. "Because you never *asked*."

Corrado heard Ginevra first. Her soft, tinkling laughter—unmistakable to his ear—seemed to stand out from the feminine laughter of others as it filled the hallway he walked down with Alessio at his side. It did something to his heart, still racing hard and a little too heavy in his chest, but he didn't wish it away.

A part of him had been wishing too much away.

Right then, he wanted to *feel*.

Corrado wasn't pleased with the way Alessio did this, but he stepped back and *shut up*. He didn't go to Ginevra after she left, and he hadn't given her the chance to explain anything.

So, regardless of the heaviness on his shoulders, the tightness in his chest, or the ache in his heart … he would see her, and listen to her explain.

Because Les was right.

As he usually was.

Corrado figured if he admitted that fact a little more often, they wouldn't have as many of these issues as they did. His pride was a real bitch.

Time to let it go.

A good portion of the main entrance, the first dining room, and one of the sitting rooms inside the mansion became a haunted house for the kids that was now … well, empty of children, anyway. A few adults lingered in the spaces, drinks in hand. Some still dressed in costumes, and others, not. Corrado had no interest in them, though.

Corrado rounded the corner at the end of the hallway, Alessio still at his side, and came to a full stop at the sight of Ginevra in the middle of what his parents used as a ballroom when they held parties. In the middle, a fountain with an embracing nude couple carved from stone with water pouring from their outstretched hands that seemed to reach for each other.

And right in front of it?

Ginevra.

Like him, and Alessio, and most of the other people in the room, she wasn't dressed up in any costume. Instead, she wore a black dress that hugged her curves with a slit down the middle that showed off all kinds of leg, and black, strappy heels that made his throat tighten again.

She smiled at something his mother said next to her, nodding back at the younger girl standing close to her. Cara leaned in closer to Ginevra, her gaze conspiratorial as she said something in a whisper, pointing to someone across the room.

Ginevra, though, looked *happy*. Perfectly content in her place, enjoying the party, and not at all bothered by the fact she was in the middle of the room, the center of attention next to his mother where they stood just a few feet away from the rest of his brothers, and father.

Like she was meant to be there.

Because she was.

Corrado had known from the start—sensed it in his heart the very second she looked him in the eyes that day she fell into his car in New York outside of the church. It'd been him and his *pride* that fucked this up.

The same way it messed with everything.

"Ginny!"

Corrado watched an older girl, although still younger than Ginevra, dart across the ballroom floor, away from a young man who was staring after her like his favorite thing had been ripped out of his hands. Ginevra turned away from his mother, laughing at whatever the older teenager rushed to tell her, while the younger girl who had been beside her the entire time rolled her eyes.

"Her sisters," Alessio explained next to him. "Greta is the older one—she'll be eighteen in two months. Giulia, the youngest, is fifteen."

Right.

Her sisters …

Corrado felt like shit.

That was the best way to describe it. He didn't have the right words, otherwise. He said it—*entirely selfish.* So caught up in his own wants, that he never even considered the people around him, or what they needed to handle.

Like Ginevra.

And her sisters.

"I do not deserve you or her," he murmured.

But fuck him if he didn't want them, and he would make damn sure both understood for the rest of his life *they* came first to him. Always, no exceptions, *ever.* That would be Corrado's promise from this day forward, he would make sure.

Once he fixed this …

Alessio glanced at him from the side, letting out a quiet sigh. "You're not wrong, but … we still want you."

"Have you figured out why that is?"

"Love," Alessio said. "It's because of love."

Right, because even until this point, Corrado's own love had still been—in many ways—an extension of his own selfishness. It came back to *him*, and what would best serve his needs to wants.

No more.

Ginevra gave her sister—Greta?—a nod before turning away. Her gaze skimmed over the crowd. She bypassed him not expecting him to be standing there with Alessio, but she tensed, her stare darting back to him.

She *smiled.*

Soft, sure, but still …

Corrado smiled back.

He didn't wait for her to make the first move to cross the distance between them. He figured she and Alessio had been doing enough of that for all of them, and he had to try now. Alessio trailed behind Corrado when he closed the space keeping Ginevra too far away from him, and not as close as he wanted her.

She took only *one* step forward. Just enough to say she finished the conversation behind her and entered a new one. Not that it mattered because her sisters and his mother watched him and Alessio come closer with curious gazes that also seemed too *knowing* for his liking.

"Ginny," he said when he came to a stop in front of her.

Not close enough, though.

A foot away.

He itched to touch her, but he didn't reach out to do it. *That* would be her choice, always.

Ginevra's gaze darted from Alessio a foot behind him and then back to Corrado in a flash. "No costume?"

"Where's yours?"

"Big wings—they wouldn't let me bring them on the plane."

Corrado smirked. "Really?"

"No."

"Damn, that might have been nice to see."

Ginevra shrugged the delicate line of her shoulders, saying, "I didn't have time to grab something for me and the girls. Alessio didn't give me much notice about this. He told me when to be at the airport, and that's it."

He swallowed hard.

And she just *came*.

She didn't question it.

"Thank you for coming," he said.

Ginevra smiled in *that* way again. "I love you, Corrado. Why wouldn't I want to be with you ... wherever you are?"

He had a million reasons she *shouldn't* want to be with

him. The same way he could list the whys that Alessio shouldn't be his, too. And yet, here they all were.

They didn't fit alone.

They only worked together.

"Corrado, right?"

Behind Ginevra, he found which of her two sisters asked the question. The tallest, and oldest, of the two.

"Greta, right?" he returned.

The girl flashed her teeth in a smile. "That's right." She jerked a thumb toward the girl next to her, saying, "And this is Giulia."

Corrado nodded. "Very nice to meet you."

Greta arched a brow. "You're very different from the other one."

"*Greta*," Ginevra admonished.

"What, he is. I thought he would be like Les, Ginny."

Alessio chuckled behind him. "Where is the fun in two people who are the same?"

Giulia's cheeks turned red, but Greta glanced between the two men like she wanted to take in all their differences, from the different style of clothing, to even the cut of their hair.

Corrado understood, then. Ginevra must have explained about this situation to her sisters, and they had to process all of it. That meant awkward questions, or comments at the wrong time.

He didn't mind.

"Alessio is the fun one," Corrado told Greta.

"Is he?"

Alessio scoffed. "*Yes*."

"Girls," Cara called behind them, saving Ginevra from saying anything, "do you want to see which rooms you'll be using for the weekend?"

Just like that, Ginevra's sisters were thoroughly distracted. It let Corrado take all her attention again.

"You're staying?" he asked.

She nodded. "I left some unfinished business here. So, yes, if you'll have me."

"We both will," Alessio said.

Corrado tipped his head in Alessio's direction. "What he said, of course."

CHAPTER 31
ALESSIO

"The girls—"

"Are fine in the mansion with Cara and Gian," Alessio said quickly.

Corrado unlocked the front door to the Guzzi guest house, adding, "My mother *rarely* has girls she can spoil, so you'll be lucky to get them back tomorrow."

Ginevra let out a little laugh, but Alessio could still hear the stress there. Corrado didn't miss it, either, if the look he shot Alessio over his shoulder when he pushed the door open was any sign.

Sliding an arm around Ginevra's waist, he pulled her in close while keeping the overnight bags he held back so they didn't get in the way. Then, he pressed a quick kiss to the side of her temple, saying, "Really, they're good. And if they need you, then you're not very far away. But better for us to do all the talking we need to *away* from everyone else, right?"

She smiled up at him.

Alessio winked back.

"Right," she whispered.

He didn't fault her for wanting to keep an eye on her sisters, though. She had been forced away from them for so long, now, that she tried to make up for lost time. Already, Greta was now in her senior year of high school, and Giulia asked to go to Siena's almost as much as she wanted to stay with Ginevra.

Alessio didn't think Ginevra was jealous of the girls' affection for their half-sister, but change could be tough. And in some ways, people had a habit of holding onto the past.

It would get easier.

Eventually.

Alessio supposed him and Corrado could help with that occasionally. By being there, or with whatever else she might need to make her life easier. And the girls, too. He liked her sisters, even with their desire to make sure he understood not to touch their things on the bathroom counter, and including all their attitude first thing in the morning.

He'd forgotten what it was like to be a teenager. Then again, he had never been a *proper* teen, anyway. A moody prick, sure, but he hadn't had the same experiences as Ginevra's sisters.

Ginevra took a minute to admire the inside the Guzzi guest house, which frankly … was larger than most normal homes, but as Alessio had spent time in it before, he was more interested in watching her.

Well, her and Corrado.

"So, you're where Les has been, huh?" Corrado asked.

Ginevra turned away from the painting she had been admiring over the fireplace to give Corrado a sly grin. "For a couple of days, but then he left a day early to come here."

Corrado gave Alessio a look.

He shrugged. "I thought people here might like a heads-up on what I was planning, that's all."

"I see."

"Are you *jealous?*" Alessio asked.

Corrado arched a brow. "Over what?"

"That I was with Ginevra."

"I slept *alone*, Les."

Right.

And he so hated that.

"But that was my fault," Corrado muttered, facing Ginevra again. "I wish you hadn't left—at least, not without telling me *something*."

"I thought Marcus would explain," Ginevra replied.

Corrado laughed darkly. "He would have, likely—except I didn't answer my calls."

"And then you broke your phone," Alessio added, "before you headed off to … where was it?"

"The lodge in Quebec."

"And then Vegas," Alessio said. "Where you still didn't bother to answer anyone's messages."

"I know what I did, Alessio," Corrado murmured. "I understand how I made it worse, thank you."

"Always helps to have it pointed out, though."

"It also doesn't matter," Ginevra said, "because we're *here*."

Alessio drifted past Corrado, tipping his head toward him as he shrugged off his jacket to set it along the back of the couch in the main room. He dropped the three small overnight bags he'd carried for them all over the side. "She's right."

Ginevra laughed. "Women are *always* right. I can't help it that neither of you are used to that—having a woman between you as the voice of reason."

Corrado chuckled.

"Nice," Alessio told her.

She winked.

Alessio dropped into the corner of the couch, settling himself on watching the two of them work their shit out. After all, he had two days to do that with Ginevra, and he was good. He knew what he wanted from all of this. They were the only ones left, now.

"A drink?" Ginevra asked.

Corrado nodded as she neared the small wet bar next to the couch. "Sure, why not?"

Ginevra didn't even ask which drink he wanted. She already knew and reached for the bottle of whiskey before pouring three fingers of the tawny-colored liquor into a low-ball glass. As she passed it over to Corrado, her gaze on him like she was waiting for their talk to continue, she didn't forget about Alessio by reaching over with her other hand to let it drift through his hair, and then her fingertips ghosted over the side of his cheek.

Second nature.

He'd realized it a while ago, but this woman was perfect for them. There were parts of her that were better suited to handle Corrado, and other pieces of her soul seemed to just fit Alessio. She was the calm to the storm, and the light to the darkness.

He'd used to think the thing between him and Corrado —whatever that was, as strong as it was—needed to be the sun in their life. Something they revolved around. The thing that kept them *alive*, and together.

He was wrong.

Ginevra was the sun.

They just hadn't found her until now.

"I'm where I want to be," Ginevra said before Corrado could speak. "Here, *with you*. And with Les. I am where I want to be, and where I should be, so let me say that first. Is this where you want me to be, Corrado, regardless of the rest?"

Corrado didn't hesitate. "Yes."

Alessio tossed an arm over the back of the chair. "That settles that, doesn't it?"

"But not *all*," Corrado returned. "What happened at the club scared you, and you ran off, Ginny. Which would have been fine, except it seemed like you kept running."

"I don't like what you sometimes do," she said simply. "That scares me for a lot of reasons, and it makes me question who I thought I was when I have to face the fact I love people who also do bad things, but I am where I want to be. And that's what matters."

"Is it?"

She stared hard at Corrado. "*Yes.*"

"Even if it happens again?"

"Even then," she whispered.

She was still touching Alessio, her fingers skimming over his jawline as she took a minute to consider whatever it was running through her mind. He knew it was something in her mind keeping her quiet because that knot formed between her brow which said she was thinking too hard.

She always did that.

Ginevra focused on details.

Alessio dwelled.

And Corrado ... well, he *shut down.*

They were three imperfect people who had somehow found a way to fit together. Life would be far more boring without them there to share it with him, though, flaws and all. Of that, Alessio was most sure.

"I always take care of everyone else," Ginevra said, her hand leaving Alessio so she could fix the bottle on the wet bar. "I was the friend my mother didn't have because she had been so isolated and dependent on a man who only used her for years; a caretaker for my sisters, and even when our mother was still alive, I filled in where she couldn't. And I was willing to marry a man I didn't know and didn't want to protect the people I cared about. In every other aspect of my life, I still take care of other people because it's what I do. It's who I am. I want to say sorry for making you think I was leaving you behind, but I can't because someone else needed me more for a bit."

Corrado cleared his throat. "You shouldn't have to apologize for being selfless, Ginny."

"Except you didn't see me that way, did you?"

"What do you mean?"

Ginevra frowned. "*Selfless*. You didn't see me the way I am because I don't have to be that with either of you—I never have to sacrifice for you or Les. You don't ask for more than I give, and you take care of me far more often than I take care of you."

"Debatable," Alessio spoke up, "but I think the way you *take care* of us, as you say, is so ingrained in who you are, and how you fit us, that you don't feel like you have to do it. It just is, but we notice it."

Corrado nodded. "We do, and when it was gone, well … it went badly, didn't it?"

Alessio glanced Corrado's way.

A crooked smile answered him back.

Where was the lie?

"So, how do we fix that?" Corrado asked. "This, I mean, how do we make sure it doesn't happen again? Because this is where you want to be, with us, and you are where we want you to be … so we need to make sure this is where you stay, Ginny. I love you, and I need you to *stay*."

"A rule," Ginevra said.

Alessio made a noise under his breath.

She looked to Corrado for an explanation, and he grinned when he murmured, "Those are what got us into trouble."

Exactly.

Alessio stayed quiet.

"All right," Ginevra said, "an *understanding*, then. Better?"

Alessio tipped his chin down to agree.

"We don't shut out people we love, and we don't shut off from them, either," Ginevra said. "*Ever.*"

"Just like that?" Corrado asked. "That's all you want from us?"

She met Corrado's gaze, unafraid and *so sure*.

Alessio smiled—life was right again.

Or it was getting there.

"And we stay together," Ginevra said quieter. "*No matter what.* Because I'm not me without the two of you, and I might be selfless to everyone else, but I am selfish enough with my happiness that I want to keep both of you."

"Do you?"

"How could I not when I love you?"

Yes, Alessio thought, *life was most definitely right again.*

Corrado stilled at Ginevra's statement, his gaze skipping to Alessio for a split second. Alessio hadn't missed it, and he was quick to ask, "What?"

"I just …"

"Corrado," Alessio murmured.

"Weren't you the one who said we put too much weight into those words?"

"*I* did."

"And yet," Corrado hedged.

"The impact is still unlike anything," Alessio said. "And doesn't it sound so fucking good coming out of her, though?"

"It does."

Ginevra passed a soft smile back to Alessio. "You are something."

He winked. "And you love it."

"Lucky for you."

"It is," Corrado said, "lucky for him, I mean … for both of us."

Ginevra's laughter colored up the space, but just as quickly, it was drowned out by Corrado closing the distance between them to kiss her. A few steps had separated them, then she moved around the edge of the couch to stand in front of Alessio, when Corrado caught her. Alessio had the privilege of being able to see it when the two let down the rest of those walls.

He understood Corrado's need—that undeniable urge to just *kiss* Ginevra and have her close—because he sensed it, too. He'd felt it when he first saw her in her New York apartment, and it had taken *everything* in him to wait long enough for her sisters to be gone before he closed the distance one fucking step at a time to get what he wanted.

Hell, Corrado had lasted longer.

Props to him.

There was something stirring to Alessio to watch the two —it didn't matter if they were cooking side by side, kissing like they were now, or waking up to see them fucking next to him in the bed. It all brought on the same hurricane of emotions. It still thundered deep in his chest, something that went beyond his heartbeat.

Love.

Lust.

Need.

Want.

Amazement.

Terror.

Appreciative.

Selfishness.

Because that was all his—both people. And that thing between them they shared. It was his, too. Individually, with each of them on a one-to-one basis, and them together as a unit with him.

People who are lucky get one great love in their life. Many more never even get the chance to meet theirs.

Alessio?

He was given two.

Two.

The hand Corrado had tucked clasped onto Ginevra's side drifted away from her to reach for Alessio. He didn't question the want for touch, simply answered it by reaching back, his fingers threading with Corrado's before he leaned forward enough to press his forehead against the side of their clasped hands.

For a single second before this moment turned into something else—he figured it would; they needed the physical side, too, with each other—he soaked that in, refusing to let anything seep into his mind so he wouldn't forget it.

That feeling.

Would it ever be the same again?

He wasn't sure.

It didn't matter.

He'd never forget it now.

But he also wasn't wrong on what he believed, either. All it took was a soft, "I need you—both of you." That whisper from Ginevra was so quiet, and yet, there was an unmistakable heat in her tone. A *want.*

And he swore it was second nature for he and Corrado … an uncontrollable urge they both had to *give* this woman what she wanted, when she wanted it. It didn't matter what it was, pancakes at nine in the evening, or fucking at two in the morning, they would give it to her because she asked.

A lot like each other, too.

Ginevra fell back into Alessio's lap, her loose hair spilling over his shoulder as his arms locked around her waist. He took that chance to dip his hands lower while Corrado pulled his suit jacket off and worked on the buttons of his shirt. Alessio wasn't the least bit surprised to find Ginevra hot and wet under the lace panties hidden between the skirt of her dress. He bunched the skirt around her hips. His hand under her panties moved fast, stroking through the seam of her sex to take the wetness he found there up to her clit.

All she needed to get off were the pads of his fingertips against her clit in fast back-and-forth strokes at a steady pressure, and he would make her come like *nothing at all*. He did exactly that, wanting her worked up. No flavor was better than Ginevra's pussy right after she came, no doubt about that.

There was something sweeter tasting to her skin, he would *swear* on it.

"Yeah, *fuck*," Corrado said when he buried his face into Ginevra's neck to breathe her in as she squirmed against his hold, "make her come, Les. Let me see it."

"Oh, my *God*," Ginevra choked out, the sound raw enough to make his cock impossibly harder beneath his jeans. And with her tight little ass grinding against his groin to get more friction of his hand against her clit, he damn near blew his load like a fucking teenager. "Please, don't stop. *Please, Les.*"

He laughed against the heat of her skin, and her pulse thrummed under the spot where his lips grazed her throat. "Not this time, sweetheart."

Alessio realized Corrado had kneeled down between the two of them when the warm roughness of the man's tongue lapped at his fingers running across Ginevra's clit. The heady moan that Corrado let loose was enough to have Alessio clenching all over—but in the *best* way.

"Do you hear that, Ginny?" Alessio asked her, his mouth drifting up the side of her trembling jaw before coming to a stop at her ear. He found the flavor of salt on her skin already, but also that strange sweetness, too—it would be a good fucking night all around. "That sound means he likes the taste of you on me, woman. Do you want him to eat your pussy while I make you come?"

A whine echoed from Ginevra. A clear *yes* following right behind it. Corrado did what she wanted, and Alessio intensified the pressure and pace on her clit for her. Everybody had that button to push, and this was Ginevra's. As soon as he hit it, and Corrado was feasting on her pussy she shouted loud as she came.

Trembling all over.

Hot to the damn touch.

Sobbing their names.

Fuck.

It was sacrilegious.

It had to be.

If sin was a physical thing like people believed it to be, it had to be the sound Ginevra made when she was coming like that with both of them touching her. And if heaven truly existed, it was also this.

Alessio grabbed a fistful of Ginevra's hair to turn her head enough to kiss her. His tongue clashed with hers, their kiss a familiar war he found had his heart pounding even as his fingers slowed between her thighs. He wasn't sure when Corrado stood up, but the rustle of a bag had Alessio pulling away from the kiss to find what was happening. He didn't wonder for long, though.

Corrado was back, leaning over Ginevra to take a kiss, too, his hands locked onto her thighs. Next to Alessio on the couch, he found what Corrado had been digging for. One of their small, black travel bags where they kept anything they might need to stay overnight. And as a *just in case*, condoms and packets of lubrication.

"Turn around," Corrado demanded.

Ginevra hurried to obey, letting Alessio drag those ruined panties off her legs before she twisted around on his lap to straddle him. He dragged the straps of her dress down her shoulders, thankful she'd picked the tight bodycon one he'd liked in her closet because the material had give.

Once he had that dress pulled down enough to get his hands on the lace bra that was covering her chest, she arched into his touch. Her lips fell open, and her tongue snaked along the outer edge as Corrado lifted her higher so that her ass was thrust out for him.

Alessio, though, focused his attention on getting his palms under Ginevra's bra. Skimming his fingertips over the tops of her nipples, he hardened them into peaks. He took one in his mouth, his teeth teasing her nipple as Corrado worked behind her. The rustle of the bag echoed again, and the sound of foil ripped open.

He knew when Corrado slipped his cock into Ginevra's pussy because her body jerked against his, and another soft whimper fell from her lips. Alessio stared upward, Ginevra's nipple still tight between his teeth to see Corrado biting the top of her shoulder as the echo of skin slapping skin sounded in the room. He got his hand between her thighs long enough to graze the hard length of Corrado sliding into Ginevra's wet heat before he moved higher to work her clit between his fingertips with a massaging motion.

Different from before, but more intense.

His other hand came up to grab her jaw as he let go of her nipple, tipping his head higher to watch her face when she came a second time.

"Almost?" he asked her.

Ginevra swallowed hard. "*Almost.*"

"You want more?"

She nodded once.

Good.

Because what she wanted, they gave.

Corrado tipped his head to the side, making Alessio aware he thought the same thing and was ready for it whenever he wanted to move. Alessio pushed his hands against Ginevra's thighs, and Corrado slowed behind her, removing himself from her body, and helping her to stand against the couch. It was long enough for Alessio to move over, and Corrado put Ginevra back on her knees on the couch, already slipping his cock back into her to fuck her from behind while Alessio stripped of his clothes.

He took all of thirty seconds to get rid of the shit in his way and find a condom in that bag to put on. Bottle of lube in hand, he handed it to Corrado as they let him resume his previous position, except this time, Ginevra's hot pussy came down on Alessio's cock.

The groan that came from him sounded foreign to his own ears, but he'd forgotten how much he loved this woman's cunt. He let Ginevra ride him at the pace she wanted for, his hands skimming around to her ass to spread her wide. It gave Corrado easy access to work her from behind.

First, with his fingers. Stretching her wide and wanting to fill more and more with each twist of his digits inside her ass. The lube would ease the tension curling her shoulders as her breaths came out a little faster with each finger Corrado added. Her rhythm on him never changed, though, because *damn*, she wanted that.

It vibrated through her.

In every single inch of her.

"Tell me," Corrado said where he kneeled behind Ginevra. "Tell me what you want, kitten."

"*Just …*"

Air rushed from Ginevra.

Alessio leaned in and kissed her hot mouth. "Say it for him. He wants you to use words, kitten."

And so did he.

"Fuck my ass," she whispered. "I need ... I need ... *Please.*"

Corrado's next moan came out *thankful* and husky at the same time. He stood, his hand finding Ginevra's shoulder as he fit in behind her. Alessio's fingers squeezed on Ginevra's ass, slowing her to a stop. He could tell by the tightening of Ginevra's muscles and the low cry that fell from her trembling lips when Corrado pressed his cock into her ass.

Alessio distracted her with kisses, swallowing all those sounds she let loose, and soothing the tension in her body. But that noise she made when Corrado fit tightly against her, cock buried deep, and she sat all the way down on Alessio again ...

Primal, he thought.

So fucking raw, really.

Her pussy flexed all around him, taking his breath away when she mumbled, "Please move ... *fuck me.*"

Corrado's hand found one of Alessio's on Ginevra's ass. Their fingers wove again, tight together as they both found a steady, fast rhythm that allowed one to flex into Ginevra as the other pulled off her. He used the hand he still had on her ass to lift her on his cock, and to yank her down harder with each thrust.

But her like this?

Perfect.

Undoubtedly.

Free with her back arched, and ass curved out. Head thrown back, and waves of dark hair falling over her shoulders. Those tits of hers pert and pink nipples hard from his handling. She'd have their marks by the morning, both seen and invisible. She'd ache from them, even sitting down, they would linger on her ... and that drove him fucking crazy.

He loved it.

Ginevra's hand on his shoulder grabbed harder, those

nails of hers scoring lines across his skin as she came with a broken cry. He didn't catch that one with a kiss like he had the others, but he didn't mind.

He'd needed that.

It made him come, too.

Corrado followed close behind.

Alessio saw stars, his breath gone as one by one, each of them stilled. He wasn't sure which one trembled, but it echoed in his *bones*. Ginevra fell forward, her forehead pressing against his chest as Corrado leaned over her to press a line of kisses up her spine. Gaze lifted, Alessio met Corrado's stare as their still-woven fingers squeezed together again.

"Chamomile, right?" Alessio asked.

Ginevra hummed a sweet sound. "What?"

"That's the tea you like before bed. They have some in the mansion, I'll go get you some and bring it back, hmm?"

"It is, but—"

"And a warm bath," Corrado added.

Ginevra sighed. "Is it spoiling me time now?"

Alessio chuckled.

Corrado smirked at him.

"For the rest of your life," Alessio said, "if that's what you want."

Ginevra made that happy, pleased hum again. "It is."

"Then, that's what you get," Corrado murmured.

EPILOGUE
GINEVRA

Almost two months later ...

"Greta?"

"What?"

Ginevra peeked over at her sister in the passenger seat of the SUV. Behind the wheel, she couldn't take her eyes off the road for too long, but all she needed was that quick look to know Greta was more interested in whatever she was looking at on her social media stream than whatever her older sister had to say.

"Could you come back to the real world for a second?"

Greta sighed, but set the phone down. "Better?"

"Slightly. Last day of classes before Christmas break, so try to make the best of it, and not get too bored. Also, did you finish that essay last night that you needed to hand in?"

"Yes."

"Last night at one in the morning," Giulia grumbled in the back seat.

"At least I did it."

"I could hear you clicking keys through the wall."

Ginevra focused her attention on the horrible traffic in front and wondered why she didn't just send the girls to their school in a fucking cab. She didn't remember bickering with her sisters as much as the other two did. Oh, she loved them to death, to be sure. Sometimes, they still got on her last nerve.

Especially when she was running late for her extra college class, had gotten halfway through her coffee that morning, and hadn't seen *either* of her men in two weeks. Ginevra needed a hell of a lot of things and listening to her sisters fight was not one.

"Can we hold off on the arguing until I drop you off?" she asked, not hiding the sarcasm in the slightest.

Greta rolled her eyes. Giulia stuck out her tongue when Ginevra checked the other girl in the rearview mirror. Nothing unusual for either of them, really.

Truth was, they were good girls. Normal teenagers, all things considered. They had their moments, and sometimes a bad attitude that made Ginevra squint. At the same time, they didn't get in trouble, took care of their business, and over the last couple of months, somehow realized on their own time that Ginevra had her own life she was trying to start and take care of them.

They were sensitive to that, never trying to take time away from Ginevra with Corrado and Alessio when they were around, even though they didn't have to worry about doing that at all. The guys *never* tried to take time from her sisters.

Thankfully, the girls quieted for the rest of the drive. Which was another forty-five fucking minutes for three goddamn blocks—New York traffic was terrible, and it reminded Ginevra daily that allowing Corrado to buy this stupid SUV was pointless. Oh, she loved it, to be sure. People got out of the way when something bigger was coming through, but that meant nothing when traffic was almost at a gridlock.

Every single day.

Ginevra was just pulling into the drop-off line when she noticed a familiar black Porsche parked along the side of the street. Cutting back out onto the street, she turned a hard left, and swung in beside Alessio's car. Standing beside it looking like absolute sin and *love* in his usual black jeans, and leather jacket overtop a plain tee, he winked at her when she cut the engine.

When had he gotten back?

Where was Corrado?

"Siena is picking you two up today, I'll drop off your overnight bags for the weekend later," she told the girls as they all unbuckled. "Don't forget, okay?"

"Got it," Greta said, pushing out of the front of the vehicle.

"Yep," Giulia echoed.

Their similar greetings to Alessio sounded as Ginevra got out of her side of the SUV, and rounded the front, tightening her tweed jacket to keep out the late December cold from seeping into her bones. The beanie on her head with the pompom on top helped too, at least, keep her ears warm, but she'd forgotten mittens in her rush to leave. Her fingers felt like icicles, so she hid them by tucking her hands inside the pockets of her jacket.

Greta and Giulia, despite being almost late for school, seemed to forget all about classes at the sight of Alessio. They chatted away as Ginevra stood a few feet back, giving him the inquisition about where he had been, and what new thing they had planned to do with him this time.

Because … that's what they did.

Ginevra didn't understand how it happened, but she loved it. She couldn't be more grateful that Corrado and Alessio spent time with her sisters when they were with her. Alessio took them out—movies, a day out, whatever they wanted. Corrado was the one who always brought something back for them, be it a small item from wherever he had been, or a story to tell.

They loved it.

Ginevra realized, after a month, that the boys were kind of like big brothers the girls never had because they were certainly nothing like their dead half-brothers. But less annoying, and a hell of a lot more fun.

"The new Marvel one, then?" Alessio asked.

"Can Siena come?" Greta asked.

Alessio chuckled. "Of course."

"Deal."

"And Corrado will come for it, too," Alessio added.

"Is he back, too?" Ginevra asked, the first time she had spoken at all, actually. Alessio's gaze turned on her, and she swore that her heart stopped for a split second when he grinned, and all of his attention was only on her. "Hey."

"Hey," he murmured, "and if he isn't already, he will be. A surprise for us, I guess. All I was told is that I'm supposed to take you to a certain address he texted me this morning at a specific time."

"A surprise for what?"

That wasn't like Corrado at all. He planned *everything*. And everybody needed to be made aware of those plans. That way, everything would go off without a hitch. Alessio was the spontaneous one, doing things just because he wanted to, and he figured it would be fun.

Alessio shrugged. "I can only say what I was told, babe. And don't these two have classes?"

Greta opened her mouth to reply with something smartass, likely, but the ringing bell across the street at the high school stopped her from saying anything at all. He gave the two a look, they sighed, and said a quick goodbye before darting across the street.

That's all it took.

Just the girls to be gone.

Alessio closed the distance between him and Ginevra in a

flash. She forgot all about the cold December wind, and her frozen fingertips when he locked her in his embrace and dotted her mouth with kisses.

Ginevra hummed against his mouth. "Missed you."

"Shit, me, too. Congo was good, though … quick."

That's about all he or Corrado ever gave about a job for The League, and she tried not to ask for more details. It was simpler that way, and she worried less. Not that she didn't worry at all because she still did.

Still, the Congo assignment he had just come back from would be his last for a few months. He chose to take time off, a spread of months to spend with Corrado, and *her*. Corrado had already started his time off, but he'd needed to head back to Vegas for a couple of weeks to do things there.

Her tiny apartment would be *full*.

This thing of theirs wasn't easy.

No doubt about it.

They did their best, though.

And she couldn't ask for more.

"So, when is this surprise?" she asked.

Alessio smirked sinfully, using the tip of his finger to slide along her bottom lip as he murmured, "After your classes at the college today."

"Damn, I hoped for an excuse to get out of them."

"I can think of a few," he replied, "but then Corrado will bitch because *you chose education, and you should have it.*"

"He's not wrong, though."

"But we don't tell him that, Ginny. It makes his ego grow."

Where was the lie?

∾

CORRADO

"I can take the job," Corrado said to his brother on the phone. His voice echoed throughout the empty hall he walked down.

Although, it was partly a lie. He *could* take the job that Andino Marcello called through to The League, but for one, he didn't give a fuck about that man. And for two, it meant the break he took to focus on Ginevra and Alessio and their *life* would have to be put on hold.

Corrado wouldn't do that.

Les and Ginny didn't come second.

Not now.

They came first.

No exceptions.

"But I knew you wouldn't," Chris said, "and Dare called me with the offer because extractions are my specialty."

Corrado cleared his throat, coming to the end of the entrance hallway where he would wait closer to the front door for his lovers to arrive. It was just about the time when they needed to arrive, and Alessio had a habit of being on time, if not early.

"How long has it been since you took an independent job from The League?"

"Four years," Chris said.

"A while, then. Do you think—"

"They have the auctions coming up, from what Dad explained. And Cree's team is heading to Syria for a job I wasn't allowed to get the details for."

"Government involved," Corrado replied.

The League had their hand in everything.

"Anyway, they would have pulled someone from somewhere else to do the extraction job for Andino down in Mexico, but I happened to be there with Dad when Dare called, and when your name got brought up, I offered."

Corrado smiled.

His twin, still looking out for him.

"Thanks, man."

Chris made a dismissive noise under his breath. "Yeah, well … gives you some time to figure things out over there in New York, huh?"

Right.

The shadowy figures approaching the frosted glass of the front door drew Corrado's attention there instead of his phone call. As the door opened, and he said goodbye to his brother to give his time to the people who needed it, the only thing to drift through his mind was, *I don't need time to figure this out, I know what I want.*

Alessio and Ginevra.

Until the day he died.

∾

ALESSIO

"Why is this stoop twice the size of a normal brownstone?" Ginevra asked.

Alessio opened the door without knocking—as per Corrado's earlier instructions. Although, he hadn't known until they pulled up to the place that it would be a brownstone, so he still wasn't sure why they were here. "I'm not sure, you'll need to ask Corrado that."

"Ask me what?"

Corrado stood just beyond the doorway, leaning against the wall like he had watched the two of them walk up the stoop together. He probably had. Smiling at the two, he winked.

"The stoop," Ginevra said, leaving Alessio's side to greet Corrado with a quick kiss, and a soft pat to his cheek with the tips of her fingers. "It's double the size."

"Because this brownstone is also double the size."

Ginevra looked around the empty hallway, the hardwood floors gleaming under their feet. Then, she peeked back at Alessio with an arched brow. "And *very* ... lonely without furniture, or anything on the walls."

Corrado chuckled. "Well, that's because you'll have to decorate it, or hire someone to do that for you."

Ginevra stilled.

Alessio looked to Corrado. "What?"

"It's double the size because double the people need space here what with the girls, and all of us. It's empty because I closed on it yesterday, and the only thing we can keep is the big oak desk in the office upstairs because the movers weren't able to take it apart to get it out of the door without compromising the structural integrity."

"You bought this?" Ginevra asked.

Corrado lifted a shoulder. "Well, I had to use private accounts separate from Les's, so he wouldn't have a clue what I did either—it's not often I get to surprise him, too."

He wasn't wrong.

Ginevra's apartment happened to be a good size for a New York place, but it still wasn't *that* big. And when you had two teenage girls, two grown men, and Ginevra trying to share the same spaces, it became ... crowded.

"Three bathrooms," Corrado murmured, "five bedrooms,

a little backyard, and an underground garage that can fit three vehicles."

"How much?" Ginevra asked.

"A lot," he returned, "but worth every single penny."

"Corrado."

Having money that was disposable still seemed like a foreign concept to Ginevra. She couldn't throw away money like them, but she was getting better at accepting *they* would spend money.

A lot.

"You need a bigger space," Corrado said, "you can't keep studying in bed, or trying to find space at a tiny table when the girls have their books all over it. I don't like you're in an apartment building with hundreds of other people. And Les and I ... we're moving everything around to be here with you until we figure out something different, Ginevra. Because this is where we want to be—starting a *life*. That starts with somewhere to live."

She made a soft noise under her breath.

Alessio smiled. "This is a good surprise."

Corrado laughed. "You think?"

"Not what I expected."

"But it's perfect," Ginevra whispered, letting Alessio pull her in close to press a kiss to the middle of her forehead.

"A big enough grand gesture for both of you, then?"

Right.

Corrado had always been the one willing to take a step back from telling them what he wanted for the sake of his pride. Heaven forbid they understand he needed them as much as they needed him.

Not now, though.

He made it perfectly clear.

Ginevra left Alessio's embrace to lean in and press another quick kiss to Corrado's grinning lips. Alessio stepped forward, too, finding Corrado's hand with his own to squeeze tight before he wrapped his other arm around Ginevra's back.

They were better together.

"Yeah, more than big enough," Alessio told him.

Ginevra smiled at both. "I want a tour."

She said the magic word.

Want.

They were always quick to give.

BETHANY-KRIS

Bethany-Kris is a Canadian author, lover of much, and mother to four young sons, two cats, and three dogs. A small town in Eastern Canada where she was born and raised is where she has always called home. With her boys under her feet, a snuggling cat, barking dogs, and a spouse calling over his shoulder, she is nearly always writing something ... when she can find the time.

Find Bethany-Kris at her:
www.bethanykris.com

Sign up to Bethany-Kris's New Release Newsletter here:
eepurl.com/bf9lzD

BOOKS BY BETHANY-KRIS

The Guzzi Legacy

Corrado

Alessio

Chris

Beni

Bene

Marcus

Renzo + Lucia

Privilege

Harbor

Contempt

Andino + Haven

Duty

Vow

John + Siena

Loyalty

Disgrace

Cross + Catherine

Always

Revere

Unruly

The Companion

Naz & Roz

Guzzi Duet

Unraveled, Book One

Entangled, Book Two

DeLuca Duet

Waste of Worth: Part One

Worth of Waste: Part Two

Donati Bloodlines

Thin Lies

Thin Lines

Thin Lives

Behind the Bloodlines

The Complete Trilogy

Filthy Marcellos

Antony

Lucian

Giovanni

Dante

Legacy

A Very Marcello Christmas

The Complete Collection

Effortless

Inflict

Cozen

Captivated

Dishonored

Find more on Bethany-Kris's website at www.bethanykris.com.

www.ingramcontent.com/pod-product-compliance
Lightning Source LLC
Chambersburg PA
CBHW072311020726
47501CB00002B/469